The Weird Picture

John R. Carling

Illustrated by Cyrus Cuneo

THE WEIRD PICTURE

THE
WEIRD PICTURE

By

JOHN R. CARLING

Author of "The Shadow of the Czar,"
"The Viking's Skull," etc.

Illustrated by Cyrus Cuneo

Boston
Little Brown, and Company
1905

THE
WEIRD PICTURE

By

JOHN R. CARLING

Author of "The Shadow of the Czar,"
"The Viking's Skull," etc.

Illustrated by Cyrus Cuneo

Boston
Little, Brown, and Company
1905

Copyright, 1905,
BY LITTLE, BROWN, AND COMPANY.

— —

All rights reserved.

Published May, 1905.

Printers
S. J. PARKHILL & CO., BOSTON, U. S. A.

CONTENTS

CHAPTER

    I   The Red Stain

   II   The Veiled Lady

  III   The Wedding Morning

  IV   Waiting!

   V   The Artist paints a notable Picture

  VI   The Man at the Confessional

 VII   What the "Standard" said of the Picture

VIII   High Mass and what happened at it

  IX   The Artist fails to secure a Model

   X   Ghost or Mortal?

  XI   More of the Picture

 XII   The Figure in the Grey Cloak

XIII   What the Artist's Portfolio revealed

XIV THE MYSTERIES OF THE STUDIO

XV   THE DÉNOUEMENT!

LIST OF ILLUSTRATIONS

"Before my uncle could prevent her she had snatched the letter from him"   Frontispiece

"The figure turned to meet, but not to greet me. It was my brother's face I saw"

"'I opened my eyes, and there was a black thing bending over me'"

"His head sunk forward on his breast and his crooked fingers clawing at the air"

CHAPTER I THE RED STAIN

"BELGRAVE SQUARE, *November 28th.*

"DEAR FRANK,—Surely you are not going to spend a third Christmas at Heidelberg! We want you with us in good old England. My marriage with Daphne is fixed for Christmas Day, and I shall not regard the ceremony as valid unless you are my best man. So come—*come*—COME! No time to say more. You can guess how busy I am. Write or wire by return.— Yours,

"GEORGE."

Such was the letter received by me, Frank Willard, student in Odenwald College, Heidelberg, on the first day of the last month of the year. The writer of the letter was my brother, a captain in the— something. I take a pride in not remembering the number of the regiment, for I am a man of peace and hate war and all connected therewith, excepting, of course, my soldier-brother, though my affection for him had somewhat waned of late years, for a reason that will soon appear.

The letter was accompanied by a portrait of George, an exquisite little painting in oils, representing him in full-dress uniform. A glance at the mirror showed how much I suffered by comparison. He looked every inch a hero. I looked—well, no matter. In the lottery of love the prizes are not always drawn by the handsome. The Daphne referred to was our cousin, a maiden with raven hair, dark blue eyes, and a face as lovely as a Naiad's.

Her father, Gerald Leslie, was a wealthy city merchant, who, after the death of our parents, became the guardian of George and myself, bestowing on us a warmth of affection and a wealth of pocket-money that made the transference to his roof seem rather desirable than otherwise, my own father having been of a somewhat cold and undemonstrative temperament. However, *de mortuis nil nisi bonum.*

My first impulse on reading the above letter was to pen a refusal to the invitation.

The Weird Picture

"What!" it may be said. "Refuse to be present at your brother's wedding? Refuse to return home to old England at Christmastide? — a season dear to every Englishman from its sacred and festive associations. 'Breathes there the man with soul so dead,' etc."

Exactly. My soul *was* dead, both to the joys of Christmas and of Daphne's wedding. Four words will explain the reason: I myself loved Daphne. And I had told her so, only to find that she had given her heart to my brother George.

I am not going to fill this chapter with the ravings of disappointed love. Suffice it to say that in my despair I left England, determined to see Daphne no more, and betook myself to the university of Heidelberg with the hope of finding oblivion in study.

Greek choruses, strophes, antistrophes, and epodes, are, however, all very well in their way, but they are a sorry substitute for love. At any rate, they did not make me forget Daphne. Her sweet face continued to haunt me, and, in the despairing and romantic mood of a Manfred, I spent many a night on the mountains around Heidelberg, watching the stars rise, and brooding over my unrequited love.

Thus my brother's letter was far from being a source of pleasure to me, though it was kindly meant on his part (for he was ignorant, so I subsequently learned, of my own love for Daphne). His invitation, translated into the language of my thoughts simply meant, "Come and be more unhappy than you are!"

Deep down in my heart I had cherished the belief that something unforeseen would happen to break off George's engagement. The sands of that hope were now fast running out. The 25th of the month would remove Daphne from me forever.

For several days I fought with my despair, but at last I resolved to be present at the wedding.

"I may as well play the stoic," I muttered, "and accept the inevitable. Perhaps the fact of seeing Daphne actually married to another will cure me of this folly."

Curiosity, also, to see how Daphne would behave on the occasion was an additional motive for going; and, poor fool that I was, I thought of the trembling handclasp, the blush, and the sweet glance that a woman seldom fails to bestow on the man who has once expressed his love for her.

Christmas Eve, midnight, found me on board the packet-boat steaming out of Calais Harbour. The sea was singularly smooth, and there was in the air that which gave promise of a heavy fall of snow ere long. Wrapped in my cloak, I leaned over the side of the vessel, listening to the silver carillon of the church-bells pealing forth from every steeple and belfry in the town the glad tidings that the sweet and solemn morn of the Nativity had dawned. Faintly and more faintly the chimes sounded over the wide expanse of glimmering sea, till they were finally lost in the distance.

At first my thoughts were gloomy. To play the stoic is never a very pleasant task. Yet I was not totally abandoned to despair. A ray of hope played over my mind, and, as the distance that separated me from Daphne diminished, this hope gradually became stronger and stronger. *Nil desperandum* should be my motto. The wedding had not taken place yet; weddings have been broken off at the very altar: why should not hers be? Foolish though it may seem, I began to nurse the pleasing idea that Fate might yet transfer Daphne to my arms. As if my wish had become a certainty, I trod the deck of the Channel steamer with exultant step, refusing to go below, although the wintry flakes were falling now in steady earnest. Such is the power of hope over the human mind; or is it something more than a poetic fiction that coming events cast their shadows before?

I was roused at length from dreamland by the sight of Dover Harbour looming through the snow-dotted gloom of night.

At the pier-head a lantern shone, and among the persons assembled beneath its light a soldierly-looking figure in a long grey coat was visible. It was my brother George. His presence on the pier seemed, in my excited state of mind, a confirmation of the daring hope I had begun to entertain.

"The dear fellow!" I murmured. "He has come down expressly to meet me, and to resign Daphne to me."

As our vessel drew alongside the pier I waved my hand to him, but at this greeting he instantly vanished. This was certainly a surprise. Why did he not await my landing?

The Weird Picture

I was the first to quit the steamer, and, emerging from the inspection of the Revenue officials, I looked eagerly around for my brother. He was not to be seen on any part of the pier.

Was I mistaken as to the identity? The figure, the face, the very carriage—all seemed to be his. Stay! Was this an ocular illusion! Had my mind been dwelling so earnestly on my brother as to stamp on the retina of my eye an image that had no corresponding objective reality outside myself? Would this account for the peculiar manner in which the figure had vanished?

I would soon put this theory to the test. If George had come by train from London, the servants at the station would surely retain some remembrance of him. If others had seen the figure in the grey cloak, it would be a proof that my sense of sight had not deceived me. I entered the station and sought knowledge from the first porter I met, a tired-looking youth, with a sprig of holly stuck in his buttonhole, who gaped vacantly at my questions till the glitter of a silver coin imparted a certain degree of briskness to his faculties.

"A military-looking gent, sir? Yes, there was one on the platform a few minutes ago."

"Describe him," said I bluntly, as my fellow passengers from the boat began to crowd into the station. "What was he like?"

I was desirous of drawing a description of the "military-looking gent" from the porter's unassisted memory rather than of suggesting personal details, to which, in his half-sleepy state and in his desire to get rid of me, he would doubtless subscribe assent.

"Well, sir, he wasn't very tall—at least, not for a soldier; but then Bonaparte wasn't——"

"Oh, hang Bonaparte! Go on," I said snappishly, for I was cold, hungry, and tired—conditions that do not tend to improve one's temper.

"He was wearing a long grey cloak and had a travelling-bag with him, marked with the letters "G.W." I noticed the bag particularly, because it came open as he was stepping from the carriage. My! didn't he shut it sharp! quick as lightning, as if he didn't want any one to see what was inside. I offered to carry it for him, and he told me——"

"What?"

"To go to the devil!"

"You didn't go, I see," said I, attempting to be facetious. "Well, go on. What about the man's face?"

"Face? He looked rather white and excited; perhaps because he was in a passion with the carriage-door; it didn't open easily. He had a dark scar on his temple, and——"

"Left or right temple?"

"Left."

George had a dark scar on his left temple, the relic of a fall from a cliff at Upsala. His initials too were "G.W." Good! The figure on the pier was not an illusion, then. The porter's words convinced me that the man he had seen was my brother.

"How long is it since he was here?" I inquired.

"How long?" repeated the official, jerking his head backwards to get a glimpse of the Station clock. "Only ten minutes since. He came down by the express from Charing Cross. It was a few minutes late owing to the snow."

"Do you know if he had a return ticket?"

"That I can't say."

"What's the next train to London?"

"One just on the move now, sir. The next in two hours' time. Better travel by this one. The next is sure to be a slow one, this snowstorm is so heavy. Going by this one, sir?" he continued, swinging open a carriage-door as he saw my hesitation. "Only a minute to spare."

"I—I don't know yet. Hold my portmanteau for a moment."

I quickly ran the whole length of the departing train, but the grey coat was not in any of the carriages. This train was the one I should have travelled by, its departure being timed for the arrival of the Continental boat; but I now resolved to delay my journey till the next, in order to travel in company with my brother, for George must return by the latter train, otherwise he would be barely in time to meet the wedding-party in the Church at half-past nine. I returned to the porter, who was surveying me with a curiosity, the reason of which soon became evident, and said:

"I shall travel by the next train. Take charge of my portmanteau until then."

"Right you are, guv'nor! What's he done? Forgery? Murder? He looks quite capable of it."

"Done? Who?" I said, astounded at this sudden familiarity.

"Why, the military cove!" returned the youth. "It's no go; I can see you're a 'tec with half an eye."

I suppose the half-eye that had discovered so much was his right one, for he proceeded to diminish it by screwing it up into a wink expressive of the penetration of its owner.

"The gentleman whom you think capable of forgery and murder is my brother, Captain Willard, of the—the never you mind; and if you give me any of your insolence, I'll report you to the authorities," I said, wrathfully.

The porter, who had evidently been drinking, was a little taken aback, to judge by his ejaculation of "Oh lor!" and as I walked off with my grandest air, I heard him mutter:

"His brother! yes, and like him, too! The one sends me to the devil, and the other threatens to report me to the station-master. Oh, they're brothers, sure enough! By your leave, there!"

A multitude of questions came surging over my mind. What was George doing at Dover only a few hours before his wedding? Obviously his purpose was not to meet me, since he had avoided me. Why? Could it be that for some strange reason he was deserting Daphne on her bridal morning?—a thought that caused my pulses to throb quickly. Was it shame, or guilt, that had kept him from facing me? Oh, if I could but find him, and learn the truth from his lips!

"On the platform ten minutes ago."

The Weird Picture

Absurd as the idea may seem, I resolved to walk the streets of Dover during the next two hours, on the chance of meeting him.

The weather was of the character that popular fancy rather than historic fact has ascribed to the Yuletides of bygone days under the name of "an old-fashioned Christmas." The snow was lying several inches deep in the streets, deadening the sound of my footfalls. The big flakes, still falling, blinded my vision with their whirling eddies. Not a soul was to be seen out of doors. Not a sound was to be heard save the sea splashing faintly against the harbour walls. The town lay draped in white, a city of the dead. Not knowing in what direction to proceed, I walked on as chance directed, without seeing the person I was in quest of. Presently, as I was turning a corner, a figure, white as a ghost from head to foot, came into sight, startling me for the moment. It was a constable, and I questioned him.

"I saw a man in a grey cloak go by just three minutes ago."

"Carrying bag marked 'G.W.'?"

"Carrying *a* bag, sir," he replied, with marked emphasis on what the grammarians were wont to call the indefinite article. "I didn't notice any letters on it. If you hurry you'll catch him up. He went that way," pointing with his hand. "Is anything the matter? Can I be of assistance?"

"I don't understand you," I returned sharply, wondering whether he, too, like the railway-porter, thought that my brother was a fugitive from justice.

"No offence, sir, but your friend seems to need looking after. He is either mad or dying. His eyes burned like live coals, and his face was as white as this snow here. I called out 'A rough night, sir!' but he glided on, looking neither to right nor left, and taking no notice of me."

These words increased my misgivings. I thanked the constable and, declining his proffered services, rushed on in the direction indicated by him. A line of footprints in the snow served to guide me, and following their course, I presently found myself in a street whose semi-detached villas were fronted with quiet unpretentious gardens separated from the pavement by stone balustrades.

There he was! Half-way down the street, standing beneath the light of a gas-lamp, was a cloaked man apparently taking a survey of a house facing the lamp, while shaking the snow from himself. I hurried forward to greet him, my feet making no sound on the soft snow.

"George!" I cried eagerly and breathlessly when within a few paces of him. "George!"

The figure turned to meet, but not to greet me. It was my brother's face I saw, but so haggard and disfigured by lines of pain as to be scarcely recognisable. His eyes frightened me as they gleamed in the lamplight; so glassy, so unnatural was their stare.

With dread at my heart I tried to clasp his hand, but he waved me back with a gesture suggestive of surprise, despair, terror, shame, grief—any or all of these might have prompted the singular motion of his arm. If I had come upon him in the very act of murder, he could not have shown greater agitation. The fingers of his left hand relaxed their grip, and the valise they were holding dropped silently upon the snow. His action said more plainly than words: "Go back! go back! There is that happening of which you must know nothing."

To my mind there could be but one cause of his emotion, a cause as awful to me as to him, and it burst from my lips in a hoarse cry.

"Good heavens, George! Surely—surely Daphne isn't dead?"

There was no reply. The laxity of his limbs and his reclining attitude against the iron column showed that he had scarcely strength to stand. Then a sudden gust of wind blew aside both his cloak and his coat, exposing his white vest to view. And there upon that vest, plain to be seen, was a red stain large and round! For one moment only was it visible in the fitful light of the gas-lamp; the next, the folds of his cloak enveloping him again, concealed it from view.

"What is the matter? Why don't you speak?" I cried, and overcoming the vague terror that had possessed me, I stepped forward.

But before I could touch him, he gave a swift glance around, apparently seeking some way of escape, and suddenly snatching up the valise, he darted through the gate-way opposite him. Hurrying up the garden-path, he ascended a flight of steps, and while I was

The Weird Picture

still gazing after him in amazement, he disappeared within the portico that gave entrance to the house.

Here was a strange affair. George, on his wedding-morn in a town far distant from his bride, trying to avoid me, his brother, after having invited me to be his best man! A second explanation of his conduct occurred to me and found its way to my tongue.

"He is mad!" and I hesitated to follow. It is not an infrequent thing for the insane to think their dearest friends their foes. And this thought begot another, more fearful still to me;

> To be wroth with one we love
> Doth work like madness in the brain.

His wild air and the red stain on his breast might well be testimony to some tragedy; in a fit of insane jealousy he had killed Daphne! Paralyzed by the idea I leaned, as he had leaned before me, against the lamp-post, with the words, "Daphne dead!" ringing in my ears.

I broke from the spell of terror imposed on me by my own fancy, and prepared to follow my brother. Putting aside the fears for my own safety with the thought that in case of an attack my cries would summon the inmates of the neighbouring houses to my aid, I cautiously groped my way to the dark portico, not without a dread that his wild figure might spring out upon me; but, on mounting the snowy steps I discovered that the portico was empty, and the front door of the house securely shut.

I had heard no noise of knocking—no sound of the opening or closing of a door; and yet, if George had not passed the threshold, where was he? This was the second time the figure had eluded me. Was it after all an apparition?

The improbability of seeing my brother in such a place and at such an hour, his obstinate silence to my appeals, his weird aspect, the mysterious manner in which he had vanished, seemed to favour this hypothesis. Was this his wraith sent to apprise me of his death? The next moment I was smiling at the idea. A being that is merely a figment of the brain cannot be credited with the power of making footprints in snow, yet deep footprints there were leading up the steps, and terminating at the threshold of the door; footprints newly-formed, whose shape and size assured me were not my own.

I drew back to take a survey of the house in which George had evidently taken refuge. A brief inspection of the dwelling failed to afford any clue as to the character of the occupants. The blinds were drawn at every window, and, as might be expected at so early an hour, no light was anywhere visible. I knocked at the door once, twice, thrice. There was no reply. Then, seizing the knocker with a vigorous grasp, I executed a cannonade with it, loud enough to rouse not the inmates of that house only, but those of the whole street. At length my summons met with recognition from within. The door slowly opened. Fully expecting to meet my brother, his eyes aglow with passion, I drew back with arms upraised to protect myself from his rush, but nothing more terrible met my gaze than a venerable old man with silver hair, who shivered visibly as the cold wind drifted the snow into the passage. The lamp that he carried in his left hand, while he shielded it from the draught with his right, shone full on his face, which had such an air of quiet dignity that I felt quite ashamed of myself for having knocked so loudly. The disorder of his dress told me that he had but just risen from his bed.

The contrast between his grave demeanour and my excited bearing would have amused the spectator, had any been present. It struck me as a reversal of positions. I had expected to see a madman; he certainly took me for one, standing there as I did, breathless and silent in the wild snowy night, with my arms extended in front of me.

Too surprised to speak, I looked along the length of the passage as far as the kitchen, and then glanced up the staircase, but could not see George, nor any trace of him.

"Well, sir, may I ask why you rouse me thus in the dead of night?"

My eager impatience gave me no time for apology.

"I want my brother," I cried brusquely. "He came in here, I think."

"Your brother!" exclaimed the old man in a tone of surprise, that, if not genuine, was certainly well feigned. "Young man, you have been too long at the taverns this morning. There is no one in this house but myself."

It was difficult to refuse belief to this statement, for the old man had so grave and reverend an air that he might have stood for an image of Truth—of Truth in these later days, I mean, when, as is well known, he has become a little old and antiquated.

The Weird Picture

"You are mistaken," I replied, after listening vainly for some sound to proceed from within that might disprove his words. "Some one entered here only a minute or two ago, unknown, it may be, to you. These footprints are not mine."

But on looking downwards I found that a snow-wreath had drifted over the pavement, effectually covering the footsteps of myself as well as those of the refugee.

The old man smiled at my perplexity—a smile that was annoying, for it implied that he regarded me as a sad wine-bibber.

"Who is your brother?"

"Captain George Willard, of the—the——"

And then I stopped. I could perhaps have given him the titles of Cæsar's ancient legions, but of the name of my brother's modern regiment I was totally ignorant.

"I really don't know the name of the regiment." The old man smiled again, as well he might. "He's in India now—that is to say, he is when he's there, you know," I stammered, conscious that I was blundering terribly.

"Captain Willard? I have never heard the name before. He is not here. You have mistaken the house."

"Would you allow me to search the place?" I asked. "It is a bold request for a stranger to make, especially at this unearthly hour, and nothing but the certainty that my brother has concealed himself within induces me to make it. You see, he's a madman, and might do you harm." I thought this last would move him, but it only made matters worse. "I am certain I saw him enter this house. I am willing to pay you for your trouble if—if——"

I paused diffidently, for his reverend air did not harmonise well with the taking of a bribe. The old man's voice now assumed a tone of asperity. He was evidently getting tired of shivering half-dressed in the cold night air, and no wonder.

"I shall certainly *not* allow you to search the house. Your brother is not here. This door was double-locked when I went to bed. You heard me unlock it. How could he enter without the key. I must bid you good-night, for I see it's no use arguing with you in your present state of mind."

And, without more ado, the door was closed and locked, and I could hear the footsteps of the old man receding along the passage and ascending the stairs.

CHAPTER II THE VEILED LADY

Completely mystified, I stood motionless for a few moments. I was certain that my brother *had* entered the house. Perhaps, despite the old man's assertion as to the door having been closed and locked, he had really left it ajar, and George, perceiving this, had, in a fit of desperation, seized the occasion to enter and hide, resolving to remain there till I had taken my departure. He might even now be stealing a look from one of the windows to see whether the coast were clear.

I looked at the time and found that I had an hour before the departure of the London train. I determined to watch the house for a short time, and then, if my brother did not appear, to betake myself to the station. The portico of the adjoining house was the spot I selected for my vigil, a place which, while concealing my own presence, gave me a full view of the strange dwelling.

"I like that old man's face," I muttered, as I shook off the snow from my cloak, preparatory to folding it closer around me. "It's a noble one and a truthful one, or I am no judge of faces. I believe he knows nothing of George's entering; but, for all that, I am certain George *is* within. Much good I do by stopping here! George can easily leave by the rear—perhaps has left already. No matter. If he is going to London he must travel by the same train as I shall, and therefore I am sure to see him on the platform. If he is not going to London—well, so much the better for my hopes. I wonder who the old man is, and why he is all alone? Perhaps he's butler to a family who are spending their Christmas from home."

The cold was intense. The wind blew keenly. The drops of perspiration caused by my violent run seemed slowly turning to icicles on my chilled skin. I took a deep draught of the brandy and water in my flask.

Taking a cigar from my case, I contrived to light it after some difficulty, and puffed away vigorously. Then I referred to my watch. "Only ten minutes elapsed? I thought it was half an hour. Time lags. Who was it that said 'Time flies?' If the ass were here to-night in my place I rather fancy he would revoke his saying. Am I really awake, I

The Weird Picture

wonder? Can this be Daphne's wedding-morn, and am I here, at 3:30 A. M., in the snow at Dover, keeping watch on an absconding bridegroom? It must be a dream. I shall wake up presently at old Heidelberg, and hear the chapel-bell tinkling for matins."

Twenty minutes elapsed. "Nothing happening so far." I muttered "I'm a fool to stop here. This is growing ridiculous. I shall freeze if I remain much longer. I believe I *am* freezing—falling off into one of those sweet Russian slumbers that one reads of in books—or is it the brandy? Aha! what's that? Something is happening in the strange house, that's certain."

A light had appeared at an upper window, and was shining faintly out into the night. My curiosity was raised to a high pitch, and I stole from my hiding-place to get a nearer view. The old man had not been burning a light previously to my arrival, and if he had gone to bed, what did he want with one now? Excitement drove all the cold from my body, and a tingling warmth succeeded, as with a quickly-beating heart I waited for some development of this apparent mystery; and no words of mine can describe my feeling of surprise as I saw the shadow of a woman glide across the blind of the lighted window. The dark silhouette stood forth for a moment distinct on the illumined white, and then vanished.

Now there is nothing surprising in the shadow of a woman crossing a blind in the early hours of the morning; but when you have been assured a few minutes previously by the tenant of the house that there is no one within the building but himself, it *does* become a matter of surprise, and in the present case everything tended to invest the event with a mysterious air. The woman, to judge by the outline of her shadow, was habited as if for a journey, and this, added to the fact that the light was now extinguished, induced me to extend the duration of my watch. No one came out, however, and as the London train would be departing in fifteen minutes, I deliberated as to the wisdom of staying longer. If I missed the train I should not be in time for the wedding, using the word wedding in a provisional sense; for, from the strange proceedings of the last hour, doubts began to seize me as to whether it would ever come off.

I was loth to depart, but the desire of witnessing the scene that would take place at my uncle's house in the event of George's non-appearance decided my course of action. I determined to wait no longer, and, having applied both eye and ear to the keyhole of the strange house without learning anything thereby, I set off for the station at a running pace.

Having completely lost my bearings, and being a stranger to Dover, I knew not which way to turn, and would have fared ill but for the guidance of a friendly constable. I arrived two minutes before the departure of the train. On receiving my luggage from the porter, I said:

"You have not seen the gentleman?"

"No, sir. He's not in this train. Not been here since you left."

Having satisfied my curiosity by walking along the platform and scrutinising the occupants of every carriage, I returned, and said:

"Find me a first-class compartment, all to myself."

"One here, sir, with the brightest lamp in the whole train."

If mine were the brightest, I pity those who were cursed with the dullest.

"Put it in specially for you, sir."

The lies some people will tell for a few paltry pence! Taking a corner seat, and calling for a foot-warmer, I leaned out of the window, keeping a sharp look-out in case George should turn up on the platform at the last moment.

"I suppose my bro—the gentleman cannot now get to London before me?"

"Not unless he has gone by the other line."

"What other line?"

"The L. C. and D."

"What's that?"

"The L. C. and D.?" repeated the porter, apparently astounded that any one should be ignorant of the meaning of those initials. "Why, the London, Chatham and Dover Railway? Their last train left twenty minutes ago."

The Weird Picture

Here was a pretty piece of news! I could have written a long article on the numerous paved *viæ* that radiated from ancient Rome, but I knew next to nothing of the lines of railway that emanate from modern London, and the idea that there might be an iron road to the great city other than the one I was travelling by had never occurred to me.

"I have had my long watch for nothing," I muttered savagely. "While I was shivering in the cold, George, for all that I know to the contrary, may have left the house by a back door, and may now be bowling on his way to London. Well, anyhow, I am close on his heels. I shall arrive before the wedding, and you don't marry Daphne, George, till you have given an explanation of your strange conduct. Something wrong has been going on, else why should you avoid me?" And, with the usual sophistry employed by mortals when their self-interest is concerned, I tried to convince myself that in requiring an explanation from George I was actuated by a consideration for Daphne's welfare, and by no other motive.

The guard's whistle had sounded, and the locomotive in front had given a warning shriek, when the figure of a lady appearing within an archway just opposite the compartment I was in darted hurriedly across the platform.

"Ticket, if you please, miss. Thank you. Charing Cross—first-class. Jump in, please. Not a moment to lose."

The carriage-door was flung hastily open, and the lady, partly by her own exertions and partly aided by a gallant porter, entered, and seated herself at the other end of the compartment on the side opposite to me.

Now, although by no means so handsome a person as I could wish myself to be, I am nevertheless not quite so ugly as to inspire aversion in the mind of any dame, be she old or young; and yet the lady had no sooner set eyes upon me than she stared at me with terror, as if mine were the most repulsive countenance that had ever disgraced the Chamber of Horrors—conduct which somewhat nettled me, for, being a not ungallant youth, I was hoping for a charming *tête-á-tête* all the way to London.

She glanced at the door, as if desirous of quitting the compartment for another, but if such were her purpose it was baffled. The train was now fairly on the move, and we were steaming out of the station into the cold snow-dotted air of night. Willing or unwilling, the lady must submit to be my companion for the next two hours. Her obvious glances of distrust and alarm put me in a false position, and I at once determined to open a conversation for the purpose of showing what a good youth I was, and how little to be dreaded; but ere proceeding to this course I took, while pretending to read the newspaper, a steady view of my fair companion.

She was slender, graceful, lady-like, and tall, as a woman should be. With Byron, "I hate a dumpy woman." Her features seemed regular and handsome, but I could discern little of them through the thick veil she was wearing, save a pair of splendid dark eyes—the colour being a trifling deviation from my ideal of beauty, since Daphne's eyes were of a dark blue. A close-fitting bonnet covered her dark hair, and a fur boa was wrapped round her throat. A pair of little red leather shoes peeped out from beneath the skirts of a long fur-lined cloak. A muff contained her gloved hands.

"A handsome brunette," was my critique. "I shall be most happy to introduce myself. How shall I begin, and what shall I talk about? Ha! tell her I'm going to a wedding. Nothing unlocks a woman's tongue so easily as a wedding—barring, perhaps a sensational divorce."

Now, while I was casting about in my mind how to begin the conversation, my attention was suddenly attracted to something that she had thrust beneath the seat immediately on entering the compartment. Down from my hands dropped the newspaper at the sight I saw. That sight was nothing more than a valise partly hidden from view by her dress. But the portion that did display itself was marked by the letters "G.W.," thus corresponding exactly with the initials on the bag that my brother had carried! Was the bag, now peeping out at me from beneath the carriage-seat, the identical one that had disappeared with George into the mysterious house? My staring eyes were transferred from the lady's face to the valise, and from the valise to the lady's face, in swift alternation.

Then I suddenly recalled the silhouette on the blind, and, as I studied the lady's head-dress and figure, I thought if she were to pass between a light and the blind the contour of her shadow would not be very dissimilar from the one I had seen. Could she have issued from the strange house as soon as I had left it, and would that account for her haste and breathless state on entering the train? Her obvious mistrust of me, then, arose from a cause totally different from that of womanly timidity at being exposed alone to the company of a stranger. Yet, since we had never met each other before, how did she know I was a person to be avoided?

"Who are you," I muttered to myself, "and what relations do you hold with my brother? for some dealing you have with him, else—why that bag? Are you his first Daphne, I wonder, travelling to London to tell the second Daphne that you are an insurmountable obstacle to a certain wedding that's to come off this morning? A sort of sister-in-law to me, whose relationship has not been sanctioned by the Church? Has George been compromising himself? Let me try to find out."

I had a high idea of my own ability to "draw" people out. The sequel will show what a dexterous cross-examiner the law has lost in me.

"Do you object to smoking, madam?" I asked, by way of beginning a conversation.

In lieu of a verbal reply, the lady responded by a quick horizontal motion of her head, which sign presumably implied that she did not object.

Ours was not a smoking carriage. Perhaps it was this fact that suggested the idea of a cigar. Youth is defiant, and "Thou shalt not" is often the parent of "I will." So, with a sovereign contempt for the company's by-laws, I proceeded to light a cigar, remarking as I did so:

"It is a rough night for travelling."

Assent was given to this proposition by a vertical inclination of her head. No words as yet had passed her lips. This was certainly not very encouraging, but then perhaps I ought not to have spoken until after I had been addressed by her. It occurred to me that while courting the Muses at Heidelberg I had perhaps neglected the Graces, and had lost all notions of etiquette; and unlike the damsel in the opera of *Ruddigore*, I did not carry an etiquette-book about with me to consult in cases of doubt, or I might have referred to it, in the present instance, under the head of "Whether it be allowable for a gentleman travelling in company with an unknown lady to try to draw her into conversation?" Whether it be allowable or not, it is certainly the duty of every one to be considerate, so I pushed the foot-warmer to the feet of my fair companion, remarking:

"Your need is greater than mine."

I thought that this famous quotation from Elizabethan history would be sure to elicit some words. But no. Her thanks took the shape of a graceful inclination of her head, and at the same time the dark eyes sparkled through the veil, seeming to say: "You want to make me speak, but you shall not succeed." She had evidently recovered from her terror. Perseverance is an essential feature in my character. I determined to continue my crusade against her silence. I took from my portmanteau some English illustrated magazines that I had brought with me from Heidelberg to beguile the tedious hours of travelling, and, extending them to the stranger, said:

"May I offer you these?"

Now this proved a bad stroke of policy on my part, for the papers were accepted with a grave bow, and the lady at once immersed herself in their contents, and took no further notice of me.

"Well, if this doesn't beat all!" I muttered. "You're a cool one! Rude, too, for surely an act of courtesy is deserving of a few words of thanks?" It then occurred to me that perhaps she was aware I was suspicious of her, and had determined to baffle me by presenting a firm shield of silence to my conversational shafts, even when those shafts consisted of casual and trifling remarks.

In ordinary circumstances I should not, after so many rebuffs, have continued to press my attentions, but I regarded the singular events of the night as a justification for my persistency. I therefore seized the occasion when she chanced to look up from her reading to make another trial to elicit a word:

"Are you travelling far, madam?"

The Weird Picture

The magazine was laid aside, and, producing a card-case, she seemed to be making a selection from its contents. Presently she handed a card to me. It was inscribed with the following words, written evidently with a view to emergencies such as she was now in:

> "Pardon me if I have seemed rude. I thank you for your kind attentions, but being dumb from birth, I am unable to carry on a conversation.—DORA VANE."

Dumb from birth! This, then, was the key to her extraordinary silence. But immediately the thought succeeded, "Perhaps she is only fooling me." The words on the card might describe the actual state of the case, or they might be but the resources of a woman determined not to yield an inch to my curiosity—an adroit device to ward off all further questions.

"You evidently heard my last remark," I thought, "even above the roar and rattle of this train, and yet I was always given to understand that people who are dumb from birth are likewise deaf. You must be an exception. If you are dumb, as this card states, you must know the dumb alphabet. I'll try an experiment, and put you through a few paces."

I was quite familiar with the finger alphabet, having been taught it by my school friend Tracey, who used to hold many a silent conversation with me when lessons grew tedious. So, after attracting the lady's attention again, I held up my fingers and proceeded to frame a sentence expressive of my sympathy for her affliction. But she stared at me with absolutely no appreciation of my meaning, and the only conclusion I could draw from my experiment was that my companion was no more dumb than myself, but that for reasons of her own she did not want to have any conversation with me, and had hit upon this device for rendering any impossible.

"Tracey's system of dumb language doesn't seem to work upon the South Eastern line," I muttered, ruefully relinquishing my efforts. "Perhaps Tracey's was one of his own invention. Not likely, though; he hadn't the brains to invent anything."

Thus do we libel the absent!

Manifestly it was out of the question to attempt to gain any knowledge of the lady by compelling her to lift her veil and to reveal the part played by her in the mysterious business, though I was more than once tempted to commit this rash act. Such a proceeding, besides being very ungallant, might have resulted in my transference from the train to a police-cell. It was equally out of the question to seize on the valise and examine its contents. To press her with further questions would be as little to the purpose; for if, accepting her plea of dumbness, I committed them to paper, she would doubtless refuse to answer. All I could do was to sit in silence, resolving in my own mind not to lose sight of her on reaching London, but to follow her and find out if possible the place of her abode.

So I whiled away the rest of the journey in reading, or in trying to read, some Christmas annuals. Dora Vane, to give the lady the name she had claimed, having glanced through the magazines, was now apparently asleep in her corner of the compartment. It was only a feigned sleep however, for whenever I moved, she would give a start, plainly showing that she was suspicious of me.

The train was delayed considerably by the adverse weather, and it was not till past seven o'clock that we entered Charing Cross Station. I opened the carriage-door, and, emerging first, assisted the veiled lady to alight. Two points were noticeable in her behaviour while stepping from the train—the care with which she guarded the bag, and the care she took to avert her face from me. As there was not a soul on the platform to welcome her, I was on the point of proffering my services to escort her to her destination, but with a friendly nod to me she flitted off without a moment's delay to the end of the station, and then hailing a cab, was driven off. And it seemed to me that, instead of handing the driver a card with an address on it, as a dumb lady might naturally be supposed to do, she had conveyed her orders to him by word of mouth; but I was too far off to be certain of this. However, the moment the vehicle had disappeared beneath the archway I flung my portmanteau and person into a hansom, calling out to the driver:

"Follow the cab that has just left. Don't lose sight of it for a moment. Don't get in front, but keep behind it. I want to see where the lady gets out. You understand?"

The man nodded with a grin and a mystical remark about being "up to snuff," then he touched his horse's flank lightly with the whip, and we bowled out of the station in gallant style, following in the wake of the cab.

London lay beneath the murky gaslights wrapped in a winding-sheet of snow, not sufficiently deep, however, to stop vehicular traffic, though it retarded it to a considerable extent. The snow was an advantage in one respect, since it deadened the sound of the wheels of my hansom, and the wintry flakes still falling served as a sort of veil to conceal the fact that the cab was being followed.

The destination of the veiled lady appeared to be some place in North London, for the vehicle she was in proceeded along St. Martin's Lane, and turned up Long Acre into Drury Lane. Thence its progress was across Oxford Street, and up Southampton Row, till it finally turned into the Euston Road.

"I have it!" I cried. "She is going to Euston Station!"

All hope of tracing the mysterious lady to her final destination must now be abandoned. If she were going by train to some distant part of the country it was out of the question to follow her. I must be at the wedding. But I was wrong in my hasty surmise. The cab did not proceed to the station, but turned to the left along the Euston Road, stopping at last in front of an obscure public-house; and the cabman, flinging down the reins, descended from the box and entered the building.

"She surely isn't going to get out there," I thought. "Go on slowly," I said to my driver, who, peeping through the lid in the roof, asked whether he should proceed. We drove past the cab, and one glance sufficed to show that the vehicle was empty. My surprise found vent in language which the most charitably disposed of my friends could not have construed into a doxology.

"You've followed the wrong cab!" I cried savagely to my driver.

"Not I, governor. That 'ere is the vehicle you told me to follow: No. 2071. It's my pal's—Bill Whippam's—cab. That's him as is in the pub now—he's a rare 'un for the booze."

In a moment I was inside the public-house. The "rare 'un for the booze" was ringing a golden coin on the counter of the bar, as if to test its genuineness.

"A good 'un!" he cried delightedly, "Blow me tight if I didn't think it was a duffer for the minute! She's something like a fare, she is! A glass of the usual, Jim, with a little lemon and——"

"Where is your fare, cabby?" I demanded brusquely.

"What's that got to do with you, governor?" was the immediate retort.

"A good deal, as you'll see," I returned pulling out a notebook, and feigning to write therein. "Your number, I see, is 2071. I shall want you at Bow Street, to-morrow. Perhaps you are not aware that I am a detective, and that the lady you have aided to escape was to have been arrested this morning?"

The man assumed a more respectful demeanour.

"Axes your pardon, governor, but how was I to know that the lady was 'wanted,' and that a 'tec was arter her? The lady she says to me, she says——"

"What?" I interrupted. "She spoke to you, then? She wasn't dumb?"

"Dumb? No more than you are, governor. She says to me: 'Coachman, there's a gentleman a-follerin' o' me——'"

"That's not a verbatim report, I suppose?" I said with a smile.

"Wot's that?"

"Those were not her exact words, I mean?"

"They wos her exact words, governor," replied the cabman, with a solemnity befitting the witness-box, "so help me! 'There's a gentleman a-follerin' o' me,' she says, 'an admirer of mine pestering me with his attentions, and I want to get rid of him. Will you help me?' 'If I can, miss,' I says. 'Well, then,' she says, 'drive fast, and the moment you have turned the corner of Long Acre, draw up sharp. I shall get out there and then you drive on at once to Euston. He'll follow you, thinking I am still in the cab. Will you do this, and I'll give you a sovereign?' Of course I says, 'Yes.' She give me the quid, and directly I turned the corner at Long Acre she was out like a shot, almost afore I'd time to draw up. She darted down a side-street like winking, and I drove on according to orders."

I could not refrain from smiling at my own discomfiture. She had guessed that I would follow her, and in the long interval occupied by our railway journey she had marked out her plan of action, and had devised a pretty little stratagem into which I had readily fallen. Why should she act thus? Could this lady really be George in disguise? This idea was inspired by the belief that she had come from the same house in which he had taken refuge.

"What sort of a voice had she?" I asked. "Was it at all masculine?"

"Oh, jest!"

"Just what?"

"Maskyline."

"Do you know what masculine means?"

"Frightened-like, I expex you mean."

"You're a f— Was it at all like a man's voice?"

Cabby seemed to think this was a question that required a good deal of consideration before answering.

"Well, it might ha' bin a man's voice," he replied, speaking slowly. "Similarly it might not. It was a trifle hoarse for a woman, but I put that down to fright."

"You wouldn't swear in a court of law that it was a man's voice?"

"No, I wouldn't, governor. I'm pretty certain it was a woman."

No more was to be learned from the cabman, so, thanking him for his information, I quitted the tavern. As I entered the hansom, the driver exclaimed with a grin:

"Given you the slip, sir? Reckon she's a cough-drop, and no blooming kid!"

I turned a withering frown on this vulgar familiarity.

"Drive to Belgrave Square," I exclaimed loftily, "and look sharp."

I flung myself back in the cab in a fever-heat. "The affair is growing exciting," I muttered. "Was it a man or a woman? If a woman—who? If a man—was it George? if not—who? Did George travel by the other line, I wonder, and will he come this morning to claim his bride, or will he not? Will the veiled lady turn up in my uncle's drawing-room or at the altar-rails, and create some melodramatic scene? Patience—patience! we shall see. Daphne, you may yet be mine."

CHAPTER III THE WEDDING MORNING

The snow was lying thick upon the streets, and as I noticed the driver's difficulty in keeping his horse up, and in getting the vehicle along, I wondered how it would fare with the wedding carriages if the storm should continue. At last we reached my destination, and running up the steps I found myself being warmly greeted by my uncle, whose beaming face showed that nothing had as yet occurred to mar the happiness of the day.

"This *is* a pleasure, Frank," he said heartily. "I was beginning to think you would disappoint us after all. But you look frozen. Come to the fireside and get some food within you."

I returned his greeting, and, having been assured that Daphne was in the best of health, inquired after the bridegroom.

"When did you see George last?"

"Last night. He was here till eleven."

"And where did he go when he left?"

"To his hotel, I suppose," my uncle said, looking, as was natural, a little surprised at my question. "He's staying at the *Métropole*, you know."

Evidently George, on parting with my uncle and Daphne the previous night, had given no hint of his intended visit to Dover, but meant it to be a secret. I was in a dilemma. I hesitated to tell my uncle all that had happened, for George might have very good reasons for his mysterious journey, and reasons requiring secrecy to be observed about it. On the other hand, there were plenty of things to make me think that he was not playing an honourable game, and I did not feel justified in allowing him to lead Daphne to the altar without satisfying me that my uneasiness was not warranted by the facts. However, we were not at the church yet. So I resolved to be silent about the night's happenings until I had seen him and heard his version of them, or until the course of events should make it necessary for me to speak out.

I went upstairs to change my travelling suit for a garb more becoming the office of best man, and then joined my uncle in the large drawing-room, where the guests staying with him for the wedding were gathered.

"I had better make my way to the hotel, and go with George to the church," I said to my uncle.

"Surely that is unnecessary," he suggested. "He knows you are not likely to fail him, doesn't he?"

"Oh, yes," I answered. "I telegraphed yesterday to say I was on the way, so he won't be afraid of my disappointing him."

"Then go to the church from here," my uncle said. "You must have had all the snow you want, and if you go in the first carriage you will be in plenty of time. Let me introduce you to some of the guests."

The most noticeable of these was a young man who had been watching me with a curiously attentive gaze. He was slender and had a graceful presence. From the profusion of his dark hair, and a certain air of detachment from his surroundings, I judged him to be a genius of some sort, an artist, a poet, or a musician. I looked inquiringly at my uncle who introduced this mortal to me by the name of Angelo Vasari.

"A gentleman," he remarked, "to whom you owe some thanks."

"Indeed?" I said with some surprise, for I had never heard of him before. "Well, that is a debt I am always ready to pay. But why am I in Mr. Vasari's debt?"

"Daphne sent you a portrait of George the other day."

"She did."

"It was Mr. Vasari who painted it."

"Really?" I said, grasping his hand. "Then you must accept my congratulations as well as my thanks. The picture is a gem of art. Are you an artist?"

It struck me afterwards that to call a man's work a gem of art and then ask if he were an artist was somewhat silly, but he took no notice of the absurdity.

"An artist? Pardon me, no. But I hope to become one."

"You *are* one," said my uncle warmly. "Your picture in the Academy last year was second to none."

"The critics did not think so," he replied with a gloomy air.

"*Nil desperandum*," my uncle said cheerily. "They will think differently some day. Every great man has had the world against him at first."

"True, true," said the artist thoughtfully. "No one ever becomes great but by sorrow, humiliation, toil. Dante did not attain Paradise until he had passed through Hell and Purgatory."

He had splendid eyes I noticed, and any reference to his art made them shine like stars. Many of the women in the room looked at him admiringly, and I have no doubt that his melancholy utterances on fame, united to the attractive beauty of his face, made him a hero in their eyes. He interested me too, but all the while I was conscious of an undercurrent of antagonism to him. Nevertheless, after a martyrdom of handshaking and formal conversation with the various persons to whom my uncle insisted on presenting me, I drifted back to the ottoman where the artist was sitting, surrounded by a small circle of admirers to whom he was showing a portfolio of sketches.

"Ah, here is Mr. Willard," he said, looking at me as if desirous of attracting my attention. "These sketches may perhaps interest him. They are views of Rhineland. I think there is one of Heidelberg among them."

There was no running away from this invitation without seeming rude, so I sat down by the ottoman and prepared myself to express an admiration that I did not feel for the artist's productions.

"Oh, Mr. Vasari, what place is this?" cried a young lady, holding forward a view representing a picturesque old town by the side of a lake, with Alpine mountains rising around it.

"That? Ah, that is—er—Rivoli, a town among the Alps." He spoke with such hesitation as to give the impression that he was reluctant to reveal the name of the town. "It is my birthplace," he added briefly.

"Your birthplace? What a pretty town it is! It reminds one of some quaint poem of Longfellow's. Is it very old?"

"Centuries old. The people are quite mediæval—live in the past. Quite an old-world town, I assure you."

"The very place for an artist to be born in, then."

Vasari smiled mechanically, and seemed to be searching in his portfolio for something he had a difficulty in finding.

"Ah, here they are! Twelve sketches—heads. Friends of mine. Some of them are artists, wild Bohemians; and others are students, two or three hailing from Heidelberg. I think Mr. Willard will recognise a college-friend among the number."

I took the papers, which were attached to each other by a piece of red tape. The sketches were in ink, carefully finished, and represented twelve different faces of men whose ages might vary from twenty to forty years. Some had both beard and moustache; others moustaches only; and one there was without either. I surveyed them all critically, but failed to identify any one of them. Looking up from my task, I was startled to see Angelo's eyes fixed on my face with an expression that could not have been more painful if he had been a prisoner waiting for the verdict of the jury.

"I don't see any one I know here."

The artist's face relaxed from its set expression. My answer had pleased him.

"No, really?" he exclaimed in a tone of evident delight. "And that is your sincere belief? You do not recognise one of these heads?"

"I do not. May I inquire——?"

"Whether I have a motive in asking? Mr. Willard," he continued, with a gay laugh, to those near him, "with that profound knowledge of human nature to be acquired only within the secluded cloisters of a university, knows that the wise man never acts without motive."

"But do I really know one of these persons?" I exclaimed, irritated at this mystification.

"Eh—well, you say not," replied the artist with a most provoking smile. "I will take your word for it you do not."

And with these words he proceeded to gather up his sketches with the air of a man who wishes to say no more on the subject.

I have seen players, elate with victory, start up from the gambling-table when by one last turn of the wheel on which all depended they have won some enormous stake, and I was strangely reminded of their manner by Angelo's air as he rose after replacing the sketches in his portfolio.

"If every action has its motive," I thought, "what was that fellow's motive in asking me to study those twelve heads? Was he trying an experiment, and, if so, for what purpose? I do not know those faces, and yet one of them seemed to have a familiar look."

I had no leisure then to consider the matter further, for more pressing matters came to the front. My uncle, who had been absent from the room, came in and sought me with a troubled look upon his face.

"Here's a pretty pass, Frank!" he cried. "Stephen"—Stephen was his head-coachman—"says it is impossible for the horses to make their way through this thick snow, and I suppose he's right, as it must be two feet deep. It's out of the question to walk. What are we to do?"

I was the last person in the world to be asked this question, for, supposing I had known a way out of the difficulty, I am afraid I should have kept it a secret. For reasons of my own I was not at all averse to a postponement of the marriage, if only for one day.

A friend of my uncle's—a wealthy banker—now spoke:

"Did you not say that Captain Willard had a special license for this marriage?"

"To be sure! Of course he has!" replied my uncle, his countenance brightening: "I had forgotten it. Ah! I remember now laughing at what I thought his folly in procuring one, and at his words: 'In case of contingencies we can be married at any time and in any place.' He was right now, I see."

"Just so," returned the banker. "Let us hope that he will always have the same happy foresight. Well, if the mountain will not come to Mahomet, Mahomet must go to the mountain: If we cannot go to the church, the church must come to us. Our sweet little bride, after looking forward to this day as the happiest of her life, must not be disappointed. The marriage can take place in this drawing-room just as well as within the walls of St. Cyprian's, unless indeed Miss Leslie attaches a peculiar sanctity to a marriage contracted within the church. Let us send to St. Cyprian's, and ask Captain Willard and the Vicar to come here.

"I suppose there is no alternative," my uncle said, "short of a definite postponement of the wedding. But I'll see Daphne. It's time we should have been starting, so she's sure to be dressed. I'll go and fetch her now."

He hurried off, and in a few moments came back with Daphne on his arm, looking in her dainty wedding dress more beautiful than I had ever seen her.

She greeted me with so radiant a smile that the spectators might have taken me for the bridegroom.

So deep was my emotion at seeing once more, and on so dramatic an occasion, the face whose image for so many months had haunted my dreams, that oblivious of all my surroundings, I could do nothing but gaze at her with an earnest and wistful (some might have called it stupid) look until her laugh—how sweet and familiar it sounded!—recalled me to myself.

"Why, Frank, have you been in Germany so long that you have forgotten your native language? Speak to him in German, papa, and ask him if he is glad to see me."

I stammered out a few words of greeting. I do not remember what. The happiness of seeing her again was too great to allow of

The Weird Picture

conventional conversation and I drew back while the development of the situation was being explained to her.

She was, of course, terribly disappointed by the turn events were taking, but her courage was splendid. Although in her eyes a marriage in a drawing-room was a less sacred ceremony than one within consecrated walls, she seemed less cast down by the prospect than did her bridesmaids who were being deprived of the chance of displaying their toilettes to the fashionable congregation of St. Cyprian's, and thus, in the probable absence of reporters, they would have to forego the pleasure of reading in the society papers the description of their finery.

"Well, Daphne, what do you say?" her father asked.

"Let George be sent for," she replied. "I will do just as he wishes."

In my anxiety to see and question George I was on the point of starting for the church myself, but my uncle detained me.

"No, no," he said. "Why should you expose yourself unnecessarily to this storm? Hall can go," and I had no option but to submit, and my uncle's valet was despatched with orders to bring back both Captain Willard and a clergyman.

Meantime Daphne with fine courage went about among the guests, as if nothing unusual were happening. Presently she came up to me.

"Come and talk to me," she said. "It is so long since I saw you. I am sure you must have much to tell me."

One of the bridesmaids made room for her upon an ottoman, and I drew a chair near her.

The language of love was all but trembling on my lips as I gazed at her beautiful face—that face so associated with my life from very childhood that it seemed to belong to me by a sort of prescriptive right. It was well that others were by to check my ardour; but for their presence I believe I should have been kneeling once more at her feet. I had come back from Heidelberg with the intention of treating her with a frigid and distant courtesy—I would be an heroic martyr! But one glance of her gentle eyes had melted my icy armour, and here I was almost on the point of making love to her on the very morning of her intended marriage to another!

Daphne was her old sweet self, and chatted as freely as if we two were alone, and sitting once more at breakfast in my uncle's old home.

"You are looking very pale, Frank," she said. "When did you leave the Fatherland?"

"I left Heidelberg two days ago, and crossed the Channel last night. But tell me about George." It made me jealous to see how bright her eyes became at the mention of my brother's name. "I suppose the Indian sun hasn't made much difference in his appearance? How does he look?"

"He is very, very bronzed, and much handsomer, in my opinion, and—and—but there, you'll see him this morning in his uniform, and you'll confess he looks every inch a hero."

I had seen him that morning, though not in his uniform, with a red stain on his breast, trembling at sight of me, and I was very far from confessing that he looked every inch a hero; but, of course, I did not tell Daphne this.

"Where are you going to spend your honeymoon?"

"At Sydenham. A friend has lent us a pretty little villa there."

"And from there you are going——"

"To India? Yes. In February. Papa wants George to leave the army now, but I don't think he will."

"George is ambitious, you see," I returned, resenting in him that quality which was lacking in myself. "Medals, stars, titles, etc. Perhaps some day they'll make him a baronet—if he do but kill men enough, you know—and then you'll be Lady Willard. Ahem! I salute you Lady Willard, *in futuro*," I added with a low bow.

"Frank, don't be ridiculous! Mr. Vasari is watching you."

"Never mind Mr. Vasari! who's he! Let him watch. We are doing nothing wrong. Hang the fellow! How he stares! Vasari," I said, repeating the artist's patronymic—"an Italian evidently: and as an artist a dead failure, if I may judge by his own remarks."

"A dead failure?" returned Daphne, resenting the expression. "Well there's one of his pictures in the next room, and you can judge for yourself whether he's a failure or not. He isn't the equal of Doré or Alma Tadema yet, but he may be, for he has genius, and some day it will be recognised."

"Ah, let us hope it will," I replied drily, meaning, of course, the reverse. "Thou shalt have none other gods but me" is the language of every lover to his lady, and Daphne's interest in the artist moved my jealousy a little.

"I am not sure that Germany has improved you," Daphne said, looking at me critically, "but never mind that now. You haven't seen my wedding gifts. They are in the next room. Papa, I am going to show Frank my presents."

And holding her long train with one hand, Daphne rested the other on my arm, and conducted me beneath some heavy hangings to the next apartment. The gifts were arranged in tasteful order on a wide and spacious table.

"You see this picture? It is Mr. Vasari's gift—the work of his own hand. 'The Betrayal of Ariadne' he calls it. Don't you think she bears a resemblance to me?—her eyes and hair are just the colour of mine."

I was somewhat surprised to see a painting which, in my judgment, rose far above mediocrity. The composition was graceful and the colouring harmonious. This is what the canvas showed: Faint blue waves rippling over amber sands; a maiden kneeling thereby, with the teardrops falling from her eyes, her arms extended towards a distant galley on the sea; and a human figure advancing from a wood with a wreath in his hand.

My comprehension of the work was aided by its author, who had followed us from the drawing-room.

"Theseus deserts her," said he, "but amid the woodland foliage on the left you will see the beautiful Bacchus: he will kiss away her tears, and console her for the loss of her false hero. See! he bears in his hand a laurel-wreath: it is the crown of fame, whose sweet attraction will cause her first love to fade from her memory like a morning dream. The picture," he added with a curious smile, "is a sort of allegory to intimate that second love is preferable to the first."

Daphne gave an indignant little gasp at these words, and elevated her pretty eyebrows.

"I don't believe second love is better than the first; do you, Frank?"

Had Daphne absolutely forgotten the cause which had banished me so long from her presence that she could thus appeal to me? Or, remembering it, did she delight in reminding me of the power she held over me?

"The sun is still the sun at noon and at eventide," I replied; "but it is only in the early morning hours that his beams are supremely soft and lovely. So with love. Second love can never have the sweet freshness, the dewy fragrance peculiar to the first dawn of passion!"

"Was Ovid's 'Art of Love' included in your curriculum of this year?" asked Daphne with a smile. "You have come back from Heidelberg quite romantic. Where have you learnt to talk so prettily?"

"In the school of experience," I returned.

She glanced quickly at me, and I saw that she understood my meaning. Her eyes drooped, and a colour stole over her face and neck. Her confusion was too evident to escape the eye of the artist, but affecting not to notice it he turned on his heel and left us as quietly as he had come.

"After the rich display of presents here," said I to Daphne, "my gift will appear but as poor in comparison. I trust you will not estimate it solely by its monetary value."

I drew forth a jewel-case I had purchased at Heidelberg. The pressure of the spring revealed a golden bracelet set with violet amethysts.

"For me?" exclaimed Daphne, and the tone of her voice gave me a delicious thrill. "Oh, how sweet! None of my gifts will give me more pleasure. Shall I wear it this—this morning?"

There was a hesitation in the enunciation of the last words that touched me more than an avowal of love on her part could have done. I nodded, and aided her to clasp the golden circlet around her slender wrist.

"I will return your gift, Frank, though in a more simple way. You have no bouquet. Let me choose you one."

There was a vase of flowers hard by. Daphne selected some snowdrops, and, placing them on a pretty fern-leaf, attached them to my breast, bending so low in the act that my lips kissed the orange-blossoms and stephanotis that gleamed in her dark hair.

"Do you know what this fern-leaf signifies?" she said.

"No; what?" I asked.

"*Oblivion!*" she whispered; and then, like a beautiful fairy, she glided from the room. I understood her.

"Oblivion!" I muttered. "Well, yes; fern-leaf may signify that, but you have forgotten that the snowdrop is the emblem of hope."

CHAPTER IV WAITING

From Belgrave Square the walk to and from St. Cyprian's ordinarily takes about fifteen minutes. Allowing, say, another ten on account of the snowy weather, and it will be seen that the valet should have returned with George after the lapse of twenty-five minutes. Twenty-five minutes passed, however, thirty, thirty-five, and yet George and the valet failed to put in an appearance—a circumstance that caused the guests to look at each other in wonder.

"What can detain them?" muttered my uncle. "If George is at the church, why does he not come here? and if he has not yet arrived, why doesn't Hall hurry back and tell us so, instead of keeping us in this suspense? Confound the fellow!" he added; "I could have gone and come twice over in the time that he has taken."

He walked to the window and looked out. The snow was still falling. So thick and heavy were the whirling flakes that the air was quite darkened by them. Still the bridegroom came not. The conversation languished, the guests yawned, and Daphne's face assumed an anxious look.

"It doesn't matter about going to the church to-day," she said in a trembling voice, in answer to a question from a friend, "if I only have George here safe and well. I do wish he would come!" she said, her lip quivering. "Something must have happened to him."

"No, no, little woman, you mustn't get that idea into your head," her father said hastily. "His friends in that case would have — —"

At last!

There was a ringing of the door-bell, a rush of feet to the hall, and twenty voices exclaimed:

"Here they are!"

The plural pronoun, however, was not justified by the event, for, on opening the door, only one person was visible, and that was my uncle's valet.

The Weird Picture

"Why, what! How's this? Where's the Captain?" exclaimed my uncle. "Speak low," he added, pointing to the drawing-room, as a sign he did not wish Daphne to hear.

"Captain Willard is not at the church, sir," whispered the man.

"Not—at—the—church?" repeated my uncle, pausing with astonishment between each word.

"No, sir. At least he hadn't arrived by the time I left. I have been waiting for him, and that's what has made me so long."

"What time did you leave the church?"

"Quarter past ten."

"And he was to have been there at half past nine!" cried my uncle.

"The Vicar wishes to know what you are going to do," said the valet. "Is he or his curate to come and perform the ceremony here?"

"That's a question that cannot be settled without George," replied my uncle. "Of course he's only being delayed through the snow. It's extremely awkward. What *are* we to do?"

He paused a moment to reflect, and then said:

"Go to the church again. If the Captain is not there tell the verger to send him on here as soon as he arrives; and ask the Vicar or his assistant to step over here. Then hasten at once to the *Métropole*, and *see whether*—whether any accident has happened to my nephew. Hurry!"

We returned to the drawing-room and explained matters to Daphne, my uncle striving to put the best complexion he could upon the case.

"It's only the stress of weather that's delaying him," he remarked. "George very likely spent last night with a friend—a brother officer, probably—who lives in the suburbs. The cab ordered to convey him this morning is unable to proceed, and so he's obliged to tramp on foot through twenty-five inches of snow. No wonder he's late, then. There's nothing to be alarmed at, little woman."

I leave the reader to imagine my state of excitement. Could it be that George was actually deserting Daphne? Was Fate after all reserving her for me?—a thought that caused my blood to course like a swift

The Weird Picture

fire through vein and artery. I turned my flushed face to the bride. Poor Daphne! She sat there, silent and pale, with her hand clasping that of an aged lady-friend who was trying to assure her that there was nothing to be alarmed at. My selfish heart was touched by the sad picture. Had the time come for me to give an account of my meeting with George at Dover? Not yet. I resolved to await the return of the valet first.

Dark, and ever darker grew the gloom outside. It was impossible to keep up a pretence of conversation. Silence fell over us all, and soon nothing was to be heard but the sound of the embers glowing and crackling in the grate, and the painful ticking of the clock on the mantelshelf. The waxen tapers in the chandeliers twinkled gaily to their reflections in the mirrors, as if they enjoyed the victory they were gaining over the daylight without. And still the bridegroom came not.

Presently there was another furious ring of the bell at the hall door, and again there was a rush of feet and a score of voices exclaiming "Here they are!"

"Who is it?" said Daphne, trembling like a leaf.

"I think," replied I, "that I can hear them saying a name that sounds very like Chunda."

"Chunda? That's George's native servant. Ask him to come here, Frank."

The visitor, having shaken the snow from his garments, was conducted—almost pushed—into the drawing-room, and turned out to be a dusky Hindoo in English garb. He was followed by my uncle's valet, who had met him on the way.

"Chunda," said Daphne, addressing the Hindoo, "where is Captain Willard?"

"I do not know, Miss Daphne," returned he, in a tone in which surprise and perplexity were blended. "Is he not here? He has been absent from the hotel all night."

"Absent from the hotel all night?"

The Weird Picture

"Yes, Miss Daphne. He left the *Métropole* about seven o'clock last night, saying he was going to spend the evening in Belgrave Square, and would be back about eleven. He never came back."

"Then he must be at Sydenham," said Daphne.

"So I thought," continued the Hindoo; "and as he had told me that he had some orders which he particularly wished me to attend to before the wedding took place, I set off for Sydenham, and waked up the housekeeper. But the Captain wasn't there, she said. I walked back to London—cold work it was, too, through the snow. But the Captain was not at the hotel when I got there; and had not been in while I was there, the hall-porter said. I found his bed untouched. I waited some time, and then, thinking there must be something wrong, I came here."

The artist now stepped forward into the circle which had been gradually forming around the Hindoo.

"I am afraid," he said, "that I must make a statement now that I would have made before but for the fear of agitating Miss Leslie; it is this: Last night, about twelve o'clock, happening to be at Charing Cross Station, I saw Captain Willard take the express for Dover. Before I could get near enough to speak with him the train was off. I was surprised to see him taking such a journey only a few hours before his intended wedding. 'But perhaps,' I thought, 'he has some urgent business to do at Dover connected with the marriage, and will return by an early train.'"

"It is true," I said in a voice too low to reach Daphne's ear. "As I was landing from the packet-boat this morning I saw George on the pier at Dover, but not to speak to. He avoided me—fled from me, in fact."

My wondering uncle gazed at Angelo and myself, as if not quite comprehending the import of our words.

"Do you mean to say that George has deserted her?" he gasped. "I will not believe it."

Once more the hall-bell rang, causing an additional wave of excitement to pass over the company. Alas! it was not George who rang, but that bearer of joy and sorrow, the postman, with a letter directed to "Miss D. Leslie."

The Weird Picture

"It is George's handwriting," said Daphne. "Read it for me, papa."

My uncle took the letter, and turned it over as suspiciously as Cardinal de Medici may have done with an epistle from Pope Borgia in the old Italian days when clerical dignitaries enlivened the monotony of their ecclesiastical duties by taking off their enemies with poison concealed in a glove, a flower, or a letter. At length, breaking the seal amid a deep silence, he proceeded to unfold the letter, and as he mastered its contents his face darkened.

"What does George say?" asked Daphne, with her hand pressed to her beating heart.

"He says," replied her father, not wishing to let the whole truth burst on her at once, "that he regrets having to defer his wedding for a few days, but as soon as——"

"That's not it! You are deceiving me, papa! Give me the letter. I will have it—it is mine!"

With difficulty she rose to her feet, trembling all over, and before my uncle could prevent her she had snatched the letter from him, and, oblivious of the company, read out each word aloud:

> "DEAREST DAPHNE—Break not your heart over what is as sad to me as you. That has occurred which compels me to leave you forever. What the terrible circumstance is that forces me to this step I dare not say. It has occurred only within the past hour. I can never hope to look upon your face again. We must part forever. By the time you receive this I shall be crossing the Channel. Do not seek for me: you will never find me. In some secluded part of Europe I shall live out my days a lonely recluse. Try to believe that this is all for the best, and forget that there ever lived such a one as
>
>   "GEORGE WILLARD."

Daphne would have fallen to the floor if some one had not caught her in his arms. She lay cradled within the artist's embrace, her fair face resting on his breast, and his arms wound round her slender figure. Brief as was this embrace, it was nevertheless of sufficient duration to make me hate him—for a time, at least.

Tenderly he laid the figure of my cousin on an ottoman. The ladies of the assembly crowded round, and applied such remedies as were at hand to restore her from her swoon. Angelo stood by the couch with folded arms, gazing at the prostrate form with a wistful look.

"Beautiful! What a model for an artist!" he murmured.

He must have had a strange taste in the selection of his subjects if he could have found pleasure in painting Daphne as she was just then. Her face had parted with its bright, fresh beauty, and had assumed the sharp and careworn look of age. Her bridal dress seemed almost to have lost its sheen: the white flowers in her hair to have become emblems of death.

Presently the artist raised his eyes with a light as of triumph in them; they met mine, and for a few seconds we stood looking at each other; and then I learned that some one besides myself had been wishing that George would never return. At length Daphne opened her eyes and spoke:

"It can't be true, it can't be true! George would never treat me like this. Oh, what shall I do?" and at last she broke down in a passion of tears, terrible to witness, and we men, conscious of our impotence in face of such overwhelming grief, stole from the room and left her to the women.

Much as the guests would have liked to relieve my uncle of the embarrassment of their presence in these unforeseen circumstances of sorrow, they were prevented from doing so by the storm, which, having raged for many hours, rendered locomotion out of doors extremely difficult. My uncle made no excuses for his withdrawal from the company, and as soon as I could do so, I too followed him to his library, where I found him sitting with Angelo Vasari.

"I suppose," the latter was saying, "that Captain Willard is not very well known in Paris or London?"

A curious question this! What could it possibly matter to the artist whether George was or was not well known in Paris or London? Yet here he was putting the question with a similar show of eagerness as when asking me to study the twelve facial sketches.

The Weird Picture

"I doubt," replied my uncle, "whether there are six people in Europe who know him—know him intimately, that is. As a young man he graduated at Upsala——"

"In Sweden, you know," I interjected, for the enlightenment of the artist, who seemed to resent this attempt of mine to teach him geography.

"And then," continued my uncle, "after a brief interval in England he sailed for India, where he has been ever since till the last two months."

"And it was during that brief interval in England, I suppose," said Angelo, "that he became engaged to Miss Leslie?"

"Just so."

"And Captain Willard did not return to England, you say, till the preparations for his marriage brought him over?"

"You have it. Daphne and I took a voyage to India last winter, and spent several weeks with George at Poonah; and a very happy time we had of it, too. None could ever have guessed that their engagement would come to such an ending as this."

"*Ah!*"

My uncle's replies seemed to have given great satisfaction to the artist.

"You are quite a prophet," I said to the latter. "Your wedding gift, the picture, seems like a prediction of what happened to-day. Were you prepared for the event?"

"To a certain extent—yes," replied Angelo.

"Had you any reason for your belief other than George's strange appearance at Charing Cross last night?"

"Well, a day or two after I was introduced to Captain Willard, I congratulated him on his approaching marriage. His face changed at once from gay to grave. 'Don't allude to it,' he said; 'it may, perhaps, never take place.' I thought this strange language from one who had come all the way from India to be married, and asked him to explain himself, but he was silent. Since then, on one or two occasions when

I have alluded to the wedding he would become melancholy in an instant; and I began to surmise that all was not right."

"Your surmises were only too well founded," I said.

And I began to tell the story of my night adventure. For a long time we sat discussing the affair, and devising all kinds of theories to account for George's flight.

"I can't understand it at all," said my perplexed uncle. "There was nothing strange or unusual in his manner last night when he left us. He talked in the most natural way of the wedding—said he would be at the church by 9:30 prompt. And yet he must have written that letter soon after he parted from us, for he left here about ten o'clock, and it is dated, you see, just an hour later."

"And he must have posted it before midnight, too," said Angelo, "or it would not have arrived here by the morning post. Strange things must have happened in those two hours to change the current of his life."

Shortly afterwards he rose, saying with a smile, "Art is long, and time is fleeting."

"Il Divino cannot leave his easel, you see," remarked my uncle, after the departure of the artist, "not even for one day."

"Il Divino? Who's he?" I returned stupidly.

"Angelo, to be sure."

"Is that his *nom—de—de—*brush?" I couldn't think of the French word, so I used the English one instead.

"It's a nickname his enemies have given him by antiphrasis, because he's so unlike Raphael."

"Can't leave his easel," I said, repeating my uncle's words. "Do you mean to say he is going to work on a gloomy day like this? Why, he won't be able to see, let alone paint."

"*Nulla dies sine lineâ*, you know. He lives in his studio, and can hardly be persuaded to leave it. It's a marvel he remained here so long this morning. He's dying to make a name."

"Do you think he will?"

"Can't say, I'm sure. It will not be for want of toil and study if he doesn't. He is occupied now on a great work which he fondly hopes will reverse the previous judgment of art-critics respecting his abilities."

"What is this great work?"

"'The Fall of Cæsar' I think he calls it, or 'The Triumph of Cæsar,' or—or something of the sort. I know it's a classical subject."

And after this we relapsed into silence.

I shall never forget the melancholy and gloom of that day as we sat, my uncle and I, in the darkening room, each occupied with his own thoughts. The non-return of my brother did not afford me the happiness I had expected, for it was counterbalanced by Daphne's exquisite grief, which was a source of real pain to me. Having wished so earnestly that the marriage might not come off, I felt as if I were in some way responsible for my brother's non-appearance.

Next day I took an early train for Dover, with the intention of calling at the strange house, and of questioning its silver-haired occupant, who, I was now inclined to believe, knew more of the mystery than he had cared to reveal. Not till I had reached the Kentish sea-town was it suddenly forced upon me that in my haste and excitement I had forgotten to note the name of the street in which the strange house was situated; nor did I even know which way to turn on leaving the station.

The cranial development known to phrenologists as the bump of locality is not my strong point. For several hours I walked the streets of the town, knocking at the door now of this house and now of that, vainly believing that at last I had discovered what I sought. I lived at the hotel a week, and spent a considerable portion of each day in the streets, and on the pier and cliffs, thinking I might meet the old man taking his walks abroad; but all my endeavors to discover him were attended with failure. The silver-haired old man, the mysterious house, the veiled lady, my brother George—all were gone, and seemed now to have had no more reality than the shadows of a dream. Once they were, now they are not.

I will not weary the reader with an account of the investigations carried on for many weeks by my uncle and myself. It will be sufficient to say that our endeavors to discover the cause of George's flight and to trace his whereabouts were fruitless.

"Heaviness may endure for a night, but joy cometh in the morning." Daphne's morning, however, was a long time in coming and my uncle proposed to hasten its advent by foreign travel.

"A Continental tour will do her good," he remarked to me. "We will visit France, Spain, Italy. The glitter of foreign cities will perhaps help to remove her grief. You must come with us, Frank; we shall need you. A young fellow like you will be able to enliven and interest her more than any lady companion could do—certainly more than her old father, who is often prosy and dull, I fear. Being her cousin, you can talk to her with a freedom and an ease that in any other young man would be familiarity. And for heaven's sake try to make her forget her grief. Her sad face and thin wasted figure cut me to the heart. You do not mind giving up Heidelberg for a time?"

It would require no great sacrifice on the part of any young man to leave the cloisters of a university in order to escort a beautiful girl through Europe, so I gladly assented to my uncle's proposition, resolving, for my own sake, to try to make Daphne forget her grief. She yielded a willing acquiescence to the project of a Continental tour. Poor girl! She was in so dull and passive a state of mind that if we had proposed a voyage of discovery to the North Pole she would have offered no objection. So, late in March, we left England, and by the end of the summer had signed our names in half the hotel books of Europe.

CHAPTER V THE ARTIST PAINTS A NOTABLE PICTURE

Night was just fading from the Alpine heights that girdle the quaint old town of Rivoli in the canton of Ticino. Two men, issuing from the entrance of a châlet perched like an eagle's nest on the jutting crag of a mountain far above the valley, paused to admire the grandeur of the scene. These persons were my uncle and myself, and we had risen at this early hour in order to witness that most beautiful of sights in Switzerland, sunrise. From the terrace of the châlet we watched the dim Alpine panorama gradually emerge from the shadowy reign of night. Silent and majestic from out the dark "sea of pines" the mountains arose to view, their icy peaks glittering with rosy-tinted hues in the soft, beautiful light that was now suffusing the sky.

"By Jove, what a glorious sight!" I exclaimed enthusiastically.

"Yes, for a poet or painter," replied my uncle, who, amid the loveliest scenery of Switzerland, sighed for the shady side of Pall Mall.

"That's a pretty little town down there," I continued, gazing at the spires of Rivoli. It lay at our feet in the valley beneath, so far down that it seemed like a toy city. "How the mountains seem to isolate it from the rest of the world! Rivoli? Rivoli?" I muttered. "I have never heard of the place before," unconsciously telling a falsehood. "I suppose it's quite out of the track of the ordinary tourist?"

"Quite. We shall not see many specimens of that genus in the everlasting suit of grey tweed."

"What's that rough stone building to the right of us?" I said. "There! just by the cascade. A hermit's grotto?"

"Looks like it. A rather damp quarter for his saint-ship, eh? I suppose in this secluded part of Europe many hermits must have lived out their lonely days, and— —"

He paused, stopped by the curious look on my face. "What is the matter, Frank?"

"Do you know that your last remark is singularly like an expression in George's letter of last Christmas?" and I repeated the passage, for every word of that epistle was engraved on my mind.

"Hum! so it is. A singular coincidence of language. 'Some secluded part of Europe,'" he added, quoting George's words. "It would be difficult to find a more secluded spot than Rivoli."

It was now August, and the object for which our tour had been undertaken—the removal of Daphne's grief—seemed to be accomplished. We had visited France, Spain and Italy. In the early days of our tour nothing could move her from the dull lethargy which had been her normal state since that ill-starred Christmas morning; but gradually, as week after week glided by, she began to take an interest, faint and languid enough at first, in the historic places through which we were passing, till at length she seemed to have become her old bright self once more. The colour had returned to her cheek and the smile to her lip. Whether this happier condition arose from a determination to forget her trouble and adapt herself to changed circumstances, or whether it was due to the secret hope that George might yet return to her with his name cleared from the dark shadow resting on it, I could not decide; she never alluded to him, and on our part, my uncle and myself made it a point not to mention his name in her presence. She treated me with the same sweet familiar freedom as of old, so that I found it difficult to believe that for three years I had been exiled from her at Heidelberg.

During our tour I had never betrayed by word or by act the state of my feelings toward Daphne. Satisfied with the pleasure of daily companionship with her, I was quite content to bide my time patiently, and wait for some clear indication that George had passed—not from her memory, for that could never happen, but from her affections, before venturing to express for the second time the love I had never ceased to bear.

We had arrived at Rivoli only the preceding evening, and were staying at a châlet belonging to a Swiss gentleman who had let it to us for a month. He had left behind one member of his household to supplement our own servants—an agreeable, talkative old woman, who had received us with an effusive hospitality.

The Weird Picture

A light step now sounded on the terrace and Daphne's sweet voice greeted us.

"I shall not say good-morning, for you don't deserve it. Why didn't you call me earlier, papa, that I too might have seen the sun rise?"

Her father kissed her hands as though she were some princess.

"Because I knew you would be tired after the jolting of that horrible diligence yesterday," he said; "and so I let you rest. But you have no hat, and the mornings here are chilly."

I ran indoors, and returned with a heavy wrap which I drew round her head and neck.

"Well, Daphne," my uncle said, waving his hand towards the châlet, "what do you think of our home for the next month?"

"It is lovely," she said, moving backward from the house to survey it better. "Just the place to dream away a summer holiday in."

It was indeed as picturesque a structure as could be found on a day's march through Switzerland. It was composed of fir-wood painted red, and the pretty low gallery which ran completely round it, together with the projecting roof, was adorned with the richest carvings.

"I see," remarked my uncle, "that the piety of the architect has decorated the facade with Scriptural texts—a common custom about here, I have observed. All in Latin—from the Vulgate, I suppose. Now, Daphne, show us your scholarship by translating them. What does the word over the entrance mean?"

"Over the entrance?" said Daphne, turning her eyes upon the carved porch. "'Reveniet;' that means 'He shall return.'"

Only one Latin word, and yet it had the power to make me tremble! During our Continental tour I had been continually haunted by the idea that in the next city or castle, or cathedral or palace, or ruin or theatre visited by us we should come face to face with George—an issue fraught with peril to my love enterprise. Though I was unable to assign any definite reason for it, this opinion had gained strength since our arrival at Rivoli.

The Weird Picture

He shall return!

Yes; there in letters of gold, that gleamed like fire in the rays of the morning sun, was the startling answer to the one question forever haunting my mind. A white cloud floating upwards from the valley at this juncture cast a cold shadow over us, and gave me an eerie sensation, as if George himself in ghostly form were passing by.

"He shall return!" repeated my uncle, in a vein of pleasantry that jarred on Daphne's feelings. "And who is it that shall return?"

"O papa! how can you? You know it refers to the millennium. I declare you and Frank are quite like two pagans! I don't believe you have entered a church for the purpose of worship since we first set foot on the Continent."

"Frank and I never go to church in Catholic countries. It's our way of showing our Protestantism."

Daphne turned from her irreverent parent, and became absorbed in the contemplation of the scenery.

"What peak is that to the left, Frank?"

"That," I replied, "is the Silver Horn of the Jungfrau."

And I proceeded to deliver a topographical lecture, interwoven with graceful legends and poetic quotations, specially prepared for this occasion on the previous night, in order that I might shine in Daphne's eyes as a hero of knowledge. A sudden exclamation from her, however, put a period to my eloquence.

"Who is this coming up the mountain-path? I have been watching him for a long time."

Whoever the person was, he ascended the mountain with the freedom of one to whom the path was perfectly familiar, selecting his way among the mossy boulders and grass-hidden pools without a moment's hesitation, and springing from crag to crag with the agility of a chamois-hunter.

"'*Excelsior*' evidently is his motto," said I. "Longfellow's young man, perhaps, 'mid snow and ice.'"

The Weird Picture

"Minus the 'banner with the strange device,'" returned my uncle. "Hanged if it isn't Il Divino! How comes he to be here?"

It was indeed the divine one, looking in the picturesque costume he was wearing more handsome and romantic than ever. A sombrero was slouched with easy negligence over his broad white brow, and a long cloak dropped gracefully from his shoulders. He had all the air of a man who, conscious of his personal charms, is determined to make the best use of them.

The look of pleasure that mantled Daphne's face had so disturbing an effect on my spirits that it was as much as I could do to treat the artist with ordinary civility.

"Angelo," cried my uncle after the first greetings were over, "I'm delighted to see you! But tell us how you came to be here, for I thought that outside of Switzerland few beside myself knew of the existence of this secluded valley."

"Rivoli the Beautiful is my native place," replied Angelo. Why had not Fate fixed his nativity at the sixth cataract of the Nile?

"I thought you were an Italian," I remarked frigidly.

"My parents were both Italians," replied the artist, "but I was born in that cottage;" and he pointed far down the valley to a tenement on which Daphne gazed with interest, while I, staring in a different direction, tried to catch a glimpse of a steel-blue lake through a veil of floating mist. "I have no parents nor any relations left. My old nurse still lives; and I make a point of visiting Rivoli each year to breathe the mountain air, and to see that the old dame does not want."

"A very pious and proper proceeding on your part," I remarked.

This was meant for sarcasm, but it did not seem to disturb the artist in the least. The look of disapproval on Daphne's face did not tend to tranquillise my mind.

"I arrived here only last night," Angelo continued, "and, hearing that a lady and two Englishmen had taken up their residence at the Châlet Varina, I guessed at once from the description who they were. I determined to call in the morning to present my compliments to

Miss Leslie and her father"—he omitted me from his congratulations—"and to ask her to accept these flowers."

And with a graceful bow he presented to her a beautiful bouquet. I thought Daphne quite ridiculous in her admiration of it.

"O, how pretty!" she cried. "Thank you very much, Mr. Vasari. I am so fond of flowers. Smell how sweet they are, Frank." And she actually held the odious gift close to my nostrils for my appreciation. "Aren't they sweet?"

"Very," I said drily.

"Aren't these violets lovely, papa?" she said, appealing to her father for the appreciation she had failed to elicit from me.

"Purple," replied her republican parent, who was accustomed to spell king with a small *k*, and people with a capital *p*, "is my aversion, being the colour and emblem of tyrants and kings."

"How absurd you are, papa!" returned she. "What is your favorite colour, Mr. Vasari?"

"That which sparkles on the cheek of Beauty," replied the idiot, with his eyes fixed on my cousin's face. And certainly no colour could be more beautiful than Daphne's sweet blush at that moment, and my jealousy redoubled toward the person who had called it forth. "Do you understand the language of flowers, Miss Leslie?"

"Only a very little; do you, Frank?"

"Not I," I answered curtly. "I consider it an absurd study, if you wish for my opinion."

"You must permit me to teach you," said Angelo to Daphne, completely ignoring my remark.

"I shall be very glad to learn," was the reply.

I gasped for breath. The fellow was actually making love to her before my very eyes! The cool assurance with which he spoke and the graceful serenity with which he ignored my presence were quite maddening. Here was I, who had been Daphne's sole companion for five months, completely thrown into the shade by a foreigner who had been in her presence only as many minutes.

The Weird Picture

"And so Rivoli is your native place," said Daphne. "Why, of course, I have heard you say so many a time. How stupid of me to have forgotten! I remember now to have seen a sketch of it in your portfolio. How lucky, papa, that you hit on this spot! You must be familiar, Mr. Vasari, with every stream and crag and cascade about here—with every turn and wind of this valley; you must serve us now and then in the capacity of guide."

"I shall esteem it an honour to do so," he returned.

Matters were growing worse. The lamp that had so long illumined Daphne's path was now under a bushel.

"Look at those wreaths of silvery mist floating across the valley!" said she.

"'As if some angels in their upward flight
Had left their mantles floating in mid-air,'"

said I. I quoted this to show that there were other poetic souls in existence besides Angelo; but my quotation was lost on Daphne.

"And what a lovely violet hue those distant mountains have!" she continued. "I wonder, Mr. Vasari, you never tried to transfer this scene to canvas."

"Canvas? Ah, that reminds me," said my uncle. "I have been very remiss in not complimenting you upon the success of your picture. We shall yet have the Pope requesting your aid in adorning the Vatican with painted frescoes. I understand that your 'Fall of Cæsar' is *the* picture of Paris this season."

This allusion did not seem pleasing to the artist, for a peculiar expression darkened his face for a moment, like the transient sweeping of a shadow over a sunny landscape.

"It is true," he murmured, with real or simulant modesty, "that my picture has been very much admired. It was exhibited one day; the next, my name was in all the newspapers. Like Byron I woke up one morning to find myself famous. I have realized a considerable sum of money by exhibiting the picture, and as a consequence have become courted by people who discover virtues in me now they never perceived before."

The Weird Picture

"'Give me gold, and by that rule
Who will say I am a fool?'"

murmured my uncle. "Just so. Gold is a lamp that lights up virtues that without it are unseen."

I regret to say that I did not view Angelo with any more favour for his rising reputation as an artist, and Daphne's evident delight at his success added fresh fuel to my smouldering jealousy.

"What, Mr. Vasari! Have you painted a picture that is creating a sensation at Paris? Why did you not tell of this before, papa? This is the first that Frank and I have heard of it."

It was, but it was far from being the last we were to hear of the artist's memorable masterpiece.

"Well, you see," my uncle replied apologetically, "I did not know it myself till last night, when I saw it in the *Standard*. You were asleep at the time, and I take it you didn't want me to call you out of bed to tell you of it."

At the mention of the word *Standard*, there appeared on the artist's face the same peculiar expression that I had previously noticed.

"*Standard, Standard!*" he muttered reflectively. "Why, that's the—" He stopped, and added abruptly, "Do you have the *Standard* sent to you?"

"It *has* been sent to me. Why?"

"O, nothing, nothing," replied Angelo; "nothing at all. It's a—a Conservative journal, and I know—at least, I believe—you're a Radical."

"A Radical. Noble profession!" responded my uncle.

"Yes; that's all it is—profession!" laughed Daphne, whose political ideals differed from those of her father.

"The *Standard* is not my paper, as you very well know," said my uncle, grandly ignoring his daughter's remark. "It's the butler's fault that it is here. I wrote telling him to forward to Rivoli a file of newspapers for June and July. As I forgot to specify what paper, the rascal has sent me the *Standard*."

"For, being a good old Tory," said Daphne, "he thought it well to administer an antidote to your Radicalism. I think his act deserves commendation."

"June and July," muttered Angelo. "What did you think of the critique on my picture?"

"Didn't know there was a critique on it. In fact, I haven't read the papers yet. I was simply untying the parcel last night, when my eye was caught by a paragraph to the effect that 'Intending visitors to Paris should not fail to visit the Vasari Art Gallery, and view Vasari's magnificent production, "The Fall of Cæsar," the great picture of the year, already visited by—' I forget how many thousand persons."

Angelo smiled.

"That is my agent's advertisement. Yes, the number of persons to see it has been enormous. You haven't read, then, the criticism on it in the issue of July 2nd?"

"That's a pleasure I have in store."

"Nor Mr. Willard?" he added, turning to me.

"Not yet. I may read it," I replied, as if the act would be one of magnificent condescension on my part, whereas, if the truth must be told, I was inwardly burning to peruse the article in question.

"A—ah!"

And the prolonging of this little syllable was marked by a decided tone of satisfaction.

"And have you really made a great name?" said Daphne, looking admiringly at the artist. "I am so glad! I always knew your efforts would meet with success. But tell me all about your picture. What is the subject?"

"The 'Fall of Cæsar.' It represents the hero, as we may suppose him to have been a few minutes after his death, lying at the base of Pompey's statue. There are no other figures in the picture besides the two I have mentioned, Cæsar and Pompey. Some columns in the background complete the scene. It is a very simple tableau, and no one has been more surprised than myself at the encomiums that have been lavished upon it."

"Did the work take you long?"

"The actual canvas-work—no; the elaboration of the idea which led to the work—yes; for it has been the outcome of a lifetime of thought." He spoke with all the air of an octogenarian. "I began the work about a year ago, a year this autumn, and finished it last—last Christmas," he hesitated at the word, as if reluctant to renew Daphne's sad memories, "and exhibited it at Paris in the beginning of spring."

"At Paris? We were at Paris in the beginning of spring. It is strange we should have missed you."

"When did you leave Paris?"

"March 31st—wasn't it, Frank?"

"Ah! *we*—" he stopped to change the plural pronoun to the singular, but, rapid as the correction was, it did not escape my notice—"I did not arrive in Paris till April 1st."

"The very day after we left. How odd! But why did you exhibit your picture in Paris, and not in London?"

"A prophet hath no honour in his own country," replied Angelo. "I think I may speak of England as my country, from the length of time I have lived in it. London has disappointed me so often that I resolved to try Paris this year. So I hired a gallery, and exhibited 'The Fall of Cæsar,' with some other pictorial compositions of mine. The people of Paris seem more appreciative of my talent—if I may be pardoned for using the word—than the Londoners."

"I have always considered the French a superficial people," I interjected.

"Oh no, they are not," returned the artist quietly.

"Of course they are not? How can you say so?" said Daphne, defending the artist with more warmth than was pleasant to me. "We must see your picture, Mr. Vasari, when we come to Paris."

"I am afraid it is impossible for you to see it, Miss Leslie," he replied, "unless you are acquainted with the Baron de Argandarez, an old hidalgo of Aragon. He purchased it from me for a sum far surpassing my wildest expectations. It now adorns the walls of his ancestral castle, and I have no more to do with it."

"Oh, what a pity!" cried Daphne, in a tone of sincere regret. "I *am* disappointed. Why, it seems as if, after achieving a brilliant success, you are determined that your best friends shall not share in your triumph!"

"Yes," chimed in my uncle, "you are not very patriotic towards your adopted country, Angelo, in letting Spain carry off the great masterpiece. Now if you had let me see it, I might have exceeded the Baron's price."

"O papa, cannot you write to the Baron What's-his-name and offer him double the price he paid for it? Perhaps he might be induced to part with it."

"We'll see, little woman. It's your birthday in a month's time. How would you like it as a birthday gift?"

Daphne expressed her delight at the idea, and, turning to the artist, said:

"Haven't you any photograph or engraving of your picture to give us some notion of what it's like?"

Angelo shook his head.

"I would not permit any one to make an engraving. The engraver would but misrepresent my art. What engraving can ever realise the beauty, the finish, the colouring of an original oil painting?"

"I prefer engravings to oils," said I.

"Probably; but then you're not a judge of art, you see," replied Angelo coolly.

"I suppose your success has brought you many orders for pictures?" said my uncle, interposing quickly in the interests of harmony.

"Very many. An English baronet has employed me to paint him a picture on any subject I choose, paying me half the price in advance."

"And what subject have you chosen?" asked Daphne.

"'Modesta, the Christian Martyr,' is the title of my new work, but I am delayed somewhat by the want of a suitable model."

"'Fall of Cæsar,' 'Christian Martyr,'" murmured my uncle. "You seem fond of death-scenes."

"Yes, I have discovered wherein my talent lies. My pencil is better adapted to illustrate repose than motion. Hitherto I have attempted to portray action, and failed. Now, still-life is my study."

"Well, I hope your next picture will become as famous as the last," said Daphne, "and that you will let us have a glimpse of it before parting with it."

"If you care to view a minor performance of mine," said Angelo, "visit the cathedral at Rivoli. It contains a Madonna painted by me while on a visit last year. It has given great satisfaction to the people here, if I may be permitted to sing my own praises. They have even said I was inspired by the saint. Perhaps I was," he added with a curious smile. "I should like you to view it, Miss Leslie, before you leave Rivoli, for a reason that will at once become apparent when you see it."

"A reason? What reason? Tell me now," said Daphne, turning her eyes upon him with a look of wonder.

"Not now. The Madonna will speak for me."

"You are talking in riddles. I shall visit the cathedral this very day, and discover your meaning for myself."

"You do me too much honour. You will receive a surprise—a pleasant one, let me trust."

Daphne's curiosity was raised to the highest point and she cried:

"You hear, papa? We must visit the cathedral this very morning, and solve Mr. Vasari's enigma."

"Very well," replied her father, rising. "I think I have solved it already, and, as I begin to feel hungry qualms 'neath the fourth button of my waistcoat, suppose you run indoors and see what progress is being made with breakfast. Angelo, you will join us, of course?"

Of course he would!

Our breakfast-room was a small prettily furnished apartment, whose latticed windows commanded a fine view of the mountains.

The fresh morning air had imparted a keen edge to my appetite, and nothing but the sense of Angelo's rivalry prevented me from doing full justice to the substantial fare that old Dame Ursula, the housekeeper, had spread before us. The look of admiration in the artist's dark eyes, his tender, respectful homage, spoke of a feeling for Daphne far stronger than friendship. He completely ignored me, and, for my part, I did not address any remark to him during the course of the breakfast. Intuitively we felt that we were rivals, between whom interchange of ideas was impossible. When, in reply to some question of my uncle's, I held forth at great length on German theology, he listened without saying a word. When he grew eloquent over the Old Masters and their works, I treated his tinsel verbiage with freezing silence. He exerted all his arts to please Daphne, and the colour of her cheek and the sparkle of her eye showed that if such attentions did not inspire the sweet sentiments he desired, they were, on the other hand, not at all distasteful to her.

On the seat of one of the latticed windows lay a brown paper parcel, partly opened, containing the files of the *Standard* to which my uncle had alluded. Angelo cast frequent glances in this direction. I supposed he was burning to read to Daphne the eulogium on his picture, but as she seemed to have forgotten it, his vanity was not gratified.

After breakfast was over Daphne repeated her wish to visit the cathedral without delay, and ran off to change her dress for the journey. My uncle withdrew for a similar purpose, leaving me to entertain the artist. The entertainment I offered him was certainly not marked by variety, for it consisted simply of an unbroken silence—a silence that did not seem to disconcert him in the least. He occupied himself with the files of the *Standard*, turning them over with deft fingers, as if selecting a certain one from among the number.

"Looking for the critique, I suppose, in order to read what a great man he is," I thought. "What conceited asses these geniuses always are!" And I mentally congratulated myself that I was not a genius, a fact that I doubt not the reader has discovered long ere this.

Daphne and my uncle now reappeared.

"We are bound for the cathedral, I presume," said Angelo, assuming his sombrero and cloak with a graceful air. "Will Miss Leslie mind if I smoke a cigar? No? Thank you. And as I see no matches here, Mr. Leslie will perhaps not object if I tear off a small piece of this newspaper"—he did not wait for leave, however, but suited the action to the word—"to light it with."

"No matches?" repeated Daphne. "Here is a box on the mantelshelf."

"So there is. Hem! Curious I didn't see it! I have been looking everywhere for a match." I had not seen him so occupied. "No matter. This will serve my purpose equally well—or better," and with a peculiar smile he ignited the twisted piece of paper at the fire.

There was in his lighting of that cigar a curious air of triumph that puzzled me very much, and set me wondering as to its cause.

CHAPTER VI THE MAN AT THE CONFESSIONAL

My uncle took Angelo's arm and led the way down the mountain path, leaving me to follow with Daphne. For some little time we walked in silence, and then she led me to the subject that was uppermost in my mind.

"What is the matter, Frank? You have not been yourself this morning."

Her statement was correct; I had not been myself. Jealousy had wrought a change in my character, causing me to act and speak in a way that, upon consideration, I admit to have been the reverse of amiable.

"It seems to me," I replied in an aggrieved tone, as if I had some solid ground of complaint, "that since our departure from England we have been playing *Hamlet* with the part of Hamlet left out."

"Why, Frank, what do you mean?" she asked.

"O, nothing much. That slave of the palette seems to have taken out a patent for the monopoly of your conversation, that's all."

Daphne assumed an air of dignity, an air that I had never before seen her assume—with me, at least.

"If I have talked with Mr. Vasari more than with you this morning, I think I had good reason. I saw a sneer come over your face as soon as he appeared, and so I took his part at once. What has he done to offend you, and what fault have you to find with him?"

I suppose if I had been perfectly truthful I should have replied that he had painted a picture that had made him famous, whereas I had done nothing to make myself famous, that he was handsome and I was not, and that as he was altogether a more attractive rival than myself I wished him at the devil. Perfect truthfulness, however, is not always observed in ordinary conversation, so I paraphrased my real meaning.

"He is too much of a genius to please me. He is a man with only one idea in his head, and that is Art. On any topic outside that circle he is mute. You think he admires your beauty, whereas he is thinking only what a good model you would make. He stands enraptured at the sunshine, and you cry, 'What a lover of nature!' whereas he is only thinking of the effect it would make on a canvas. He would paint a rose and swear that the copy was more lovely than the original. In everything Art comes first with him. According to him Art was not made for the world, but the world for Art. The world is only a place to paint in, to obtain pictorial effects from. Ask him to choose between living forever in this lovely valley of Rivoli and living forever in his studio studying a picture of it, and he would choose the canvas daub in preference to the reality. He is a monomaniac. I *do* like a man to have a comprehensive breadth and depth of mind."

An excellent way this of detracting from a man's abilities! Mr. A. is a great poet: exactly, but he knows nothing of science. Mr. B. is a great scientist: exactly, but he knows nothing of literature. Estimate a man, not by what he knows, but by what he does *not* know, and you can draw up a formidable indictment against him: as though, forsooth, it were possible for one mind to master the whole of the cyclopædia!

"In short," I concluded, "his conversation smells too much of the brush. He talks of nothing but 'shop.' I hate a fellow who is always talking 'shop.'"

Daphne evidently did not know how to reply to this tirade. She merely said: "You did not speak a single word to him at breakfast."

"Well, you see," I replied in an injured tone, "when a fellow has been a lady's companion for five months, he naturally feels that he has some claim upon her attention and he doesn't like being ignored."

"Did I ignore you?" she replied in a conciliatory tone; and then with a pensive, retrospective air she added. "Five months! And is it so long since we left England? It was too good of you to leave your university——"

"Where I was earning quite a reputation," I murmured. It would have puzzled me to say for what.

"—In order to escort me through Europe. I am sorry for my neglect of you this morning."

The Weird Picture

The look that came into Daphne's eyes was so pretty, wistful, pleading, that I, who had really no cause of complaint against her, began to feel what a hard-hearted tyrant Love sometimes makes of his votaries. I was just wondering whether she would object were I to seal our little concordat with a kiss, when my uncle and Angelo chanced to look back, so I could but give her arm a significant pressure in token of my magnanimous resolution to forgive her.

Near the foot of the mountain we came upon a beautiful pool, its waters being supplied by a slender streamlet that wound down the mountain-side almost in the line of our walk. Rude stonework bordered with moss ran all round the fountain, imparting to it a circular shape. On one side arose a steep rock containing a tall rectangular niche, which had been hewn for the reception of an image, though at present it was apparently devoid of any such ornament.

"Please, Mr. Willard," said Daphne, dropping a mock courtesy, "have I your permission to ask Mr. Vasari what place this is?"

"Mr. Vasari," I called out, "Miss Leslie would like to know the name of this spring."

"This," replied the artist, coming to at once, "is the haunted well of Rivoli."

"Why do they call it haunted?" said Daphne.

"From certain mysterious things that have happened."

Daphne became interested at once, while my uncle, a disbeliever in the supernatural, shrugged his shoulders.

"What things?" said Daphne.

"Mr. Leslie will smile at what he deems a superstitious story," said Angelo, by way of prefatory apology, "but it is a story that no one in Rivoli doubts."

"I hope you do not class yourself among the believers in humbug," my uncle remarked.

"From time immemorial," said Angelo, ignoring the protest, "this place is said to have been haunted, though I never could discover by what. Was it a pagan god, demon, or *fata*—the spirit of a murdered man or of some wicked mediæval baron—that lurked within the shades of this fountain? No one could tell me. 'It was haunted,' was the only answer to my questionings. Such a belief might well have been dismissed as superstition, were it not for certain events that have taken place within my own knowledge. The bishop of the diocese, with a view of removing the ghostly fears of the people around here, resolved to exorcise the spirit. A procession of priests came to the well, the forms of exorcism were gone through, and a crucifix—a life-size image of the Saviour—was consecrated by the bishop, and placed in that niche which you see before you. The place was thus to become holy ground. Next morning the crucifix was found hurled from its position. Who had done it? None of the peasants; they would not be guilty of such impiety. And besides, none of them would have had the courage to venture to the haunted well in the night-time. The crucifix was restored to its place. Next day it was again found hurled from the recess, and this time it was blackened as if by fire. I leave you to imagine the excitement in Rivoli at this. A bold priest—I knew him well—resolved to spend a night here, for the purpose of exorcising the dark power so antagonistic to the Church's sacred emblem. He came alone, equipped for the task in full canonicals, with bell, book, and candle to boot. Next morning, when we came to look for him—I say we, for I was one of the search-party—we found him, apparently exhausted, lying asleep by the fountain. We woke him, and—"

"And he gave an account, I suppose," said my uncle, "of an awful figure he had seen, adorned with horns, tail, and hoofs?"

"He related nothing of the sort," replied Angelo with quiet dignity, "for he had become——"

He paused, to give greater effect to his words.

"What?"

"Insane!"

"What had he seen to make him so?" said Daphne.

"No one will ever know, Miss Leslie. He died the same week."

"What a strange story!"

"And a true one," returned Angelo gravely. "No one in Rivoli dares come within a mile of this fountain after dark; and no priest, or body of priests, has had the courage to try the powers of exorcism since that fatal day."

Daphne was silent and my uncle, taking Angelo's arm, resumed the journey, saying:

"Your story is a mysterious one, but it admits of an easy explanation on rationalistic and psychological principles. Now Professor Dulascanbee——"

And while I was enjoying sweet confidences with Daphne on the way to Rivoli, Angelo had to listen to a prosy lecture from my uncle, directed against belief in the supernatural.

"What do you say, Frank?" he called out to me. "Shall we imitate the bold cleric, and try to solve the mystery by passing a night at the fountain?"

"I'm perfectly agreeable," I responded. "I long to see a ghost."

It was a superb day. The mists had vanished before the glowing sun, and the sky was now one clear expanse of delicate blue. A soft breeze fanned our temples. Through the sunny air the mountains shimmered, faint violet airy masses topped with snow, their various peaks reflected in the surface of the lake, on whose margin stood the quaint old town of Rivoli.

The women of the place, having little else to do, assembled at their doors to see the rare spectacle of foreign visitors. All interest, however, was centred in Daphne: fingers were freely pointed at her, and she seemed to be an object of animated conversation after we had passed by.

Arrived at the cathedral, Angelo paused by the holy water at the porch, and, after making the sign of the cross, led the way into the building. To my surprise, Daphne allowed her High Church tendencies to carry her so far as to imitate the artist, dipping her pretty finger in the lustral font, and tracing a wet cross on her forehead, while she whispered with a smile to me, "When one is at Rome, one must do as Rome does."

It was on the tip of my tongue to say that if the water had not been previously consecrated, it certainly was now after the touch of *her* hand; but this action of hers was a going over to the enemy, so I frowned under pretence of being a Protestant consumed with a zeal for orthodoxy.

"You will be taking the veil next, Miss Leslie," I remarked loftily.

"Miss Leslie? Just hear him, papa! Not Daphne," she whispered with a sweet smile, holding up her little gloved hand, with the second finger crossed over the first, to indicate that it symbolised my frame of mind at that particular moment, as there is no denying that it did.

We rejoined Angelo within the precincts of the cathedral. The interior was a marvel of art, and with its dim magnificence mysteriously coloured by the subdued light of the stained casements it seemed more like the splendid dream of some Gothic architect than an actual reality in marble and mosaic.

"There is my picture!" exclaimed the artist; and, hastening forward to a painting of the Madonna suspended from the cathedral wall and before which waxen tapers were burning, he assumed a kneeling attitude.

"From the days of Pygmalion downwards," I whispered to my uncle, "what artist has not fallen in love with his own work and—worshipped it?"

Daphne's thoughts were more charitable than my own:

"I always think Catholics are more devout than we are."

"Externally, perhaps, they may be," said my uncle; adding aside to me, "but, if I mistake not, neither art nor religion is claiming his thoughts at this moment. Do you not recognise the face of our Lady? No wonder the people in the streets stared so at Daphne."

Surprise for the moment kept me dumb.

Angelo had given to his Madonna the face of Daphne! Very sweet and saintly the portrait looked, too, I must confess, and yet, withal beautiful and womanly, totally different in character from the stiff unnatural productions of the mediæval school. The background was of bright gold, and a deep blue coif veiled the fair throat and hair.

The drooping eyes seemed to be contemplating the kneeling devotee, and the fringe of long dark lashes lay, a vivid contrast to the purity of the snow-white cheek.

Angelo's gaze was fixed in rapt adoration on the lovely face above him. The expression of his eyes and the significance of his attitude were not to be mistaken.

Anger flamed in my breast. The artist's motive for wishing Daphne to visit the cathedral was now clear. It was to flatter her vanity by representing her as a sort of saint, to whom good Catholics paid their vows—another of his steps toward weaving the silken threads of love around her. Oblivious of the timid, retiring delicacy that characterises the spirit of true love, he thus by a bold profanation of religious art dared to flaunt his passion for Daphne in the face of others, so sure of victory did he feel.

"They call this the Iron Age," I whispered in my uncle's ear. "It should be the Brazen."

"Ah," he returned in a tone which did not indicate whether he was pleased or annoyed at the tableau before him, "a custom this of the old Italian artists—a beautiful face, I suppose, materially aids one's devotions."

I turned to Daphne. The colour had mounted to her brow, but her face was no index of the thoughts passing within her mind. Did she divine the meaning of Angelo's kneeling attitude, or did she regard the portrait as a compliment only—an over-bold one, perhaps—to her beauty, and see in his pseudo-devotion nothing more than the spirit of a devout Catholic?

The artist, having gone through the beads of his rosary, rose to his feet and addressed Daphne.

"I trust, Miss Leslie," he said with a smile, "that you will forgive me for having canonised you without either papal sanction or your own."

Like a good Catholic, he put the papal sanction first and Daphne's next.

The Weird Picture

"Last autumn," continued Angelo, "I was requested by a priest of this cathedral, Father Ignatius by name, to paint a Madonna. Not thinking that you, Miss Leslie, would ever visit this place, I took your face as my model, for, pardon my boldness, I could not find a more beautiful one."

Daphne looked extremely grave.

"It is sacrilege," she said in a tone of awe. "What would your priest say if he knew of this?"

"He would pardon the sacrilege—if sacrilege it be—that gave him so fair a Madonna. If the divine Raphael introduced the heads of beggars in his delineations of patriarchs in the frescoes of the Sistine Chapel, may I not employ the living face in my picture?"

Daphne did not reply to this question, but, still very grave, continued:

"To be recognised by staring, gaping crowds in the streets of this town as the original of their cathedral Madonna is a kind of fame I could very well dispense with."

"They will say that the saint has left the skies to shed the sunlight of her presence on earth," he answered.

He accompanied this extravaganza with a smile, but it was a melancholy one. Clearly Daphne was not pleased with the act that had elevated her into a saint. The artist was not slow to perceive the light of triumph in my eyes, and his face darkened.

"I have committed an error," he said with a deferential bow. "I must ask pardon. I could not know when I painted this Madonna that you would ever set foot within this edifice."

"But you could at least have told me before setting out what to expect."

The artist was the picture of despair.

"I have done wrong in your eyes—English Protestants perhaps regard it as a sin, but believe me, the practice is not unknown among us Italian artists. Let the example set by others exculpate me to some extent."

The Weird Picture

The melancholy of his face and the humility of his manner softened Daphne's displeasure, and, resuming her wonted air, she said quickly:

"Let us say no more. What is done cannot be undone. You have my forgiveness, and as a proof you shall show me round the cathedral, if you will."

A look of delight mantled the face of the artist, and he offered her his arm, which she readily took. My uncle, saying that he preferred to rest in some quiet spot, and that he would await their return, had already taken a secluded seat, and I moved off to join him.

"Are you not going to accompany us, Frank?" said Daphne in a tone of surprise.

"Thank you, no," I returned loftily. "Mr. Vasari will not mind if I remain here till your return."

She made no reply, and, escorted slowly by her cicerone along an aisle adorned with statuary and pictures, was soon deep in the mysteries of ecclesiological lore.

We have it on the authority of a gentleman who lived at Stratford-on-Avon that jealousy is green-eyed. If so, my eyes must have resembled emeralds as they followed the pair. Of the two candidates for her smiles, which was the favourite? During breakfast I fancied it might be Angelo; while escorting her to the cathedral I felt certain it was I; now once more my rival's star seemed in the ascendant.

"And probably," I thought, "she will smile sweetly on me at her return. Verily woman is an enigma!"

"What are you thinking of?" asked my uncle, as I took a seat beside him.

"Of inditing a sonnet on the mutability of women."

"Ah! take my advice, and never attempt to understand a woman or her motives. You will never succeed."

"Daphne's motives are pretty obvious," I replied, glancing darkly at the distant figure of the artist.

My uncle's only reply was a smile, that resembled his opinion of women, inasmuch as it was very oracular and quite impossible to understand, and he resumed his reading of Goethe's *Faust*—a work of which he was extremely fond, carrying it about with him wherever he went, and favouring us hourly with quotations appropriate to any state of circumstances we happened to be in.

Presently he looked up from his reading, and said: "Has it never occurred to you that Daphne may have a motive in giving a little encouragement to Angelo—a motive, totally free from any love for him?"

"I am afraid I don't understand."

"Did you not—er—well, make love to her once?"

"Yes," I said gruffly. "I did. But it's more than three years ago."

"And you have not breathed a word of love to her since then."

"Certainly not," I said.

"Very well, then. Supposing she wants to find out whether you still retain your love for her, how is she to do it? Do you expect her to ask you outright? No? Well, one way of finding out is to seem to encourage a rival and note the effect on you. I don't say it's a noble way, but it's a woman's way. And if she sees that you are jealous she can draw her own conclusions."

"Do you honestly mean that that is her motive in encouraging that fool of an artist?" I cried eagerly.

My uncle put up his hand.

"How do I know? Woman is an enigma, to which I don't pretend to know the proper answer. I merely make a suggestion."

That I found the suggestion palatable requires no saying, but if I accepted it I was immediately confronted by the further question why Daphne should wish to know whether I still loved her, and therein I found matter for not a little meditation.

My uncle seemed disinclined to carry on the conversation, so I whiled away the time by taking a survey of the cathedral. It was a Saint's day on the morrow, and preparations for the festival occupied most of the attendants. There was much moving to and fro. Now and again peasants would enter with baskets of fruit and flowers for the adornment of the columns, shrines and altars, until the place began to assume the aspect of a flower market. Tired of gazing at the decorations, I directed my attention to a confessional box not far off. Unlike most confessional boxes, the front of this one was quite open to view, and within there sat an aged priest, corded and sandalled, while outside, with his lips applied to an orifice on a level with the priest's ear, knelt a man whispering a confession. The penitent was aged too, with hair that gave him quite a venerable appearance.

I watched the "little sinner confessing to the big sinner," to use a favourite phrase of my uncle's, and noted the troubled expression on his face and the nervous humility with which he clasped one hand over the other. If looks were to be taken as evidence the father confessor was deeply interested in the recital of the other's frailties. Suddenly I saw his eyes turn to a far corner of the cathedral, and following his gaze I saw that the objects of his attention were Daphne and Angelo, who had just come into view from behind the pillars of a colonnade. She was laughing gaily, and the artist was bending over her in an attitude suggestive of tender affection. Long and earnest was the look that the priest fixed upon the pair—so long and earnest that my curiosity was aroused as to its cause. Was he envying Angelo his happiness? Was he thinking of the maidens who might have loved him in the early days before his vows of celibacy were taken?

A quick motion of the priest's cold grey eyes recalled me from this train of thought, and to my surprise I found him regarding *me* with a keen gaze that was in no way abated when he saw that I was conscious of it. Then he turned his gaze once more upon Daphne and her escort, who had again become visible between the columns of the cloister. And so long as he sat there, coffined in the confessional box, he continued to manifest this singularity, that when he was not looking at Daphne and Angelo he was looking at me, and when he was not looking at me he was looking at Daphne and Angelo, so that I could tell simply from the motion of his eyes when the artist and my cousin were visible, and when the pillared walk concealed them from view. Although he appeared to be putting a number of questions to the aged penitent he nevertheless did not abate one jot of his steady gaze.

It occurred to me that he had recognised in Daphne the original of the Madonna, but that did not explain his scrutiny of me,—a scrutiny that sprang, I was sure, from something more than casual curiosity. Could the confession of the penitent have anything to do with it? Once more I surveyed the person of the old man, and it began to dawn upon me that I had seen him before, but when and where and in what circumstances I failed to recall. I closed my eyes in order to aid my powers of reflection, but still could not solve the problem of his identity. Just as I opened my eyes again to take another view of the confessional box I witnessed a remarkable tableau.

The penitent was still proceeding with his whispered story when the priest started to his feet with an impulse that apparently he could not control. Horror was painted in vivid characters on his face as he stood erect and stiff, with his eyes fixed on the distant cloister, while the other man, with his white head bent and his hands piteously clasped, sank low on his knees, a study of humiliation. What terrible secret had been imparted to the priest that he should betray such emotion? For a full minute he remained as rigid as a statue, and then hurriedly quitting the confessional box he beckoned the penitent to follow him. They passed through a small archway leading to some sacristy, and the oaken door concealed them from my view.

Then it was that memory came to my aid, and I trembled all over at the revelation it imparted. I turned to my uncle who, absorbed in his book, had not observed the singular scene.

"Uncle," I said, and even in my own ears my voice sounded strange; "did you notice an old man kneeling at that confessional box over there?"

"I have been at Nuremberg all this time," replied my uncle in tones aggravatingly dry and measured, "and therefore could not see what was passing here. Why do you ask?"

"Who do you think he was?"

"Answer your own riddle and let me return to the wit of Mephistopheles."

"He was the tenant of the mysterious house at Dover."

My uncle found my words more interesting than those of Mephistopheles.

"You are dreaming, Frank."

"No. I am sure that it was he."

"So far from Dover? Is it likely he would turn up in this out-of-the-way place?"

"It isn't a question of what he is likely to do; it's a question of what he has done. He is here. That's a fact. For aught we know to the contrary he may be an Italian. Now I come to think of it his voice had a foreign accent."

"Where is he now?" asked my uncle, looking all around the cathedral.

"He went with the priest through that door-way," I answered, and I told him of what had taken place at the confessional box.

"What are we to do?" my uncle asked.

"We must not let him go without having a word from him," I answered. "Wait at the sacristy door and speak to him as he comes out, and learn—what you can. I will walk to the aisles yonder, for should he see me he will be suspicious of you. We won't say anything to Daphne about this yet."

As I was turning away I caught sight of Daphne, who, having gone the round of the cathedral, was sitting near the picture of the Madonna, with the artist by her side. They were chatting away as confidentially as if there were no one in the world but themselves. The sight of the Italian offering his homage to my beautiful cousin would have moved my jealousy at any other time, but at present my head was occupied with the tableau at the confessional.

"Your father will be with us in a few minutes, Daphne," I said, taking a seat beside her. "You have seen all that is to be seen?"

The Weird Picture

"Yes. I have to thank Mr. Vasari for a very interesting lecture. He is quite a learned antiquary, minus the pedantry."

"Ah! that last is a stroke at me, I suppose," I returned carelessly, without looking at her. My eyes were directed toward my uncle, whom I could see in the distance, keeping watch by the sacristy door.

"May I ask why papa is playing the part of a statue?"

Here was a question! But I was equal to the occasion.

"He fancies he saw an old friend of his enter that room, and he is waiting for him to come out."

"Why doesn't he go in after him?"

"Well, if you ask Mr. Vasari, he will perhaps tell you (for he knows better than I) that that is the priest's private room, and naturally your parent is reluctant to intrude."

"True, Miss Leslie. It is the sacristy of Father Ignatius."

"Father Ignatius? Haven't you mentioned his name once before?"

"Yes, it was he who commissioned me to paint my unfortunate Madonna," replied the artist, glancing at the picture above his head.

"What sort of a person is this Father Ignatius?" I asked of Angelo, who seemed surprised at my addressing him, as well he might; it was so rarely I did so. "I saw a priest just now with a very remarkable type of head, quite like an antique Roman's—bald, aquiline nose, keen grey eyes, erect, proud——"

"Yes, that was Father Ignatius.

"A high dignitary of this cathedral, I suppose?" I remarked.

"The very highest, save the bishop, whom he quite eclipses by his vigorous personality—supersedes, in point of fact, for the bishop prefers to live at Campo, and leaves the entire control of Church affairs to Father Ignatius."

"I see. The bishop is *le roi fainéant*, and Father Ignatius mayor of the palace."

The Weird Picture

"Just so. Yet despite his love of power he is a good man, and every one in Rivoli loves him. He was a second father to me in my boyhood. It was he who first directed and encouraged me in the study of painting, but of late he has looked with disapproval on my art."

"What! After your brilliant success?" cried Daphne. "He ought to be proud of his *protégé*."

"He is vexed because I have turned from the mediæval school with its 'Madonnas,' 'Pietas,' and 'Ecce Homos,' to seek inspiration from the pages of classic history. He thinks that whatever talent a man has should be consecrated to the service of the Church."

It was ever thus with Angelo. No matter what subject was being discussed he always contrived to drift down to art before long.

"What a pretty girl that is telling her beads before yonder crucifix!" said Daphne.

"Yes," replied the Italian, surveying the girl's figure with his artist's eye. "She would make a beautiful model for my 'Modesta the Martyr'—if I had not a fairer form in view," he murmured in a lower tone.

Impatiently I turned my eyes in the direction of that sentinel my uncle, and found him still on the watch at the sacristy-door. It swung open at last.

To my disappointment, however, neither priest nor penitent issued forth, but a man who had every appearance of being one of the attendants of the cathedral. He was walking over to us.

My heart beat fiercely. The mystery of last Christmas Eve was going to be cleared up!

The belief in my own mind that the attendant was going to invite me to the priest's room in order to interview the aged penitent was so great that I had actually risen to meet him—an unnecessary action on my part, for he passed by without regarding me, and, walking up to Angelo's picture of the Madonna, he removed it from the wall, and was preparing to depart with it, when he was stopped by the artist.

The Weird Picture

"What are you going to do with that picture, Paolo?" inquired Angelo, to whom the attendant was evidently well known.

"I am taking it to Father Ignatius' room," replied Paolo.

"What for?"

"Such are Father Ignatius' commands. He says it is to hang no more on these walls."

"No more! Why not? Did he give any reason?"

"None at all—to me. He seems extremely angry, and when he bade me do this his voice was sharper than I have ever heard it before. 'Take that man's handiwork down,' he cried, 'and burn it.'"

"Burn it! Did Father Ignatius say that?" said Angelo in a tone of concern.

"He did, Master Angelo," was the reply. "I told him that you were here in the cathedral sitting by the picture, and that you would be sure to ask why I was taking it down. 'Remove it at once, and burn it, I tell you,' was the only answer he would give me."

"You may tell Father Ignatius for me, Paolo, that I look upon this as an insult, and——"

"You must tell him that yourself, Master Angelo," replied Paolo, speaking with considerable freedom. "I have a sister in Purgatory whom he is going to set free next week by his prayers. He'd keep her in Purgatory forever if I gave him your message. You know the fiery stuff old Padre Ignatio is made of."

And with these words, so spoken that I could not tell whether he were in jest or earnest, the man marched off, carrying the picture with him.

The artist stared after him with so dark a look on his face that if Paolo had been in Purgatory in place of his sister, with Angelo for mass-priest, Paolo's detention would certainly have been a long one.

"What can this mean?" muttered the artist. "I shall see Father Ignatius to-night, and shall ask him the meaning of this affront."

"Perhaps," said Daphne, "the priest has seen me, and is vexed to think that the Madonna he asked you to paint, instead of being, as he supposed, an ideal face, is simply the portrait of an Englishwoman—and of an Englishwoman who is a heretic in his eyes, you know."

The artist was silent, and, turning to Daphne, I said:

"I will just ask uncle how long he is going to remain standing over there."

Walking off quickly, I overtook the attendant before he reached the sacristy door.

"You really do not know, then," said I to him, "why Father Ignatius wishes the picture to be destroyed?"

"I know no more than I told Master Angelo just now, sir."

My uncle at this juncture approached us, wondering much to see Angelo's Madonna in the hands of the attendant. Addressing Paolo, he said, while pointing to the sacristy door:

"The old man who went in here with the priest—is he still within? I want to see him."

"He is gone. Left a few minutes since."

"Gone? Left? What! both of them?"

"Both of them."

"They did not pass through this door-way then?"

"No, sir. They left the sacristy by a side-door."

"Confound it! Baffled!" exclaimed my uncle with a gesture of impatience, and stamping his foot. "After all this waiting, too! What are we to do, Frank?"

"Do you want very much to see this old man?" said Paolo. "Perhaps," and he looked around, as if to see that no priest were by—"perhaps I may be able to help you."

"Help us?" said my uncle. "Good! You will be the very man for our purpose. Ah!" he continued, as he saw the fellow's face gleam with the hope of a reward, "you worship the golden calf, I see. We understand each other. What is your name?"

"Paolo."

The Weird Picture

"Paolo, eh? None other? Perhaps you prefer a single name. The great men of Greece had but one. Well, Paolo, you must know every face in this little town. Tell us whether this old man is an inhabitant of Rivoli."

"He is a complete stranger to me," replied the attendant. "I have never seen his face till this morning."

"If, Paolo, you can find out for us what his name is, where he is staying, whence he came, and what business brings him here," my uncle continued, "I will give you more money than you can earn in a twelvemonth. There is an earnest of it," and he pressed some silver pieces into the fellow's palm. "But conduct your inquiries very secretly and cautiously. You understand? We do not wish him to suspect he is being watched. We are tourists staying at the Châlet Varina—you know it—a house perched on a crag on the mountainside, two miles from here——"

"Châlet Varina! What, Andrea Valla's house—the great tenor's?"

"Ah! the great tenor's. He sings in the choir here, I believe. I see you know the house. Ask for Mr. Leslie. But stay," he ejaculated, as the thought passed through his mind that if the fellow called at the châlet the matter would have to be explained to Daphne—"stay. I will meet you this evening at eight. Be in the cathedral square at that hour. Can you contrive to be there?"

The man nodded assent and then pushing open the door of the sacristy to its full extent, showed us that his words were true, and that both priest and penitent had quitted the chamber.

"Stay," I said, ere the door closed; "ask him, uncle, whether Father Ignatius and the old man talked before him, and if so, what they said."

My uncle put this question, and Paolo replied:

"As they pushed open the door, I heard Father Ignatius say, 'When do you say this happened?' and the old man answered, 'Last Christmas Eve:' and that's all I heard, for when they saw me they stopped talking at once, and Father Ignatius ordered me in a voice of thunder to go and take down Master Angelo's Madonna and burn it here in the sacristy, though for what reason I can't make out; and then, as I said just now, they went out by the side-door, and that's all I know of the matter, and— But there's Serafino, the deacon, looking at me; he's sure to ask why you gave me this money."

And in some trepidation Paolo closed the door and occupied himself with whatever work he had to do within.

My uncle had become the personification of gravity.

"'Last Christmas Eve,'" he muttered, speaking slowly. "Did you hear what he said, Frank?"

"I heard it, uncle."

"That old man's confession must have had some reference to George."

"That's what I've been fancying all along."

"You say the priest started up excitedly at the recital of the other?"

"Yes, with a look of unspeakable horror. I was watching him closely, and could not mistake the expression."

"What caused the priest's excitement? Some terrible crime that the old man was relating. If so, whose? His own or another's?"

My uncle stared slowly round at the stained casements and sacred pictures, as if expecting an answer from them.

"Not his own. I will never believe that old man guilty of crime; his face is too noble."

"Face is no index to character," he returned; and then he added reflectively: "and no sooner does this priest quit the confessional than he orders Angelo's picture to be destroyed. Frank, what are we to make of this?" he added, a curious expression passing over his face as he glanced at the distant figure of the artist.

"Oh, that's easily explained," I rejoined. "The priest, as he sat in the confessional-box, saw Daphne and Angelo, and no doubt he considers that Madonna a sacrilegious piece of work."

"Ah! true, true," he replied, his brow clearing instantly; and after a pause he added: "Frank, say nothing to Daphne of our discovery. It will only excite her unnecessarily, and revive memories of George."

"You may depend on my silence. But if you wish her to suspect nothing, just try to infuse a little more gaiety into your countenance, for you are looking as grave as a judge."

"I look as I feel, then. I am afraid I should make a bad detective; my face always betrays my emotions. But what shall we say to Daphne, for she has been watching us? She is sure—women *are* so confoundedly curious—to ask the meaning of this long vigil of mine, and of the bribe to the attendant."

"I have told her," said I, as we moved off to join her and the artist, "that you fancied you saw an old friend of yours enter that sacristy. So keep up the farce."

"Now, papa," were Daphne's first words, "why have you been standing by that door so long?"

"Hem!" replied her parent, clearing his throat, and pausing to collect his inventive faculties. "I thought I saw a German friend of mine pass into that vestry—the great Professor Dulascanbee—gathering materials for his learned work, *Ecclesiologia Helvetica*, but I was mistaken. A silver fee to the attendant has elicited the fact that the man in the vestry doesn't resemble my learned friend at all; he always wears blue glasses. Well, my pseudo-Madonna," he continued, touching his pretty daughter under the chin, "what say you if we quit this 'dim religious light'?"

No one offering any opposition to this, we passed out through the porch. On the top of the cathedral steps Angelo paused.

"I shall not see you any more to-day, Miss Leslie. I have an appointment to keep, and must leave you at the foot of these stairs. It is a high festal day to-morrow in Rivoli. May I hope to see you present at early Mass in the morning? You love music, and I assure you, you will find the singing beautiful; Mozart's Twelfth Mass."

Daphne with a smile promised to be present if the weather were propitious; and thus ended our morning in the cathedral.

CHAPTER VII WHAT THE "STANDARD" SAID OF THE PICTURE

We did not return immediately to the châlet, but spent the rest of the day in exploring the antiquities of Rivoli. Daphne, from her resemblance to the cathedral Madonna, drew attention wherever she went. She frequently expressed her annoyance at the staring to which she was exposed, especially when she learned from some semi-audible remarks that she was regarded as the artist's future bride!

For my own part, I was secretly delighted at all this, knowing that with the increase of her displeasure came a proportional decrease in the artist's chances of winning her. It will be readily guessed that I did not let the grass grow beneath my feet, and in the absence of my rival I used every opportunity of strengthening my hold upon her affections.

Toward the close of the day, when the purple hues of twilight were suffusing the air, and the bell of the Angelus was sounding softly from the cathedral-tower, Daphne and I set off home. My uncle, promising to follow us later, lingered behind, on pretence of awaiting the arrival of the diligence from Campo (the nearest large town to Rivoli), with its slender freight of letters and newspapers, his real object being to keep his appointment with the cathedral attendant.

Old Ursula had prepared a dainty repast for us, and when the meal was over Daphne lit the lamp, drew the curtains, and took her seat by the fire.

"Read to me, Frank. There is a whole heap of newspapers over there."

I sat on a footstool at her feet, with the file of journals beside me, in the light of the blazing fire, and wished that Angelo were looking through the casement, to see how cosy and comfortable we were.

"Where shall I begin?"

"Anywhere you like."

"Very well. 'Theatre of Varieties, Westminster; every night, at 8:30, Tottie Rosebud will sing "Then she wunk the other eye." Admission—'"

"O Frank! How horrid you are!"

"Am I? You told me to read anywhere, so I took the first paragraph that my eyes fell on. However, as you don't like that, I'll turn to something else. 'Letter from Paris.' Would you like that?"

"Yes, that will do," she replied, composing her dainty little person comfortably in the big armchair.

So, compliant with her will, I began to read the lively letter of that mysterious personality, "Our Own Correspondent," keeping a cautious eye ahead, in case I should be landed before I was aware of it on some Parisian doings whose recital might offend the susceptibilities of my fair cousin, equally with those of that staid old lady, the British Matron. I had not read more than half a column, when my eye lighted upon a name that drew from me an exclamation of surprise.

"What's the matter, Frank?"

"Here's that fellow Vasari's name."

"Fellow Vasari, indeed!" returned Daphne with mock dignity. "Do you mean the eminent artist, Signor Angelo Vasari?"

"That's it. The oil-and-colour man. Here's a notice of his famous daub. This must be the critique he was referring to."

"O go on, Frank! Read it, read it!" she cried eagerly.

The praises of a rival are never very pleasant reading. They become doubly unpleasant when the beloved object is a listener. Pity me, then at having to read the following little *Vasariad*!

"'The principal topic of conversation among art-circles at present is a very remarkable picture, called in the catalogue "The Fall of Cæsar." The artist, who till yesterday was completely unknown to the public, is one Angelo Vasari, an Italian by birth, who has, however, spent the greater part of his life in the art-schools of London. He is said to be a descendant of the sixteenth-century Vasari, the friend of Popes and Princes, who has earned considerable fame by his *Lives of the Painters*. Though but twenty-five years of age, this new artist has produced a work that, without exaggeration, may be ranked with the finest compositions of Doré or Gérome. What he may be expected to accomplish when his genius is fully matured is shadowed forth by his present picture. What causes great surprise is the fact that up to the present time Vasari has never produced a work that deserved to rank above mediocrity. Indeed, so devoid of talent have his previous compositions been that the name "Il Divino" was bestowed upon him, not from his likeness to Raphael, but from his unlikeness. We are given to understand that when the artist was informed of the nickname, he replied unconcernedly: "Ah! then I must endeavour to merit the appellation."

"'"Tis not in mortals to command success;" but Il Divino has both deserved and commanded it. His toil and perseverance have enabled him to turn the tables completely upon his critics, and from a poor, obscure, struggling artist he has become elevated to a position of fame and wealth, for the profits drawn from the crowds that have flocked to view the picture have been enormous.

"'That a young man accustomed only to paint mediocrities should, as it were, by one stroke produce a masterpiece is indeed a marvel, and there are not wanting tongues to say that "The Fall of Cæsar" is not the work of Vasari at all—an absurd statement, for it is not likely that the real author of such a remarkable work of genius would be so self-sacrificing as to give his glory to another. If there be any truth in this rumour, it is probably founded on the fact that some one may have collaborated with Vasari to produce a few minor points. If the latter be not the author of "The Fall of Cæsar," then assuredly his next work will betray him, unless indeed he has determined to rest his fame on this one picture only. But no importance is to be attached to the mysterious rumours current to account for the artist's success.

"'The Vasari Gallery is situated in the Rue de Sèvres, and admission is obtained by the payment of two francs. What the visitor first sees on entering the apartment devoted to this masterpiece is a wide doorway at the farther end draped on each side with curtains between which can be seen a court apparently open to the sky, since glimpses of a heavenly blue are visible between lofty columns. By one of these columns rises the statue of a warrior mounted on a pedestal, and at the base, with arrowy beams of sunlight streaming over it, lies a prostrate form, which requires no second glance to certify that it is a dead body, especially as the bloodstained weapons that have accomplished the deed are scattered on the pavement around.

"'The spectator (not in the secret) hurries forward, and on arriving at the end of the apartment can hardly be persuaded that no doorway exists, and that the whole scene is simply a picture painted on canvas. Yet so it is. The picture is draped on each side with curtains so disposed as to give it the appearance of a doorway. The light entering the apartment from above strikes the picture at a certain angle, and, aided by the marvellous perspective skill of the artist's brush, the picture has every appearance of being an actual scene beyond the room in which the spectator stands, and in which some terrible tragedy has taken place. The illusion is perfect.

"'We have indicated the principal features of the picture; the fallen Cæsar with his toga wrapped partly round him, the statue of Pompey rising above, a tesselated pavement stained with blood, here and there a discarded dagger, columnar architecture in the background: such are the simple elements presented by this work of art. The fidelity to archæological details displayed in all parts of the picture has satisfied the judgment of every antiquary who has examined the work.

"'The picture, as we have intimated, contains but two figures—a disappointing number, one might think; and yet it is no paradox to say that had the picture contained more it would have revealed less. Had the artist, for example, represented Marc Antony mourning over the dead body, and drawing eloquence from its pitiable aspect, the eloquence that was to excite the Forum, or had he given us the conspirators waving their swords aloft, their faces radiant with the enthusiasm of liberty, he would have drawn off the spectator's attention from the point which most deserves praise. In the multiplicity of details we should perhaps have lost sight of the marvellous manner in which the painter has triumphed over the difficulty of his subject in regard to the face of the dead Cæsar,

The Weird Picture

expressing therein all the varying emotions that must have agitated the great Dictator's mind at the moment of his death.

"'How often the painter, desirous of depicting the human countenance lit up by some sublime feeling, has had to lament the impotence of his art!

"'Timanthes, unable to express the death-emotion on the face of Agamemnon, conceals the head of the king in a purple robe; Da Vinci in "The Last Supper," despairing of diffusing a ray of divinity over the features of the Saviour, lays down his pencil, and leaves nothing but a blank oval for the face.

"'Who shall succeed where such masters fail? Echo answers—Vasari! A bold statement, but a true one!

"'Mr. Vasari might reasonably and with perfect fidelity to historic truth have adopted the method of Timanthes, since, every schoolboy knows, that Cæsar fell with his head concealed in the folds of his toga; but, disdaining the pusillanimity of such a method, the artist has permitted the whole of Cæsar's face to be seen, for the purpose of delineating with ghastly realism the expression of a dead face. The effect of the sunlight quivering on——'"

At this point I paused to look up at Daphne, whose eyes were eloquently expressive of the interest she was taking in the subject of my reading, and remarked quietly:

"To be continued in our next."

"Go on," she said eagerly. "Don't stop."

It was with a certain amount of malice that I replied:

"There is no more."

"No more? It doesn't end in the middle of a sentence?"

"Probably not. But some one has been kind enough to tear off the bottom of this sheet just at the very line I have arrived at."

"Oh, how annoying! Isn't it continued at the top of the next column?"

"Fortunately—no."

"Fortunately?"

"Yes; I'm tired of it; it's the essence of dulness. I marvel that the writer is still at large."

"Who can have torn it," she said, taking no notice of my gibe. "Not uncle, I'm sure. Oh, I know now. It was Angelo himself that did it. Don't you remember? This morning, when he lit his cigar."

The memory of this last event invested the newspaper article with an interest which it did not before possess in my eyes. I recalled the artist's uneasy manner when asking whether my uncle or myself had read the critique on his picture, his evident satisfaction when he found we had not, the triumphant air with which he had lit his cigar with a piece of newspaper; and this conduct disposed me to think that he had designedly torn off the bottom of the column containing the end of the article.

The more I dwelt on the matter the more my opinion became strengthened. I was as anxious now as Daphne to read the critique to the end.

"How curious that Angelo should tear the very paper referring to himself!" remarked Daphne.

"Very!" I responded drily.

"Can't we get another copy of this *Standard*?"

"Not at Rivoli. Rome or Paris is the nearest place to send to, and then it will be at least four days in arriving. Besides, it's an old copy, and very likely no more are left."

"How provoking! You'll send to-morrow for another copy, won't you Frank?"

"Most readily. I, too, wish to see the end of this article."

"Why, you said just now that it was the essence of dulness."

"Yes, but you know what a variable mortal I am."

"How well the paper speaks of him!" said Daphne, taking up the *Standard*, and dwelling with more pleasure than I cared to see on the flattering language bestowed on the artist. "Angelo isn't vain, that's easy to be seen. Didn't you notice how reluctant he was this morning to speak of his picture? One had to draw it out of him, as it were. I am glad he has made a name at last. 'There are not wanting tongues,'" she continued, reading from the paper, "'to say that it is not the work of Vasari at all.' What a shame to say that!" she ejaculated with considerable indignation. "When his pictures were not very good the critics sneered at him and called him 'Il Divino'; and now that he *has* produced something good they suggest that some one else painted it for him. Just like the critics! Fancy Angelo being a descendant of the great Vasari, too!"

"No great honour," I returned, as eager to depreciate the artist as Daphne was to exalt him. "His great ancestor's pictures have always been considered daubs; and as for the famous book, *Lives of the Painters*, it is supposed not to have been written by Vasari."

Critics will bear me out in these statements; but Daphne scorned criticism, and would not listen to any reflections on Angelo's ancestor.

"Ah! I suppose it's the case of Shakespeare *v*. Bacon over again. Well, for my part I believe in Shakespeare. Say good-night to papa for me."

And she danced gaily off to bed at an earlier hour than usual. Was she going to dream of the artist?

Now, ever since my interest had been roused in the critique of the picture my eyes had been fixed on the fireplace, where Angelo, after lighting his cigar, had thrown the burnt paper, and in one corner of the fender I had fancied I could perceive a charred piece of paper. Accordingly after Daphne had gone I pounced on this fragment. It crumbled to black powder in my hands, save one little unburnt piece.

This piece contained six words only; yet they were sufficient to cause my pulse to throb more quickly:

an Anglo-Indian officer to judge.

That was all; and I had some difficulty in making out even those few words, owing to the blackened aspect of the paper. I did not doubt that they formed a part of the critique, and that the paragraph in which they occurred was one that the artist was anxious to conceal from us.

The Weird Picture

The memory of my lost brother had been strangely revived by the events of the day, and the phrase "an Anglo-Indian officer" naturally and immediately associated itself with his name. It was impossible in my then state of ignorance to establish a connexion between my brother and Angelo's picture, and the various hypotheses I framed to account for the admission of his name into the art-critique would fill a chapter.

"It was a mean trick of Angelo's," I muttered, "to mutilate that paper. I am certain it contained a reference to George. I would give fifty pounds to know his reason for so doing. No matter; this little mystification can't last very long, for I'll send to England for another copy to-morrow."

From the picture my thoughts wandered to the hidalgo whom Angelo had represented as having purchased it, and with a view to learning something, however brief, about this grandee, I took down from the shelf a book on the Spanish peerage, and turned over its pages. I was still occupied thus when my uncle returned.

"Have you discovered anything?" was my first question.

"Absolutely nothing."

"Paolo had nothing to reveal?"

"Paolo was not there. I was in the cathedral square by eight, but could see nothing of him. I looked in at the cathedral, too. It was bright with lamps, being the eve of a festa; but he was not there; so, after two hours' patient watching and waiting, I gave it up in disgust."

"We are sure to see him at early Mass; his duties will take him there."

"Probably," replied my uncle, sinking into the armchair lately vacated by Daphne, and lighting a cigar. "But what ponderous tome are you poring over so studiously?"

"The *Spanish Peerage*."

"Ah! take St. Paul's advice, 'Beware of endless genealogies,' for they are dull reading."

"Not when one has a motive for studying them."

"A motive? Great Jupiter! what has made you take so sudden an interest in the hidalgos?"

"You remember to whom Angelo said he had sold his picture?"

"The Spanish baron, De Argandarez. Ah! I see, you are looking him up."

"I am; and, do you know, I cannot find the name anywhere in this book."

"You haven't looked in the right place."

"Well, here is the book; examine it for yourself. Here is the list of barons. Find De Argandarez."

"Humph! I have no wish to qualify myself for a Spanish herald. I'll take your word for it that the name of Argandarez is not here, merely remarking that the book is dated 1898, and that therefore the fellow may have been created a baron since then, which will account for the omission of his name."

"What! When Angelo called him an old hidalgo of Aragon, and spoke of his ancestral walls, or ancestral castle, or something similar! At any rate, he used the word ancestral."

"Ha! I remember something of the sort," my uncle said, and the alert glance in his eye belied the indifference in his tone. "You are certain the name does not occur in this book? Hum! Unless it be an editorial oversight, our noble grandee would seem to have no existence, save in the imagination of Angelo. Il Divino is slightly given to romancing."

"Il Divino must have had a motive for the—lie," I replied, with an emphasis on the last word, as a protest against my uncle's euphemism. "He evidently wishes the destination of his picture to remain unknown to us."

"Why should he wish that? And even if he does, it is impossible for him to conceal it. The sale of so notable a work of art would be mentioned in all the papers, together with the name of the buyer."

"Not necessarily. An agent may have bought it for a client who wishes his name to be kept secret. Or the sale may have been a private affair between Angelo and the purchaser."

"Granted," he agreed. "To tell you the truth, Frank, there's something about Angelo's success I can't understand. How, after his many failures, he has contrived, by the exhibition of one picture only, to acquire so great a name is a mystery."

"So the public seem to think. Here is the *Standard's* account of it."

I passed the paper to my uncle, who read as far as he could, and then exclaimed:

"The end has been torn off!"

"Yes, by Angelo this morning when he lit his cigar; designedly torn off, I believe. This is a fragment of the burnt piece," I said, laying it before him.

My uncle did not betray the excitement that I had expected of him.

"So you think the mutilation of this newspaper intentional?" he asked with a half-smile.

"I am certain of it."

"How suspicious you are growing of Il Divino! A lover's jealousy, I suppose," he said, knocking the ash of his cigar into the fender.

"There was something in that paper that Angelo did not wish us to see," I replied. "That something, whatever it was, was probably peculiar to this paper, and Angelo supposes that if we are prevented from taking note of it now, we shall never hear of it again."

My uncle regarded me with a look of good-humoured surprise before taking a whiff again at his cigar.

"Nonsense!" he returned. "My dear Frank, whatever was in the *Standard* cannot be a secret. It's absurd to suppose that Angelo is trying to keep from us that with which a large number of the reading public is already familiar."

"Yes, but the reading public are not, like us, behind the scenes and familiar with the artist. In a sentence they would pass over as of no note we, who can read between the lines, might discover something."

"Well, what is this something we might discover?"

"'An Anglo-Indian officer,'" I said, tracing the words with my finger. "George is an Anglo-Indian officer; so are his chief friends. 'The Anglo-Indian officer' alluded to here is either George himself—and, if so, this passage would afford a clue to his movements—or it is a friend of his, recently returned from India, and from whom information respecting George might be obtained."

"Granting your inference, what motive has Angelo for wishing to conceal the fact from us?"

"Motive? His motive is pretty obvious after to-day's revelation. He is in love with Daphne, and, being so, he is tormented by two ideas— namely, that she still retains her love for George, and that George himself may yet return to claim her. Therefore, do you think he wishes her to know where George is? Not likely! His plan is to woo and win her before George reappears to spoil his game."

"I do not think so. The tearing of that paragraph was an accident."

"An accident? Did you not notice this morning how anxious he was to know if we had read this critique; how relieved he seemed when he learned we had not? Singular that he should light his cigar with a bit of newspaper, pretending he could see no matches in the room, when all the time they were staring at him from the mantel! Singular, too, that out of fifty newspapers he should light on the very one in which this eulogy of himself is, and tear the very column containing it, leaving, however, sufficient to show what a great man he has developed into. An accident? Bah! My good uncle, give me credit for a little discernment."

"Or—a picturesque imagination. Well, well, if you think the paragraph of such importance, by all means send to England for a copy of the *Standard* of July 2nd. If there were anything of consequence in it, I feel sure that some friend would have called our attention to it before now."

I was silent, and my uncle occupied himself in reading the article again.

"I wonder," he remarked, "if there is any truth in the suggestion that some one else painted the picture?"

"Can George paint?" I asked: an unnecessary question on my part, for my uncle knew no more of the matter than I.

"Never knew him to handle the brush; though it is not unlikely he may have studied painting a little in India, but scarcely to the extent of being able to produce a masterpiece such as we have been reading about."

"You remember the date Angelo assigned for his arrival at Paris."

"I do. It was the day after we left."

"Exactly. And don't you think it strange that he should arrive there the very day after we had taken our departure?"

"I see nothing strange in it."

"And then, talking of his arrival at Paris, he made use of the plural 'we.' 'We arrived,' he said, and then, suddenly checking himself, he altered it to 'I did not arrive.' Do you remember it?"

"I can't say I do."

"But I do, though, and wondered at it. Now who are they who compose the 'we'?"

"He and his agent, probably; or he and those who were conveying the picture."

"If he meant those persons only, why should he check himself so sharply?"

My uncle shrugged his shoulders, as if he were growing tired of the subject. "I think, Frank," he said, "that you are attaching too much importance to a trivial expression."

"Possibly I may be; but I cannot help thinking that a mystery surrounds the production of Angelo's picture, and that the mystery is in some way connected with George."

CHAPTER VIII—HIGH MASS AND WHAT HAPPENED AT IT

The morning dawned more soft and lovely than the preceding one: a boon to the good people of Rivoli, for it was a gala-day with them.

Daphne, my uncle and myself rose with the break of day, and at an early hour we were standing in the market-place watching the worshippers throng into the cathedral.

Be it far from me to attempt to describe the various ornaments and robes displayed by the dames of Rivoli on this festal occasion: the silver chains and rich headdresses, the dainty cloaks and embroidered kirtles. Suffice it to say there was sufficient white, blue, and black among them to gladden the heart of his Holiness the late Pope, who has expressed his approval of these colours as most becoming to young persons. Nor were sober grey and brown wanting, hues suitable, according to the same authority, to ladies of a more advanced age.

"To be or not to be? that is the question," murmured my uncle, as the last devotee filed into the cathedral, and the great square was left to us. "Whether 'tis nobler to follow the crowd into this edifice to witness a ceremony whose superstition provokes my irreverence, or to stroll onward in the soft morning air and finish this weed? Havana *versus* church, that is the question."

"No question at all," said Daphne; and, compelling her pagan parent to fling away his cigar and assume a more decorous air, she drew him within the cathedral.

As we came as spectators only, we took up our position in a side-cloister. Looking round for the artist among the crowd of worshippers I at length discovered him in the very first line of seats, reading a Missal, with such attention that he never once glanced to left or right. His devout air and the position he had taken so near the chancel evidently implied an intention to partake of the Communion.

On the high altar seven lofty candlesticks of solid silver, each with its seven waxen tapers, gleamed on the great brazen gates of the chancel, and on the lofty casement above with its blazoned saints and angels, and fretwork of purple and gold. The splendour was sufficient to illumine the whole length of the nave, and, contrasted with the gloom of the more remote parts of the edifice, had a dazzling, not to say theatrical, effect.

We had not occupied our position in the aisle above two minutes, when forth from the sacristy issued the train of the priests and their auxiliaries. Thurifers swinging slow their golden censers, and acolytes with lighted tapers, led the way to the chancel. Father Ignatius, his eyes fixed on the ground, came last, robed in a magnificent white cope, and bearing under a veil the sacred vessels, which he deposited on the altar.

"What is the matter?" remarked Daphne presently. "Why do they not begin?"

This question found an echo in my own mind. Though several minutes had elapsed since Ignatius had entered the sanctuary, he had not yet begun the prefatory rite of incensing the crucifix, but was conversing in whispers with his deacon, and their motions and glances, which were directed towards Angelo, seemed to intimate that the artist was the subject of their talk. It was with considerable surprise that we saw the deacon leave the sanctuary and, walking over to the spot where Angelo sat, still absorbed in his Missal, hold a brief but animated conversation with him. Presently he returned to the side of Father Ignatius. Whatever the object of this intercourse may have been, it had met with failure, to judge by the perplexed looks of the deacon.

The service commenced. The organ, touched by a master-hand, rolled with grand cadence through the cathedral, now swelling high and loud to the lofty arches above, now dying away with faint echoes in far-off aisles.

From the chancel issued voices so mysteriously beautiful as to suggest the idea of a hidden choir of angels. Daphne was deeply interested, and even my anti-ecclesiastical uncle condescended to remark that it was a "well-organised noise."

As for me, the character of the worship was such that at any other time it would have enthralled my senses and filled me with dreams of mediævalism; but on the present occasion curiosity to know the nature of the communication that had passed between Angelo and the deacon overcame every other feeling, and made me inattentive to the solemnity.

The tinkling bell of the acolyte sounded, and the assembly fell on their knees as Father Ignatius elevated the sacred host for the adoration of the faithful. The sun by this time had mounted high above the rooftops and was now gilding the chancel-window with its splendour: and from the holy dove figured at the apex of this casement, arrowy beams of mystic and many coloured light slanted full on the head of the aged priest, lighting up a countenance thin and ascetic, yet bearing in every lineament the lofty spirit and iron will of a Hildebrand.

The time had come for the people to receive the Mass. Among the first to advance and kneel reverently at the altar-rails was Angelo. My position prevented me from seeing his face. I could not help wondering whether his faith was sincere, and whether, in accordance with the spirit of the holy mystery, he was in charity with all mankind, even with me, his rival.

The administration of the sacrament was conducted by Father Ignatius accompanied by the deacon, who held the paten under his host as it was placed on the tongue of the receiver. The worthy padre commenced at the Epistle side of the altar. Angelo was the ninth in order from that end. We noticed with surprise that Ignatius, while giving the host to the first eight, never once looked at them, but kept his eyes all the time on Angelo with a fixed stony expression that gave no indication of his thoughts.

I waited with painful interest for the priest to confront Angelo, absurdly thinking there might be some secret between them, and that in addition to the ritual words Ignatius might whisper others not of sacred import. I was certainly not prepared for the result. As Angelo reverently elevated his face to receive the wafer between his lips, Ignatius, affecting not to notice the action, passed him by for the next communicant, and proceeded with the delivery.

I was doubtful at first whether I had seen aright, but the looks interchanged among the assembly told me that others too had observed the action. My wonder found its reflection in the wide-open eyes of Daphne; her arm trembled on mine, but she did not speak; for a deep silence had fallen over all, and the faintest whisper would have attracted attention.

What could be the reason for this action on the part of the priest? What could Angelo have done to forfeit the privileges of the Church? Quick as a flash of light there rose before me the confessional scene of the preceding day. Was the rejection of Angelo the result of the recital made to Father Ignatius by the silver-haired penitent? Of the nature of that confession I had only an inkling, but that it was the key to this priest's conduct I felt certain.

The first line of communicants retired to their seats. The artist did not move but remained kneeling solitary and silent, his lips pressing the cold marble chancel-rails, his hands clasped nervously above his dark hair, as if he were supplicating the Church, his mother, to receive and forgive an erring child.

For a brief moment I had entertained the idea that Ignatius, in passing Angelo by, had perhaps committed an oversight. It was impossible now for him not to perceive the artist; but with a face cold and impenetrable as marble he stood erect within the chancel, openly ignoring the other's mute appeal to be noticed. It was clear that his refusal to give the Communion to him was a deliberate act. The most exquisite penalty that can fall on the soul of a devout Catholic had fallen on Angelo. A rustle of surprise passed through the assembly like the ripple of the forest-leaves swayed by the summer breeze.

Despite my jealousy I could not help pitying the artist at having to suffer this slight in the face of a great mass of people. He had crossed the sea and travelled hundreds of miles expressly (so he had told us) to be present at this solemn festa—a festa hallowed by all the memories of his childhood and youth; and the end of it all was to become an excommunicate from the Church he loved, an object of suspicion to the people among whom he had been brought up.

Several minutes had elapsed since the first communicants had retired; a second line had not yet come forward, and the artist continued to kneel in silent loneliness. Still he moved not, as if dreading to lift his head and face the wondering eyes of the faithful.

Father Ignatius was in a dilemma. Knowing—as I supposed—his old *protégé's* passionate nature, he feared that a command for the artist to retire might provoke an outburst of rage that would profane the sacred solemnity. He hesitated to speak, and so this singular tableau continued some moments longer, and people looked at each other, wondering how it was going to end.

Suddenly the deep hush and awe that lay on all was broken. Sweetly, solemnly, from some hidden portion of the chancel, in tones as clear as a silver bell, the voice of a woman arose. She was singing a sacred solo; and the words directed none to draw near the altar but those whose consciences were pure, whose lives were holy. The effect of this music was thrilling in the extreme. Whether applicable or not to the would-be communicant, certain it was that his whole figure quivered like an aspen, and his head sank still lower on the chancel-rails. The solo did not form part of Mozart's Mass, and I could not help thinking afterwards that Father Ignatius had previously directed that the words should be sung in the event of the artist's presenting himself at the altar.

Still Angelo did not stir; and the deacon glanced at Father Ignatius, as if apprehensive of a disturbance. That ecclesiastic staved off the difficulty for a time by motioning the attendants to bring forward a second line of communicants, who, advancing to the chancel, knelt some on one side of Angelo, some on the other.

Would the priest ignore the artist a second time? was the thought that filled every mind in the cathedral. Interest gleamed from every face. The sanctuary had assumed for the time being the aspect of a stage, and with bated breath the assembly awaited the result, as an audience awaits the *dénouement* of a play. The only person who showed no trace of feeling was Ignatius himself. With solemn air he proceeded to the delivery of the Sacrament. Once more he approached the artist, who elevated his face to receive the host, and once more did Ignatius pass him by.

At this second refusal Angelo bounded to his feet with a suddenness that startled every one except Ignatius, who, calm and dignified, drew back a few paces, covering with the linen corporal the paten containing the wafers as if to guard them from seizure and profanation.

The Weird Picture

With eyes of fire and lip of scorn Angelo glared round on the assembly, as if in disdain of any opinion they might have formed of him, his face proud, dark, and defiant. The cathedral attendants, observing his wild bearing, were stepping forward to remove him, but a signal from Father Ignatius checked their advance.

"Peace!" he exclaimed with lifted hand, and at his word the rising murmur of many voices was hushed. "Peace! Let there be no tumult, I pray you, my children. My conduct may seem harsh, but the occasion warrants it. My son," he continued, turning to the artist, "you have forced this humiliation on yourself. Warned yestereven by me that you had forfeited the privileges of the Church, you have yet dared to disobey her voice, and to approach her hallowed altar. Leave this holy place, I pray you in quietude; or if force be employed in your removal, on your head be the guilt of profanation!"

A wave of emotion swept over Angelo, but with an effort he subdued it, and faced the priest.

"One question, and I retire. For what reason do you thus refuse me the Mass?"

"The reverence due to the holy mysteries forbids you to participate in them. Now go. Would that my words might be: *Vade in pace!*" The voice of a judge giving sentence of death could not have been more impressive than those solemn tones issuing from the depths of the chancel. "Will you compel me to speak out?" he added, as the artist showed no sign of moving. "Let your own conscience vindicate me."

"My conscience acquits me of any action that can justify you in excluding me from the Communion."

"The saints pardon thee that falsehood, my son!"

"Falsehood!" repeated the artist, stepping up to the chancel rails with clenched hands, and with so dark an expression on his face that I thought he was going to attack Ignatius. "If it were not for your age and holy office, you would not dare use such words to me. But the priest is protected by his alb and chasuble, as a woman by her sex. You have publicly affronted me. I demand an explanation, nor will I retire till you give it."

"This is not the time or place. At the confessional will I hear thee—nay, absolve thee; but come not as thou art to the holy altar."

"I tell you,"—Angelo began angrily, but Ignatius would not hear him.

"Too long have we listened to thee!" he exclaimed with a gesture of impatience. "Attendants, remove this brawler, ere from the high altar we curse him with bell, book, and candle!"

"Touch me at your peril!" cried Angelo fiercely. "Who dare accuse me of——"

His eyes, glaring defiantly round at one and all, suddenly lighted upon us. There in that hour of his humiliation he beheld a sight calculated to call up all the bitterness of his nature; the woman whom he loved reclining in the arms of the man whom he hated! Daphne, with a frightened air, was clinging half fainting to me.

He cast a look at her as if appealing for sympathy, but in the expression of her face, and in the quickly averted motion of her head, he read the loss of all his hopes.

I was but human—it was ignoble of me, I know—but I could not repress the exultant thought that this was a splendid triumph for me!

A similar thought was evidently passing through the mind of the artist. Despair caused him to stand immovable, staring in Daphne's direction, regardless of the people's murmurs that rose on the air like the sound of many waters—regardless of the advice of the attendants to withdraw quietly. Like a statue he stood, deaf to their appeals, till at length, losing their patience, the attendants, aided by some of of the worshippers, laid hands on him to enforce his removal. Their grasp seemed to rouse all the latent fury of his nature.

"Touch me at your peril!" he cried, struggling to free himself from their grasp and actually striking out among them with clenched hands. "Who dare accuse me of guilt? I have not deserved this," he continued, panting and breathless, as he was dragged with more force than ceremony from the chancel. "Let me go. Release my wrists. I am going quietly, I tell you. Will you not take my word? Cowards! Oh, if my hands were but free! I ... let me go ... I tell you ... let me——"

The Weird Picture

The oaken door of the sacristy removed the struggling group from our view; and the scene that for the space of a few minutes had degraded a holy solemnity to the level of a stage-representation was at an end.

"Why, the boy must be mad!" cried my uncle, as Angelo's cries became lost in the distance.

Daphne lay a dead weight in my arms.

"She has fainted," I whispered to her father; and I bore her far away from the worshippers to the entrance of the cathedral for the cool morning air to revive her.

It is impossible to describe my thoughts as I held her close to me. Once before, on the very morn of her intended wedding, she had been snatched away; and now on a second occasion, when another rival seemed on the point of winning her, and of triumphing over me, events had conspired to destroy all his hopes. Was there not a fatality in this? Was not Destiny reserving Daphne for me alone?

"No one shall ever have you but myself," I murmured, as I gazed on her beautiful face.

An old woman had been slowly following us. She now offered us her assistance.

"Let me see to her," she said, as I laid her at the pedestal of a font near the porch, and, kneeling, sustained her head on my knee. "Poor pretty lady, she will soon come to."

And she proceeded to remove Daphne's hat, and to loosen her cloak and dress.

We waited a few moments, but she lay as still and white as the alabaster font above her.

"Is there no water to be had?" said my uncle, lifting the lid of the baptismal basin and peeping in. "None here. Ah! the holy water at the porch! Good!"

"The saints forbid!" exclaimed the old dame fervently. "It would be sacrilege."

"The holy water couldn't be put to a better use," I said, as my uncle darted to look for some receptacle to convey the water in.

"Is not this lady's name Daphne Leslie?" inquired the old dame, chafing the hands of her patient.

"Yes; how did you learn it?" I asked in amazement.

"I have heard it often enough," she smiled, "on the lips of my boy Angelo. You know him well. I am his old nurse. Perhaps you have heard him speak of me."

"I believe I have," I replied.

"Ah me! this lady has turned my poor boy's brain. He is mad—quite mad—with love for her. No sleep had he last night. All through the long hours he was walking his room to and fro, to and fro, to and fro, repeating her name. Ah, why did Father Ignatius frown so on him? I want to tell her that he is a good youth and can have done nothing wrong. The Father is a hard man, and the lightest trifle displeases him. I saw this lady faint at my poor boy's disgrace, and I want to tell her that it is all well with him. Jesu, Maria!" she ejaculated suddenly, looking with loving adoration on Daphne's face "how beautiful she is! A worthy match for my handsome boy."

So this, then, was her motive in attending Daphne! To pour into her ear the praises of Angelo, and to assure her of the goodness of his character!

"Your 'boy,' as you call him, shall never have Daphne," I exclaimed savagely—"never!"

And in an ecstasy of rage and love I kissed her passionately, and at the very moment my lips met hers her dark blue eyes opened wide and looked full into mine. Was it the reflection of my own eyes that I beheld in hers or did they really shine with a tender light? Did her fingers really return my pressure, or was it but the effect of my imagination? I could not tell. She had returned to her unconscious state again. The old woman had risen to her feet, and was regarding me with a superb contempt that would have done credit to the prince of darkness.

"So you, then, are the rival of whom my boy speaks in his dreams—you!" she exclaimed with a gesture of disdain. "And do you hope to win this lady from him—you? It will not be by the beauty of your face, then. Compared with you, my boy is an angel."

"I thank you for your services," I replied coldly, "but I can dispense with them, and with your compliments too. I wish you good-day, madame."

And, seeing that my uncle could not find a vessel in which to convey the water, I lifted Daphne and carried her over to him. The old dame remained standing on the spot where I had left her, and, after contemplating me for a few seconds, walked off with a stately air.

"What have you done to offend our good *bonne*?" asked my uncle, as he sprinkled Daphne's face and throat with water.

"Who do you think she is?"

"Florence Nightingale?"

"Angelo's nurse. She was instituting comparisons between your humble servant and her oil-and-colour *protégé*; so I dismissed her."

Very slowly Daphne recovered from her swoon, smiling faintly at her weakness, and very tenderly did I lead her to a seat.

As soon as she was quite recovered my uncle left us to ascertain what had been done with Angelo.

"I feel quite frightened, Frank," said Daphne, trembling all over, "at what has just happened. Why did the priest refuse Angelo the Sacrament?"

"That is a mystery I too would like to solve."

"The priest must have had some reason for his action," she rejoined. "How awful Angelo looked when he jumped to his feet and glared round on the people! Promise me that you will not leave me alone with him," she said, laying her hand confidingly on my arm. "I feel afraid of him now; I did not think he could be so wild and passionate."

I gave her the required promise, knowing that the reason she exacted it was her dread lest the artist should use such opportunity for declaring his love to her.

She drew, perhaps unconsciously, nearer to me, and her arm within mine tightened its clasp. At the same time a rose she was wearing in her hat (a flower from the bouquet Angelo had given her the previous day) fell from its stalk. Daphne affected not to notice its fall, and it lay neglected, its petals scattered and withered as the hopes of the donor.

"Well, what have they done with Angelo?" said I to my uncle, as that worthy returned to us.

"His paroxysm of fury passed off after a few minutes, so they let him go."

"Do you think," I whispered, to my uncle as we journeyed homewards, "that Angelo's Madonna had anything to do with his expulsion from the Communion?"

"I am pretty sure that it had not," was the reply. "Angelo's was a much more grave offence."

CHAPTER IX THE ARTIST FAILS TO SECURE A MODEL

On our return from the cathedral I spent the early portion of the morning in writing letters to some college friends at Heidelberg, not forgetting at the same time to send to my uncle's butler telling him to procure another copy of the *Standard* of the date July 2nd, and to forward it to Rivoli.

My uncle, occupying himself with the files of the newspaper in question, was deep in the mazes of politics, and favoured Daphne now and then with extracts from the oratory of statesmen out of office, to the effect that the country was on the eve of ruin, and that nothing but a speedy return of the Opposition to power would ever set matters right—statements which my uncle, who favoured the Opposition, regarded as profoundly true.

Daphne yawned at the impending fall of her country without seeming to be much impressed thereby; and finally, putting on her hat, she exclaimed it was a beautiful morning for a stroll, and sauntered leisurely out, expressing a wish that I would follow her as soon as my letters were finished.

This I did, and walked down the mountain path in quest of her. Not having seen her by the time I had reached the haunted well, and not knowing in what direction to look for her, I flung myself down on a grassy bank behind the fountain, beneath the shadows of the overhanging foliage, determined to devote five minutes to a cigar before proceeding further.

The day was sunny, the breeze soft and warm, the waters of the fountain rippled pleasantly, and the shadows danced to and fro on the greensward. Repose in the shade was much more agreeable than walking in the sunlight, and I found my five minutes extending to ten, and, while dreamily thinking that it was time to resume my quest, I dropped off to sleep.

How long I continued in a state of repose I cannot tell. I was aroused by the sound of voices; and, glancing out from my covert, I saw Daphne and Angelo standing beside the fountain. The artist was labouring under some deep emotion: his dark hair hung negligently over his brow and eyes; his attire was in a frayed and disarranged state; for disorder and melancholy he looked a very Hamlet.

Evidently neither he nor Daphne was aware of my proximity. I hesitated to play the spy, but by doing so I might obtain a clue to Angelo's expulsion from the Communion—a clue that probably could be obtained in no other way, since his affection for Daphne might induce him to impart to her what he would withhold from my uncle and myself. This thought acted as a salve to my conscience, and, drawing my head within the foliage, I resolved to remain a silent and hidden spectator of the interview, in direct contravention of my promise to Daphne not to leave her alone with the artist. It was not a very honourable position I candidly admit. But I paid the penalty for it, by overhearing that which made me most miserable.

"I am afraid, Miss Leslie," the artist was saying—and his voice sounded so strange and hoarse that I scarcely recognised it to be his—"that the incident that happened this morning in the cathedral has tended to prejudice me in your esteem."

Daphne's silence seemed to imply assent to this.

"If it be this that causes you to look on me with a different face, it admits of an easy explanation. Father Ignatius recognised in you the original of my Madonna. He considers me guilty of sacrilege. My refusal to atone for it at the confessional excludes me from the communion of the Church. You know what these priests are, Miss Leslie," he continued with a sneer. "Meat in Lent, absence from confessional, a thousand similar trifles, are deadly sins in their eyes."

Daphne still maintained silence. He took from his bosom a crucifix and kissed it.

"On this crucifix, image of our God in agony, holiest symbol of the Catholic faith, I swear by my hope of salvation that I speak truth when I say that my exclusion from the Mass rests on no other ground than the one I have stated."

I did not believe him; and if he had repeated his statement twenty times, and sworn it on his crucifix twenty times, I would not have believed him. A subtle stroke on his part, this: to represent to Daphne that his tribute to her beauty had cost him nothing less than—'the communion of the saints!' It might move her to pity, and we all know to what pity is akin.

"I am sorry," said Daphne, "that I am the cause—the innocent cause," with a stress on the adjective, "of your suffering the Church's censure."

And then came a long pause, during which both stood looking at each other: he with undisguised love and admiration, she with evident distrust and fear. Each seemed afraid to break the silence.

"Miss Leslie," he continued, speaking slowly, as if it were difficult to find words, and his breathing came thick and heavy, "you can guess why in painting that picture I was enabled, in the absence of the original, to reproduce your features with such fidelity?"

"I cannot tell."

This was a falsehood on her part—a pardonable one, perhaps. She knew the reason as well as he did, and dreaded what was coming. At last, after another long pause, came the momentous declaration:

"It was *love* that aided my memory."

With his hands tremulously clasped, he bent forward, his dark eyes fixed on Daphne's face. Hers were bent on the ground. I had never seen her looking more beautiful.

"Yes," repeated Angelo, speaking with more ease now, as if his avowal of love had removed the restraint from his speech, "it was love that aided my memory. It was love, if classic story speak truth, that drew the first portrait."

It was characteristic of him that even in his lovemaking he could not wholly avoid reverting to his adored art.

"Yes," he continued, "it was love that inspired the production of my Madonna. Madonna!" he exclaimed in scornful tones, as if in contempt of his religion. "I know of no Madonna save you—your worship excludes all other. The saints are forgotten when I gaze on your face. You alone are my divinity. Visit my studio, and see how many pictures there are of that face which troubles me by day and haunts my dreams by night. Look in my desk, and see how many letters there are addressed to Miss Leslie—written, but never sent.

Miss Leslie, you must know how much I love you! O, do not say that you do not return the feeling!"

His cloak dropped back from his shoulders as he extended his arms in a pleading manner toward my cousin, his bronzed, handsome face glowing as I have seen the face of a Greek statue glow in the quivering sunset. He was not ignorant of his own personal charms, and his present attitude, acquired perhaps in the *atelier* of the artist, was purposely adapted to display the statuesque grace of his figure.

Daphne did not speak a word. I knew what her answer would be, and I knew that her reticence arose from her dread of the effect which that answer might have on the passionate nature of the artist. She had seen something of his nature that morning in the cathedral, and divined but too well that his love was of the character that turns by a leap to hatred.

"I love you," he repeated—"how deeply no words of mine can tell! The months that have separated us have been to me a torture. I cannot rest apart from you. I have come from England expressly to see you. I am here now to ask you to be mine. I had intended to stay long with, or near you, and seek to win my way gradually into your heart, but I can be silent no longer. Who can forge chains for love, and say, 'To-day thou shalt be dumb; to-morrow thou shalt speak?' Forgive me if my language seems wild. We Italians do not love so coldly as your English youth; we are all passion and flame. If I am precipitate, if I am rash, if I am mad, blame not me, but blame the beauty that has made me so."

He checked the flow of his words; they seem poor and commonplace enough on paper. It must have been the tone in which they were uttered, and the aid they received from his sparkling eyes and dramatic gestures, that made them sound like eloquence at the time.

Daphne, her drooping eyes fixed on the ground, stood beside the tree overhanging the fountain, still and silent as a statue. To say "No" to any request, however trifling, was always a source of pain to her; how much more now when it would give despair to the one it was addressed to!

"Ah, Heaven! how beautiful you are! What a picture you would make!" One might have thought from the manner in which he dwelt on the word "picture" that he wanted her for no other purpose than to minister to his art. "Will you not speak, Daphne?"

She sought refuge in evasion.

"Give me time—a day—to reflect. I will reply to you by—by letter."

"No, no—a thousand times, no! Not for worlds will I endure another such night as last in an agony of suspense and doubt. Let me have your answer here and now. This avowal cannot be a surprise to you. What woman was ever loved without knowing it? Did you not understand my action yesterday when I knelt before your picture? Could you not interpret the look in my eyes the first time they saw your face? That day marked an era in my art. For years I had been seeking to paint a face that should be the very ideal of beauty, and my hand had failed to delineate the shadowy conceptions of my mind; but at last the ideal face shone upon me. My dream of beauty was realised in a living form. With that bright form by my side to inspire my pencil——"

The artist paused, stopped by the expression on Daphne's face. Surely in the presence of the bird the net is spread in vain? Angelo's desire for Daphne was prompted quite as much by art as by love. She would be a priceless acquisition to his studio, would serve as a beautiful model for his princesses, his nymphs, and his angels. So absorbed was he in his passion for art that he could see nothing objectionable or ludicrous in his avowal. Do all artists make love in this fashion, I wonder? The thought of my own beautiful Daphne posing in various attitudes, and in various stages of dressing, before this demon of an artist, in order that he might produce some exquisite masterpiece for the delectation of a gaping public, so set my nerves a-quivering that I all but rushed from my hiding-place for the purpose of hurling him into the fountain. Great was my joy to hear Daphne's reply, given in a voice that was tinged slightly with sarcasm:

"Mr. Vasari," and she inclined her dainty head, "I thank your for the honour you do me in selecting me as your model——"

"Ah, you are cruel," the artist stammered. "It is not for art alone I love you."

"But, believe me, it can never be as you wish."

"Ah, why, Daphne? Say not that you hate me."

"You forget that I am to be Captain Willard's wife."

Angelo started. So did I, for these words were a complete revelation to me. I had thought that she had all but forgotten George, and that I was gradually replacing his image. Her utterance completely dispelled this illusion.

With a strange heaviness of heart that increased each moment, I continued to listen to the dialogue. Angelo's pleading expression had changed to one of surprise and contempt.

"Captain Willard?" he exclaimed. "Surely you do not think of him now—he who deserted you on your bridal morning! He is not worthy of you."

"Deserted me?" repeated Daphne. "Yes—but not forever, I feel sure. He has left me only for a time. Whatever the crime was in which he became involved—for crime I suppose it must have been—I am certain that it was none of *his* causing. If there be any truth in my dreams he will yet return to explain the mystery of his absence, to vindicate his character, and to take me for his wife."

She spoke with such a look shining from her eyes, with so proud a trust in the faith of her absent hero, in such a tone of conviction, that I (thinking only of my own faint—very faint—prospect of winning her) trembled, lest her words should be the heralds of a stern reality. Some dark shadows dancing suddenly across the greensward between her and Angelo, accompanied by a rustling sound as of a footstep, gave me a start as great as if the ghost of George had suddenly risen up before me.

"Your faith is womanly, sublime, but—misplaced. He will never return. He has left you forever. Think no more of him. There is one who loves you a thousand times more deeply than Captain Willard ever did; compared with mine, his love was but as ice. Ah, Daphne! say that you will be mine. I will gladly wait years for you, content to hold a second place in your affections, if in the event of Captain Willard's non-return you will offer me a little hope."

"Mr. Vasari, it cannot be, even if George were never to return. Be he living or dead, I will remain faithful to his memory."

My mental gloom increased as I listened to these firmly spoken words. Daphne little thought she was wounding two hearts by her remarks.

"Daphne, I would not hurt your feelings, but have you never considered that Captain Willard may have left you for another? If I could show you that this is the case, would you still remain faithful to his memory? Will you not rather show your scorn of him by listening to another lover—me?"

There was little in Angelo's remarks to suggest the reminiscence, and yet by some inexplicable mental process I found my mind reverting to the episode of the veiled lady. Daphne's cheek grew white and her lip quivered at the idea suggested by the Italian, but she replied proudly:

"I will never believe that he was faithless."

"If I could prove that he left you for another—" began the artist.

It was now Daphne's turn to become the suppliant.

"Oh, why do you say this? You talk as if you knew something of him. If you have any knowledge of him, tell me, for pity's sake! Do you know where he is?"

"First, my question requires an answer. If I could prove that he left you for another, what would be your answer to me then?"

In the interval that elapsed between the question and the reply I could have counted sixty. The deep silence was broken only by the ripple of the fountain. I almost thought I could hear her heart beating against her breast. But the question must be answered, and drawing her dress around her with a grace which charmed while it maddened the artist, and raising her head with the proud dignity of a queen, she replied:

"Since you force me to speak out, and are determined to have an answer from me, listen to it. I do not love you, and—forgive me if my words seem harsh; better a cold truth than a sweet falsehood—it is better that you should know now, once and for all, I could never love you—never, *never*, NEVER!"

There could be no mistaking the meaning of those cold, deliberate words. It pained her to say them, and I believe she would have burst into a flood of tears; but she repressed her emotion, lest it should encourage Angelo to a more earnest persistency of his suit.

The effect of her refusal on the artist was singular in the extreme. At first he trembled, in every limb, and I could distinctly see drops of perspiration glistening on his brow. Then, as he realised all the bitterness of his position, and that the lovely woman before him was lost to him forever and ever, and that if they were to live a thousand years on the earth she would still be as cold to him as she was at that moment, he lifted his arms with a slow motion and extended them towards her, and for some moments he maintained this position, petrified to rigidity, staring at her with ghastly look and glassy eye. His attitude was the very apotheosis of despair.

I marvelled at his emotion. My own sense of disappointment on hearing Daphne express her determination to remain faithful to George was exquisitely bitter, but, bitter as it was, it was apparently but a tithe of the pain felt by the artist.

Several times he tried to speak, but no words came from his dry lips. It was painful to see him going through the mockery of speaking, yet unable to produce a sound. It was as if the dead, touched by some galvanic apparatus, were trying to assume the mechanism of life, and when at last he did speak his strange hollow voice aided the illusion.

"Miss Leslie, you surely cannot—cannot mean *that*!"

"Indeed I do," was the cold reply.

Scarcely able to keep his feet, the artist moved backward till he touched the trunk of a tree, where he leaned for support. The sight of his misery touched Daphne to the quick, and she cried impulsively:

"O Mr. Vasari, I am sorry for you; but I cannot love you. I cannot forget George. Believe me, it pains me to have to say this. Try to think it is for the best."

The Weird Picture

She placed her hand timidly on his arm; but he swung it off with so dark an expression on his face that I had almost thrown myself between them.

"I want not your pity," he exclaimed scornfully, turning the fire of his eyes on her, "if I cannot have your love!"

And, ignoble at heart, he began now to sneer at the prize he found beyond his reach.

"And so," he continued in a bitter tone, "rather than accept the love of one who can immortalise you by his pencil you prefer to be a living cenotaph whose sad aspect testifies the esteem set upon her by her first lover!"

Dropping his sneering tone for one of fierce anger, he added:

"You must have some less fanciful reason for rejecting me than this absurd attachment to—to a shadow. Tell me, do you not love another?"

"Mr. Vasari, you have no right to question me thus. You have received your answer, and this meeting may as well end, since it seems now that insult is to be my portion."

And she turned proudly to go.

"Stay!" cried Angelo, barring her passage. "You evade my question. You love another. Nay, do not deny it. I will not accept your denial. I know who my rival is. Let him beware. You may listen to his whispered words, smile at his kisses, receive his gifts; but never shall you go with him to the altar! Rather will I see you dead by my own hand first!"

"Oh, why do you talk so wildly? Leave me and think no more of me. There are many women whose love is more worth winning than mine. Try to forget me."

"Forget you?" and he laughed bitterly. "There are many artists, but only one Raphael; there are many women, but only one Daphne. O Daphne! dear, dear Daphne!"—his manner changed at once from the fierceness of scorn to the softness of love, as, dropping on one knee, he held her struggling hands in his and covered them with kisses, "do not refuse me! You——"

"Mr. Vasari, it is not right to detain me against my wish. Let go my hands."

He obeyed her, sprang to his feet, but continued his pleading tones:

"Daphne, I beseech you to recall your decision. You asked for a day to consider. Let me meet you here in twenty-four hours. I have been too precipitate. I surprise, frighten you. You were not prepared for this. Give me your final answer to-morrow."

"I have given you my answer."

He looked at her beautiful face, so cold in its firmness to resist all entreaties, and then, turning as if to address an imaginary audience, said:

"Can this cold statue really be the same maiden who but yesterday smiled at my gifts and blushed at my words? How quick a change has passed over her! Yes," he continued, observing the colour that mounted to Daphne's brow at these last words, "yes, blush at your actions of yesterday. You cannot deny that by your words and your smiles you have encouraged me to this confession."

"Mr. Vasari," she returned, speaking very humbly, with her eyes fixed on one pretty little foot that was shifting uneasily to and fro on the greensward, "I cannot deny that your attentions gave me pleasure. I am fond of admiration—perhaps too fond. I am only too sorry now that my vanity had led you to put a false interpretation on what was intended for friendship only, and must ask you to forgive me."

He looked with a wistful gaze at her fair face, but read no encouragement there. A long silence ensued during which he seemed to grow calmer and more resigned to his position.

"Enough of this supplication," he muttered, folding his cloak around him with a moody, half-scornful air.

Art had apparently humiliated itself too long in the presence of Beauty.

"Let us part friends," said Daphne.

But he turned from the little hand offered to him in friendship. Magnanimity did not form part of his character.

"Will you not come and see us to-morrow?" said Daphne, affecting not to notice the repulse.

"I leave Rivoli to-day—this hour. You will see me no more."

"Will you not say good-bye to my father and Frank?"

A scornful gesture of refusal was his only reply, and, with a dark glance, he was preparing to depart when a motion from Daphne stopped him.

"Angelo," she said in a plaintive, supplicating voice, and using the Christian name of the artist—she was loth to ask the question of him, and yet felt that she must—"Angelo, answer me truly. If you know anything of Captain Willard—and your words just now seemed to imply that you do—tell me, I implore you, and I will be—your—your best friend," she added, as if sorry she could not offer him the highest place in her regard. "Do you know where he is?"

"Do I know where he is?" repeated the Italian with a peculiar laugh. He turned back, took a step nearer to Daphne, and said:

"You are nearer to him now than you have been for months."

He seemed on the point of saying more, but, suddenly turning on his heel, he left her.

"O Angelo, what do you mean?" she called out after him.

But the artist was now plunging down the mountain side, and if he heard her words, did not at any rate reply to them. Daphne watched him sadly for a few moments, and then, turning away, began to ascend the zigzag path which led to the châlet. Not wishing to let her know that I had been a spectator of the interview, I remained where I was, and gazed after the retreating figure of Angelo, who was springing down from crag to crag in a manner that augured very little care for his own safety, his dark locks and long cloak swaying on the breeze.

I, Frank Willard, sitting there on that calm summer day amid the loveliest scenery of Switzerland, rich in youth and health, endowed by my uncle with a competent fortune, and with nothing much to trouble my conscience, will seem to many an object of envy; and yet there I was, bewailing what I called my sad destiny, and sentimentally thinking myself the most unhappy of mankind.

Daphne's avowal of her continued love for George had cast a gloom over me. Was I again to tread the Via Dolorosa of hopeless love, and, as the melancholy student of Heidelberg, to outwatch the stars once more on the solitary crags of the Odenwald?

"Living or dead, I will remain faithful to his memory."

"You are nearer to him now than you have been for months."

These two sentences continued to haunt my mind all the way to the châlet. The artist's parting words seemed to imply that George was living at Rivoli—an idea that had previously occurred to me. What would become of my love-dream if, on hearing that Daphne was at Rivoli, George should emerge from his seclusion with some strange but justifiable reason for his past conduct? Would he do this, I wondered, or would he remain hidden in obscurity? A shadow fell across my path. I looked up, and the porch of the châlet fronted me with its legend, ominous, so it seemed to me, of some coming tragedy:

"He shall return!"

CHAPTER X—GHOST OR MORTAL?

On entering the house I found my uncle looking over a packet of letters that his valet had just brought from Rivoli. Daphne was cutting open the envelopes with a paper knife. No one would have thought from her quiet demeanour that she had just been the recipient of a passionate love appeal.

"How well women can conceal these things," I thought, dropping despondently into a chair.

"Oh, papa, here is an envelope with a seal as big as a florin. Who is it from?" Daphne's curiosity gave her no time to observe the niceties of grammar. "Do read it."

My uncle settled his glasses on his nose and examined the letter.

"It is from an old schoolfellow, Hugh Wyville," he said. "He has just succeeded to the baronetcy and is now Sir Hugh Wyville, and master of a splendid property in Cornwall. Silverdale Abbey is the name of his place. He wants us to spend Christmas with him. It's a little early for the invitation, but I suppose he wants to forestall all other invitations. He says—it is shocking writing; he ought to get a Secretary—he says he will take a great interest in my slaughter. What the deuce does he mean? Slaughter? Oh, I see—daughter. That's you, Daphne."

"Much obliged to him, I'm sure, papa."

"He is now in Paris buying pictures. Says his gallery alone is worth a visit to Cornwall, and he is adding to it still. Well, what shall we say to the invitation, Daphne? Shall we accept it?"

"What do you say, Frank?" she said.

"I say, yes," I answered. "Christmas at an old abbey ought to be delightful."

"Then that is settled," my uncle said. "I'll write to him to-day." And being a man of his word, he wrote.

"There are to be all sorts of sports at Rivoli this afternoon," he announced at luncheon—"archery, musical contests, dances, and I don't know what else. Would you like to see them, Daphne, or are you too tired?"

She pleaded that she was, but would not hear of our remaining at home on her account, and as my uncle seemed to expect my company, I set off with him to the town, conscious that I was a little unchivalrous to Daphne in doing so.

On our way through the valley I paused to admire a cottage of firwood perched on a crag overhanging the road.

"That is the house in which Angelo said his old nurse lives," said my uncle, looking at it with interest. "Let us give a call."

"What for?" I asked, surprised.

"Well, I am curious to know what his explanation of that affair in the cathedral is, and he might refer to it; indeed, I don't see how he can avoid doing so."

We ascended some steps roughly cut out of the solid rock, and entering a porch over which a vine clambered, we tapped gently at the door. It was opened by the old woman who had offered her good services to Daphne in the cathedral. The moment she saw us her face assumed a hard expression, and contrary to the hospitable spirit usual in the district did not invite us inside but kept us standing at the door.

"What do you want?" she demanded curtly.

"We want to see Mr. Vasari, if he is at home," my uncle answered civilly. "We are friends of his. Perhaps you have heard him speak of Mr. Leslie. I am Mr. Leslie."

"Angelo is not here. He has left for England."

"What? Without saying good-bye to us?"

"He left by the diligence two hours ago."

"So soon? Do you know why?"

"Why?" she flashed out. "Ask this boy here!" and she turned to me with a lowering brow. "But for you he would have won the love of the English lady. But for you he would have been saved from—from—"

"From what?" I said eagerly, too eagerly I suppose, for she shook her head as if she took a pleasure in withholding the information she was about to give.

"I will tell you nothing," she said. "He can live without your pity. Go! After all, she is a Protestant, and all Protestants go to hell. Father Ignatius says so."

"That is our ultimate destination, I believe," said my uncle with a sigh, due rather to vexation at finding himself unable to get the information he wanted than to proper regret at his future doom. "We are a wicked lot."

"Can you tell us why Father Ignatius refused Angelo the Mass?" I asked. "That looks as if the good Father were not any too confident about *him*."

Her eyes blazed at the suggestion.

"I will tell you nothing," she said again, and closed her lips tightly as if she feared that her thoughts might assume material shape and make their escape against her will, if her mouth were ever so little open.

"We shall gain nothing by staying here," my uncle remarked. "Madame, I wish you a very good day," with which words he led the way down to the road again, and we resumed our journey to the town, wondering what it was from which the artist might have been saved, and how Daphne's love could have saved him from it.

"We may see your aged friend from Dover to-day, if we keep our eyes open," my uncle said presently. "The sports are sure to draw all the people out of doors."

"We may see Paolo too," I replied. "It is strange that he did not turn up last night as he promised, and strange that he wasn't at Mass this morning; at least if he was I did not see him."

"Not at all strange, if Father Ignatius has ordered him to avoid us."

"Why should he do that?" I asked in surprise.

"You remember Paolo breaking off from us suddenly, because, as he said, some deacon was watching him?"

"I do—Serafino he called him."

"That's the name. Well, it's not at all improbable that this Serafino told Ignatius that, immediately after his retirement to the sacristy with the old man, certain strangers began to question Paolo, giving him money. Thereupon Ignatius sends for Paolo. 'Paolo,' he demands *ex cathedra*, 'what did these strangers say to you?' perhaps threatening to dismiss him from his post, or, still more, threatening the poor fellow with excommunication, if he should refuse to disclose his knowledge. Paolo blurts out the truth, and lets the padre know that we are deeply interested in learning what the old man's confession was about. Whereupon the reverend Father, not at all desirous of our becoming cognisant of statements given under the seal of the confessional, delivers judgment: 'Paolo you have done very wrong. Give up those silver coins to your holy mother the Church; and as a penance recite to me next holy-day the 119th Psalm, and remember to keep out of the way till these strangers have left Rivoli.' I may be wrong, but it's my opinion that something of this sort has taken place."

We were soon within the streets of Rivoli. All the inhabitants seemed to have turned out of their homes, and by the merriment of their talk and the brightness of their gala dresses were contributing to the gaiety of the scene.

The centre of attraction was the market-place, where picturesquely-clad hunters and shepherds were displaying their skill with the rifle to admiring and applauding crowds. These sons of William Tell did not receive from us the attention that their feats deserved, for our eyes were continually wandering from them to scan the faces of the spectators. Paolo, however, and the nameless old man from Dover were not to be seen.

From the sweet singing-contests in the cathedral we wandered to the meadows outside the town, where youths and flower-crowned maidens danced, wreathing and twining in pretty figures on the greensward, and thence back again to the town, peeping in each tavern, resonant with jollity and song, and odorous with the fragrance of the fir-cones that strewed the floor. But we could not find Paolo or the mysterious old man.

The Weird Picture

Tired at length of prosecuting a search that seemed to promise no success, we turned our attention to the innocent diversions, which were protracted till the moon, rising above the shining snows of the mountain-tops, projected the shadow of the cathedral belfry across the market-place. The white light silvered the quaint gables, was reflected from the diamond panes of many a casement, and, mingling with the glare of the torches carried by some of the crowd, produced a picturesque and romantic effect.

The sweet carillon of the cathedral bells, pealing forth the quarters, warned the people that midnight was drawing nigh, and gradually the throng began to disperse. Imitating their example my uncle and I directed our footsteps homewards. Groups of peasants and shepherds passed us on the way, some singing gaily, others winding with their horns the melodious "*Ranz des Vaches.*"

As we turned to quit the road for the mountain-path, the cathedral bell chimed the first stroke of midnight.

"Twelve o'clock!" exclaimed my uncle in a deep, tragic voice. "Now is the time when elves and fairies trip it on the greensward, and spirits rise from yon haunted well. Come, let us sit by it for a time and enjoy the ghostly revels. It is an affront to Nature to sleep on such a night as this."

Slowly the silver tongue from the belfry continued to toll forth the chimes with a solemn little interval between each. As the twelfth stroke died gently away, a peculiar sound, muffled by the distance, was wafted to my ears, seeming to my quickened fancy like the cry of a woman. Whence the sound proceeded I could not tell. It might have come from the north; it might have come from the south.

"Did you hear it?" I said.

"Hear what?"

"A sound like a woman's scream."

We both listened for a few moments, but the sound, whatever it was, was not repeated.

"Your fancy," my uncle remarked with a smile. "In such a place as this you will hear many ghostly cries, if you give your imagination rein. But don't let us turn in just yet. I've some good news for you."

Wondering a good deal what the news would be, I followed him to the fountain. He found a seat on a mossy boulder close to the stonework of the well, and leaning back against the trunk of a tree, proceeded to light a fresh cigar, as an indispensable aid to reflection.

The moon was now at its zenith, riding through a veil of light fleecy clouds. Around us at the distance of a furlong towered an amphitheatre of rocks, and the jagged edges of this cliff sharply defined against the deep violet sky exhibited crags of fantastic shape like the towers and pinnacles of some genie's castle. It required but small aid from fancy to believe that the blast of a horn startling the midnight air would summon to these crags beings as wild and unearthly as ever crowded the haunted Brocken on a Walpurgis-night. No more appropriate scene could be imagined for the revelry of demons and witches.

The solemn hour and the wild legends connected with the spring contributed to invest the place with an atmosphere of mystery. The trees whispered secrets to each other: the waters rippled with a cold and ghostly sparkle. In the distance foaming waterfalls standing out in relief against a background of dark rocks glimmered like waving white-robed spirits with a never-ceasing murmur. The air seemed alive with the mystic "tongues that syllable men's names on sands, and shores, and desert wildernesses."

Who that has visited a scene of deep beauty by moonlight has not felt an awe stealing over him, as if some unseen presence were by? Such a presence seemed to be floating around us, whispering that we were on haunted ground. Was it the far-off murmur of a cascade or the faint voice of some one calling for help that was wafted to our ears?

So firm was my belief that the sound was of human origin that I appealed to my uncle, who had been strangely silent.

"Did you not hear a distant cry, as of some one in pain?"

"I thought so, but it must be fancy. Let us listen again."

We were silent for a time, but there was no repetition of the sound.

"Some shepherds calling one another," he said, resuming his cigar with a laugh. "We are becoming influenced by the superstitions of the place."

He seemed to have forgotten the communication he had promised to make, so I reverted to it.

"You were going to tell me a piece of news, I think?"

"Ah! so I was. (If you wouldn't mind turning your head from me, Frank; your eyes seem to have an unearthly gleam by this light. Thank you!) Well, here is my news. Daphne had a proposal to-day. You can guess from whom."

"Is that your news? Then it is no news at all. I know it already."

"The deuce you do! How did *you* learn it?"

"I was present during the whole interview." I gave him an account of how I came to play the spy, adding: "How did you learn it?"

"She told me directly after parting from him. Poor Daphne! she was quite upset over it—crying, in fact."

"She might have spared her tears," I grumbled. "His love was not so disinterested that she need weep. My candid opinion is that the fellow is so mad over his art that it governs even his choice of a wife, and he selects Daphne because he thinks her figure will serve as a model for some of his pictures." And I detailed to my uncle those utterances of the artist that seemed to bear out my opinion.

"A naïve avowal, certainly. His mode of lovemaking was a fine example of 'How not to do it.' And so," he continued, after a brief interval, "Daphne still hopes and dreams that George will return. Absurd! I thought she had given up that idea long ago. However, let him return. He shall never have Daphne—never!"

He said that last word in a decidedly emphatic manner, and scarcely had he said it when a startled expression crossed his face, the cigar dropped from his lips, and he looked nervously round in all directions.

"My dear uncle, what is the matter?" said I, amused at his alarm.

"Didn't you hear a laugh?"

"A laugh? No! Why, you are becoming nervous!"

Never before had I seen my uncle looking so startled as he was at that moment. The one point of his character on which he prided himself was his disbelief in the supernatural. To see him trembling at a mere sound was a surprise to me. I had yet to learn that extremes meet. Have there not lived philosophers who, denying the existence of ghosts, have nevertheless been so apprehensive of meeting them as never to enter a dark room without a light? My uncle's philosophy savoured very much of this character.

"Bah!" he exclaimed, picking up his cigar from the grass after listening intently. "You are right. I *am* becoming nervous. Well, I was on the point of saying——"

"That you will never allow George to marry Daphne. Why?"

"Why? Can you ask? Is not the reason obvious? A man who could desert her on her wedding-day, sending a cold note to the effect that she must never see him more, forfeits her by that very act. Good God! I become mad when I think of his conduct. Remember Daphne's thin, wasted figure and wan, wistful look last spring. She might have died. Grief has killed people before to-day. He must have known how much her heart would be wrung by his conduct, and yet—never a word of explanation from him. No. If he were to return this very night, he should never have her—never!"

"I have often wondered why he took his departure so hurriedly."

"His reason must have been a very bad one if it could not be stated by letter even to his nearest relatives," replied my uncle, speaking in a very bitter tone, for naturally he could not be expected to think well of the man who had deserted his daughter, even though that man were his own nephew. "His flight was accompanied by very suspicious circumstances, you must admit, seeming to point to complicity with, if not to the actual perpetration of crime. He will never return, rest assured of that; and I told Daphne to abandon the idea."

"What was her answer?"

"Tears. 'Look around you,' I said. 'You will soon find a worthier lover. Frank loves you, and you know it.' And I launched out into your praises, for between ourselves, Frank, there is no one to whom I would more willingly give Daphne than yourself."

I suppose I ought to have thanked my uncle for thus championing my cause, but I preferred Daphne's love to turn towards me without being directed by paternal authority, so I merely said:

"What did she say?"

"She said that she could not so soon forget George, but that if he had not returned by a twelvemonth from the day he left—"

"That is, next Christmas Day?"

"Just so; next Christmas Day. If he had not returned by then she would try to think no more of him."

"Next Christmas Day! What a whimsical notion!"

"Exactly. Women *are* whimsical," returned my uncle, speaking as if he had had all the experience of a Mormon. "Well, she did not seem— What the devil's that?" he exclaimed with a suddenness that startled me.

The "airy tongues," that during the whole time of our conversation had never ceased to whisper mysteriously, had now changed to a series of deep and regularly recurring sighs. They were not the creation of our fancy. Distinguishable from the murmur of the fountain was a sound as of some one breathing. It proceeded from a cluster of trees on one side of the spring.

Too much surprised to speak, my uncle and I sat staring at each other without either will or power to move. Then, shaking off the spell that lay upon us, we rose and stepped on tip-toe to the spot whence came the sound, moving cautiously and softly, as though within the grove some terrible dragon lay sleeping which loud footsteps might awaken. Within the gloom created by a canopy of dense foliage we caught the gleam of something white. Our eyes, unaccustomed at first to the darkness, could distinguish nothing clearly, but gradually the object of our attention resolved itself into the seated figure of a woman. I thought at first that it was the statue of some nymph, but the eyes, shining like stars, dispelled this illusion. Four steps nearer, and I saw that it was no Dryad of the grove or Undine of the waters, but our own loved Daphne. She seemed petrified with terror.

"Good heavens, Daphne!" cried her father. "What are you doing here at this hour of night?"

The only reply to this question was a continuation of the deep inspirations that had drawn our attention to her. Fright had deprived her of the power of speech.

"She is recovering from a swoon," said my uncle. "What can have frightened her? Daphne, dear, tell us what is the matter. All is well now. Don't be afraid. Tell us how long you have been here."

"How long? Ah! a long time," she murmured, speaking like one in a dream.

A sigh of relief escaped her father's lips, for her reply seemed an assurance of her sanity, and his first thought had been that fright had turned her brain. Her wild expression might well have given him this idea.

"Tell me what is the matter, darling," he said, lifting her, and stroking her hair with a fatherly tenderness. "My poor little girl!"

She gazed fearfully around, as if dreading some awful vision. Then closing her eyes with a shudder, she rested her head on his shoulder, and clung like a child to his embrace.

"Have you not seen it?" she asked in a whisper.

"We have seen nothing, that is, nothing to be frightened at. Come, open your eyes and look at me, darling. Tell me all about it. What has frightened you so?"

She was so thoroughly unnerved that it was a long time before she could be induced to talk at all. When at last she *did* reply her words were not a little startling.

"O, papa. I have seen George's ghost!"

My uncle shot a glance half whimsical, half nervous at me, for it was very odd that her explanation should have reference to the man of whom we ourselves had just been talking. But he affected a laugh of kindly scepticism.

"George's ghost, eh? And how could you see George's ghost when he isn't dead? How long have you been here, and why did you come at all?"

"I have been thinking of him ever since you went out," she said, after another long pause. "He has been in my mind all the time, and try as I would I could not get his face out of my thoughts. I wondered whether he were alive or dead, and at last I began to feel that he must be dead, or he would have returned before this, or would at least have written to me. To-night was so lovely that I came out partly to meet you, and I came to this well, and stopped as I was rather tired. And then I took off the ring he gave me, and—" She paused between each sentence as if it hurt her to go on, but the mere fact of telling her story seemed to do her good, and she continued. "And I thought that as he had broken all his promises and cast me off on the very day fixed for our wedding, I would cast off his ring; and at last I made up my mind, and I threw it into the well. And presently I looked up, and there, on the other side of the well was—" she hesitated again, and clung closer to her father—"don't laugh, papa dear, it really was George's ghost."

"I'm not laughing," her father said. "Tell me how he looked."

"He was wearing the same dress and the same grey cloak that he wore the night he left me. He looked so sad, as if he had understood all that I had been thinking. I tried to speak, but in a moment he was gone. And then I screamed and turned to run away, but I suppose I fainted.—It was not fancy, papa. It was George's ghost. I could see the stars shining through him."

"Well, well!" her father said, shrugging his shoulders, but still stroking her hair; "we will see whether you are of the same opinion to-morrow morning. You see, your mind has been full of him all day, and at last it has played you a trick, and you think you have seen with your bodily eyes what could have existed only in your imagination. Sitting all alone at twelve o'clock at night, in this eerie place, I only wonder that you haven't seen half-a-dozen ghosts. When you are indoors by a bright fire after a second supper, you will

The Weird Picture

laugh yourself at your fright. Do you think you can walk all right now, if I give you an arm? Come, that's splendid! The sooner you are away from this weird spot and out of this heavy dew, the better."

"Did you say you threw the ring into the well, Daphne," I asked, "or only that you were going to do so?"

"I threw it in," she replied; "but never mind, let it stay there."

"Oh, but that's a pity," her father said. "You may be sorry afterwards, and it will not be difficult to recover it. Have a try, Frank."

"Didn't you take it out of the water, again?" I asked.

"No."

"Then where is it? I am looking hard, but I can't see it."

We all peered into the fountain. There was plenty of light for the purpose, and we could see the sandy bottom of the well quite clearly, but the ring was nowhere visible.

"Can't you see it?" said Daphne anxiously.

I hesitated to reply as I did not want to add to her alarm, but as she pressed me I said as carelessly as I could—

"I don't see it in the water. You must have thrown it on to the grass;" and I began to feel among the moss and verdure that fringed the stonework of the well.

"No, it fell into the water," Daphne said. "I heard the splash, and noticed the rings of water widening out before I looked up and saw—George! It must be there."

It was not to be found, however, either in the well or on the bordering grass, and we had to give up the search and make up our minds to go home without it. Language is but a feeble thing to express the surprise we all felt, and I could guess from the expression on Daphne's face something of her thoughts. In throwing away George's ring she had thrown away the pledge of her love for him, and from the mysterious manner in which it had disappeared it seemed almost as if the dead had accepted her renunciation.

I had long been familiar with the idea that at the point of death the disembodied spirit may appear to distant friends; and the thought now held me that the figure I had seen last Christmas amid the falling snow at Dover was the apparition of my brother, who had perhaps been seized with death in a manner secret and sudden. Could it be that, owing to some telepathic influence exerted on him by Daphne's mind, his spirit had been permitted to return to earth for a brief space to assure her of his death, and by vanishing with the ring that she was now free from her engagement to him? In the light of day and far from the scene of the event one may smile at this theory, but by that well in the ghostly moonlight, with Daphne's terror fresh on me, and the ring gone, it seemed quite in harmony with the circumstances. The eerie sensation that had been creeping over my uncle and myself since we had taken our station by the haunted well deepened now to an indescribable intensity.

Our interval of uneasy silence was brought to a close by a sound of many voices stealing faintly on the breeze—so faintly that we disputed at first what it was. The sounds drew gradually nearer, and their measured rhythmic cadence would have suggested a party of peasants returning home, but that the music had more the air of a solemn litany than of revelry. Daphne, wondering what new source of surprise or terror was in store for her, clung trembling to her father. The place where we stood was elevated above the roadway, and we by and by saw winding along its course a procession of cowled and corded monks, marching two and two in solemn order, and chanting a mournful refrain. Some bore aloft flaming torches, an act that, even in the excitement of the moment, I could not help thinking to be an absurdity, seeing that the moonlight made everything as bright as day. A few of the train were boys, and their silvery trebles made sweet contrast with the deep bass of their elders.

With bowed heads and measured pace the monks advanced, seeming in their grey robes silvered by the moonlight more like ghostly figures in a dream than living beings in a real world.

Those at the head of the procession were carrying a bier upon which lay something covered with a cassock.

"A strange hour for a burial," said my uncle, "if burial it be. Or are they carrying to the town some dead body they have discovered among the mountains?"

"O papa!" cried Daphne, clutching her father's arm, and speaking in a broken voice, "can he have committed suicide?"

"Who?"

"Angelo! I remember his wild look when he left me. Oh, if it should be——"

"No, no, you are frightening yourself without reason," said her father in a reassuring tone. "It is not Angelo. Can you not see? It is one of their own order whom they are mourning. They would not make such a lament over mere secular clay, I warrant you. Stay here, and Frank and I will ascertain who it is. You do not mind being left alone for a minute or two? No harm can happen to you. We will not be long. Come, Frank." And my uncle and I descended hastily to the road.

As this is a faithful autobiography I must not shrink from recording my thoughts at this time. Full of my selfish love for Daphne, I was hoping that the dead form carried by the monks might be—George. A wicked wish, and one that I was ashamed of the minute after I had entertained it.

The monks had ceased their singing for a brief space, but as they neared us a fresh outburst of mournful harmony rose from them. It spread through the vale around, and, rolling onward, echoed and re-echoed from many a distant cliff, and, as if refused a lodgment there, mounted upward to the midnight sky:

"DIES IRÆ, DIES ILLA,

SOLVET SÆCULUM IN FAVILLA."

The deep cowl that veiled the head of each grey brother gave a singular appearance to the throng, and the peculiarly wild effect of their harmony was heightened by the solemn hour and the moonlight.

"What ghostly looking figures!" I muttered to my uncle.

"Ay! Charon multiplied by forty. How I hate these doleful Gregorians! Let us stop these sandalled friars, and ask—if indeed they will be so condescending as to tell us—who it is that has received his *Nunc Dimittis*."

The Weird Picture

As the train came abreast of us, my uncle stepped forward and lifted his hat to the monks, who at once stopped both their march and their requiem.

"Pardon the curiosity of a stranger," he said, addressing the leading brother: "may we ask the reason of this midnight procession?"

The monk regarded the questioner with a look that seemed to ask what business it was of his; but, verbally courteous, he replied:

"*Pax vobiscum, mi fili.* We mourn one who but a few hours ago was alive. Now—*sic est voluntas divina*—he is no more."

"How came he by his death?"

"By falling from the cliff on which our monastery is built. The holy Virgin—*gloria tibi, O sancta Maria*—foreshadowed the event this morning by the fall of her image in the chapel."

"Ah, the days of Urim and Thummim are not past, then," remarked my uncle, with a tinge of irony in his tone unnoticed by him to whom he spoke. "Is the dead man a brother of your order?"

"An old inhabitant of Rivoli, but a neophyte of two days only. It was but yesterday that the good Father Ignatius brought him to us, bidding us receive him as a novice. This evening at vespers he quitted the convent unknown to us. He did not return. At nocturns Brother Francis startled us by rushing in and saying that he had heard groans coming from the foot of the cliff. We descended to the spot. This is what we found."

With these words the speaker drew back the covering from the bier. And there, calm and still in death, with glazed eyes staring up at the sky, as if in reproach of the cold, silent moon that had seen him die, was the face of the silver-haired old man, the penitent of Father Ignatius. My sudden exclamation of surprise drew all eyes upon me.

"Did you know him, young sir?"

"I have seen him once in England, and once here in the cathedral yesterday. I know nothing of him, not even his name. Where are you taking the body?" I added after a moment's interval.

"To the house of Father Ignatius," replied the leading monk, as he motioned the *cortège* to proceed.

"Stop!" cried my uncle, and at his imperative voice the monks paused.

For some moments he had been closely scrutinising the corpse, and now, pointing to it with a stern look, he said:

"There must be an inquiry on the body, for this man did not die by accident. He was pushed over the cliff. See! these marks on the throat were made by a strong hand. He has been murdered."

"Murdered!" repeated forty voices.

The bier was hastily set down. The bright torches were lowered to the level of the dead man's face and, making the sign of the cross, the monks crowded around to look.

"*O sancta Maria, ora pro nobis!*"

The dark purple bruises on the throat, and the frayed condition of the clothing round it, were proofs too strong to be confuted, of my uncle's statement.

"These marks may have arisen from some other cause than the one you suggest," remarked the leading monk in tones sweetly supercilious. He seemed annoyed, probably because my uncle had discovered what his monkish dulness had overlooked.

The fingers of the dead man's right hand were tightly clenched. My uncle proceeded to force them open, and as he did so there fell to the ground something which when picked up proved to be a grey cloth button adhering to a fragment of grey cloth, and assuredly not belonging to the garments of the dead man.

"This," said my uncle, "has been torn by the dead man from the clothes of him who hurled him over. There was evidently a struggle. This button must not be lost. It may be a means of tracing the assassin."

So, while the pious monks had been lifting to heaven their prayers and psalms, a death-struggle had been going on under the walls of their convent, perhaps within the very sound of their voices. But what motive had prompted the deed, and whose was the hand that had so swiftly hurled the aged man into the arms of death?

The sight of the grey cloth button—suggestive of a military cloak—recalled to my memory the figure that Daphne had seen at the fountain; and instantly there darted into my mind a terrible suspicion. The same had occurred to my uncle. Bending his head over to me, and pointing to the corpse, he said in a whisper:

"Is this George's work?"

A warm breath on my cheek checked the reply I was about to make. I turned. Daphne was at my side, her hands raised, her eyes dilated with horror, and her figure swaying like a young sapling in the breeze. Unperceived by myself or her father, she had followed us to the road—had seen the dead man, the damnatory evidence, had caught her father's whispered words. A scream such as I shall never forget broke from her, and before I could catch her in my arms she had dropped at my feet, a white senseless heap. Her voice, like a death-cry, rang over the moonlit valley, awakening countless echoes from the sleeping rocks, and mingling with the mournful refrain of the monks:

"REQUIEM ÆTERNAM
ET LUCEM PERPETUAM
DONA MORTUO, DOMINE!"

CHAPTER XI MORE OF THE PICTURE

We had not expected to see Sir Hugh Wyville until the following Christmas, which we were to spend as his guests in Cornwall. It chanced, however, that he too was taking a Continental tour, and joined our Rhine steamer at Cologne. He was delighted to see his old schoolfellow, my uncle, and arm in arm with him paced the deck in friendly converse, talking of the old days at Eton.

Daphne's beauty made a great impression upon the Baronet, and he inquired the reason of the sad look on her face, a look that had become habitual since that terrible night at Rivoli. So my uncle related her story to him, finishing with an account of the mysterious circumstances that had attended our stay at Rivoli, to all of which the Baronet listened with deep interest.

"And so," he remarked, when the tale was ended, "the enquiry held on the body of the old man led to no result?"

"None, so far as the discovery of the assassin was concerned. All that we learned was that the old man's name was Matteo Carito; that he was a native of Rivoli, but had been absent from the town for twenty years or more, and that he had returned to it only three days before his death. It is strange that he should have been struck down so soon after reaching his home."

"The assassin had perhaps followed him there. And so the button proved no clue?"

"None at all."

"A pity, that. And the priest you have spoken of?"

"Father Ignatius?"

"Yes. Was he questioned as to the nature of the confession made to him by the murdered man?"

"Yes, but naturally he refused to divulge the secrets of the confessional. He declared, however, it had no bearing on the crime, and could not in any way help towards the discovery of the murderer, and with that we had to be content. Legal procedure is carried on at Rivoli in a fashion different from what it is in England. Father Ignatius is *the* great man of the town, and he would be a bold magistrate who would dare to question him too closely. The reverend padre would think nothing of excommunicating him next Sunday from the altar with bell, book, and candle, and the people of Rivoli would approve, so devoted are they to him."

"It is certainly a mysterious business," said Sir Hugh, "and one more so never came within my experience. At any rate, let us hope your suspicions are unfounded, and that Captain Willard was not at Rivoli as you suppose."

"Remember, Leslie," he said a day or two later, "you are not to spend Christmas at your London house. The place and the time of the year would only serve to recall your daughter's grief on the very day when she should be most happy. You must come to the Abbey and help me to burn the Yule log. There will be more than fifty guests, so you will hardly be dull. My niece, Florrie, will be just the companion for Miss Daphne, so you must make no excuses."

And he parted from us at Cologne on the understanding that we were to pass our Christmas-tide at Silverdale Abbey.

Once removed from Rivoli and its weird associations Daphne rapidly recovered her health and spirits, and we spent the summer exploring the beauties of the Rhineland.

When we returned to London, my first care was to obtain a copy of the *Standard* of July the 2nd, and I turned eagerly to the remainder of the article relating to Vasari's picture, and found the passage referring to the Anglo-Indian office to be as follows:—

"Mr. Vasari's explanation of his success is to the effect that he has rediscovered a secret known only to the ancient Greek artists, a statement that must be taken with a grain of salt. A few days ago a strange incident happened in connection with the picture. A gentleman in uniform—an Anglo-Indian officer, to judge by a description given of him—who had paid the fee for admission, was proceeding leisurely along the gallery, and had arrived at the room containing the masterpiece, when his further progress was barred by Vasari, who would not allow him to enter, but in an authoritative voice ordered him to withdraw, without, however, assigning any reason for this behaviour. The officer declined to withdraw, and an altercation ensued between him and the artist. When at Vasari's order the attendants prepared to remove the officer the latter drew his sword, but the timely intervention of the *gendarmes* prevented serious consequences. The gentleman, whose name we are unable to give, was ejected and his money returned. It is said that he intends to take legal proceedings against the artist. A curious point of law will thus be raised: Whether the proprietor of a gallery open to the public has a right, on purely personal grounds, to refuse admission to whomsoever he will? In an interview with a reporter, Vasari stated that the officer in question was drunk, that he was hostilely disposed towards the artist, and that he had sworn to destroy the famous picture with his sword. On the other hand, it is alleged that the officer was quiet and sober, and that he contemplated no such act of vandalism."

That was all concerning the Anglo-Indian officer, and what Angelo's real reason was for withholding the picture from the eyes of this man, and why he had been desirous of concealing this part of the critique from me, were insoluble questions adding fresh elements to the atmosphere of mystery in which it seemed his delight to walk.

I determined to have an interview with the Italian for the purpose of obtaining a little light on the matter. I was anxious, also, to question him on another point—namely, the whereabouts of my brother. George had evidently been living in seclusion at Rivoli, and Angelo must have been aware of the fact, otherwise his words to Daphne on parting from her—"You are nearer to him now than you have been for months"—would have had no meaning. So I called at the artist's London residence, but was told by his servant that he was in some distant part of the country, engaged in the production of a picture which it was confidently affirmed would be superior even to "The Fall of Cæsar."

Then I took a hasty trip to Paris, to the Rue de Sévres, to find, as I had expected, that the Vasari Gallery no longer existed. I visited the offices of the *Temps*, the *Gaulois*, and other newspapers, and studied whole files of journals in order to learn the details of the law-suit between Vasari and the officer, but could discover no mention of it. I found on enquiry at the law courts that the case had never been brought.

Next I tried to discover the destination of the famous picture, and learned that it had not been disposed of at public auction, but that the sale had been effected privately between the artist and the purchaser. No one could give me the name of the latter, and so, completely baffled, I returned to England, to find that Vasari was still away from town in some distant place, of which his servant either could not or would not tell me the name.

December came, and on the day before Christmas Eve Daphne, her father and myself were established at Silverdale Abbey, a fine castellated building mantled all over with ivy, and embosomed within a spacious and well wooded park. There was already a goodly company of guests present, which was expected to double its number on the morrow.

In the temporary absence of the Baronet we were received by his niece, Florrie Wyville, and spent a delightful time as she led us through the many tapestried rooms full of curious old furniture, down carved oak staircases lighted by ecclesiastical-looking casements of stained glass, along broad halls adorned with stags' antlers and suits of armour, out on to stone terraces grey with age and dark with ivy.

"Isn't it a dear old place?" she exclaimed enthusiastically when our first tour of exploration was over. "I have been here only a week, and yet I believe I know more about it even than Uncle Hugh knows. It is more than six hundred years old, and was originally a nunnery."

"And why is it called Silverdale?" I asked.

"There was a silver mine here at one time. I believe part of the Abbey stands over an air shaft belonging to it; and in olden days nuns who broke their vows were thrown down it."

"How horrible," said Daphne with a shudder.

"Not so horrible as walling them up alive like that poor thing in *Marmion*," Florrie replied, jealous for the good repute of her beloved Abbey.

The Weird Picture

"Does the shaft still exist?" I asked.

"I think so, but the passage leading to it was bricked up years ago. I lay awake last night thinking of those old days, and fancying I could hear a ghostly procession of nuns rustling along the hall and chanting— — Why, what is the matter, Miss Leslie? you look quite scared."

I diverted the conversation to more cheerful topics, and soon the girls were discussing what characters they should assume in the fancy dress ball to be held at Silverdale on Twelfth-night.

The Baronet was justly proud of his beautiful home, and when, late that night, after the retiring of the guests, we were smoking in the library, he listened with evident pleasure to my congratulations on its perfect preservation unspoiled from the middle ages.

"You must see the picture-gallery to-morrow," he said. "That is the real gem of the place. But as you take such an interest in the Abbey and its antiquities, this book may interest you." He found a key and unlocked a bookcase. "It is a complete history of the Abbey from its foundation to the present time. It has never been published. My brother had it drawn up by a first-rate antiquary. I haven't had time to read it properly yet. Why, how's this? The book is gone."

"Some other guest who takes the same interest in the Abbey that I do," I suggested, "has borrowed the book and forgotten to return it."

"Impossible," Sir Hugh replied. "This bookcase is kept locked, and I always carry the key."

"Was that the only copy of the book?" my uncle asked.

"The only copy. It was in manuscript, but the leaves were bound like an ordinary book. If the book be gone the loss is irreparable."

"When did you see it last?"

"About a month ago, I should say. Its usual place is there, third from the end on the top shelf. Whoever took it away did not wish its removal to be noticed, for he— —"

"Or she," I murmured, thinking of Florrie's enthusiasm over the Abbey.

"Or she has filled up the gap with a book identical in colour and binding, so that I thought at first it was the very book. *Athanasii Opera*," he muttered contemptuously, scanning the title of the substituted volume. "Confound Athanasius."

"With all my heart, and his creed too," said my uncle cheerfully. "But I have no doubt the other, more valuable, book will turn up all right soon."

"I sincerely hope it will," Sir Hugh replied, scrutinising every part of the bookcase as if he thought the volume were deliberately hiding from him. "At any rate, it isn't here now," and giving up the search in disgust he walked to the fireplace and flung himself into a chair, looking exceedingly annoyed. "It looks like a case of theft, but I can't for the life of me see why a thief should choose that particular book. He would only give himself away if he tried to make money by selling it. No one in the Abbey would have taken it; people don't pick locks to get what they have only to ask for, and every one here knows I have no objection to lending my books." And for some time he smoked in moody silence, uninterrupted by any remark from us.

"By the way," he said presently, "I shall shortly have the pleasure of introducing you to a genius. I'm waiting up for him now. He is coming by the last train."

"Who is the genius?" my uncle inquired with a smile.

"That Italian artist whose picture 'The Fall of Cæsar' made such a sensation in Paris last spring."

I was so surprised that I knocked over a branched candlestick by my side and nearly set the tablecloth on fire.

"You must have heard of him," said Sir Hugh, carefully replacing the candlestick.

"Oh, yes, we have heard of him," said my uncle, looking at me.

Sir Hugh did not appear to notice the meaning way in which my uncle spoke.

The Weird Picture

"He is spending Christmas here," said Sir Hugh. "In fact he has been living at the Abbey for the last two months. He went to London this week to get some artistic material. He is painting a picture for me."

"What is the subject?" my uncle asked.

"I left that to him," Sir Hugh answered. "Artists naturally prefer not to be fettered in matters of that sort, and they always do best what they like best. But he calls this new picture— —"

"'Modesta, the Christian Martyr,'" I interrupted.

"Yes," said Sir Hugh surprised. "How on earth did you know? I was not aware that he had told any one but me."

"He told me himself," I explained. "We are friends of his. At least we met him at Rivoli last summer, and he told us he had a commission for a picture with leave to choose his own subject. You must be the man who gave him the commission he was referring to."

"So you know him?" said the Baronet regretfully. "I am disappointed. I thought I had a pleasure in store for you, and I am forestalled. Yes; that's it. 'Modesta, the Christian Martyr,' is to be *the* picture of the year. He stipulated that he should exhibit it before finally handing it over to me, and of course I was quite agreeable."

"It was politic too," my uncle remarked. "A man will take more pains over a picture that all the critics will see than over one that will go straight into a private collection."

"I suppose that is true," said Sir Hugh, "though Vasari is not the man to scamp his work. I have fitted up a studio for him in the Nuns' Tower, that grey tower connected with the east wing of the Abbey by a cloister. It's a lonely sort of place, but he seems to prefer it to any other room in the Abbey, and he certainly is free from interruption there."

"Well, I hope for your sake the picture will be a success," said my uncle, suggesting that he did not care at all how it might affect the artist's career. "Do you think it will equal his last?"

"I can't say. I haven't seen it." Then, noticing our surprise, Sir Hugh explained. "You see his studio is a sort of holy shrine into which only the high priest of art is allowed to enter. The door is closed to every one—even to *me*." The pomposity with which the good Baronet emphasised the last word was immense.

"Well it is contrary to his usual practice," my uncle said drily. "We haven't found him backward in talking about his work, have we, Frank?"

"I don't think modesty is a disease with him," I admitted. "Do you know whether he was as secretive about his 'Fall of Cæsar' before he sprung it on an admiring world?"

"I believe he was. Permitted none to enter his studio till the work was finished. He claims to have rediscovered a secret known to the great artists of classical times, and does not want to reveal it to contemporary rivals. Between ourselves, I don't believe there is any mystery about it, but it suits his purpose to pretend there is. Our friend knows something about human nature, and to throw a veil of secrecy round your work while you are doing it is quite good business, provided, of course, the work is good when finished. Let me see, you were in Paris last spring. Of course you saw the great picture?"

"No, we haven't seen it," my uncle replied. "Have you?"

"Have I?" said the Baronet, looking as much astonished as if he had been asked whether he knew the alphabet. "My dear fellow, what are you talking about? Don't you know the picture is here?"

"Here?" was the simultaneous ejaculation of my uncle and myself.

"Here. In this house. In my gallery."

That which eludes the most painstaking search is often revealed by mere accident. Without any design on our part, we were at length within measurable distance of seeing that which we had been vainly trying to see—to wit, Angelo's famous picture.

"Did you buy it from the Baron?" I asked.

"The Baron? What Baron? I don't understand you. I saw the picture last summer in Paris, was struck with it like everybody else, and offered Angelo £4,000 for it."

"Which offer he accepted?" said my uncle.

"Which offer he accepted—after a delay of a day or two."

"You purchased it direct from Angelo?" said I.

"Direct."

"Strange!"

"What is there so strange in the transaction?"

"Do you know," I said, "that when we saw Angelo at Rivoli, and expressed a desire—or, to be more correct, when Daphne expressed a desire to see his picture, he told her it was impossible—he had sold it to some Spanish hidalgo."

"He must have been dreaming, then," returned Sir Hugh. "I was the first purchaser and the last."

"What could have induced him to tell such a falsehood?" I said.

"Do not say falsehood," replied the Baronet; "say error of memory, rather. He was thinking of some other picture, perhaps?"

"No, 'The Death of Cæsar;' that was the work he referred to, I am certain."

"Perhaps he confounded me with some intending purchaser. Why he should wish to conceal the destination of his picture from you I cannot tell. But there, he's a curious fellow," muttered the Baronet thoughtfully. "Genius always is eccentric, I suppose. He will stand for hours, I am told, on the cliffs, solitary and melancholy, watching the Atlantic breakers and soliloquising like a second Manfred. If I didn't know that art was his only mistress, I should fancy he was in love."

"Your fancy is not far removed from the truth," I murmured to myself. "When you were at Paris," I asked, "did you hear anything of a fracas between Angelo and a military officer in connection with this picture?"

"Yes, I remember the affair very well."

"Can you tell me the name of the officer?"

"No; he was never heard of again. I think he received an order that very day to rejoin his regiment. It was that fracas, I believe, that led to my becoming the possessor of the picture."

"How was that?"

"I had offered Angelo £4,000 for it, which he refused. He could gain more by exhibiting it, he said. However, after this affair with the officer, he came of his own accord to me and tendered it at the price I had named. He explained his change of mind by what seemed to me an absurd statement. A clique of artists, jealous of his success, had vowed to destroy his picture. He resolved to exhibit it no more publicly. He thought it would be safer in some private collection and he stipulated that I must allow him to have a sight now and again of his beloved masterpiece. I put all this down to morbid vanity, but, of course, I professed to believe him and sympathised with him, very glad to obtain the picture on any terms."

The Baronet's butler, who had entered a few minutes previously to ask whether we wanted any more wine, and was lingering about under pretence of smoothing the cloth and of arranging the decanters, now joined in the conversation with the freedom of an old and faithful servant.

"I beg your pardon, Sir Hugh, but are you talking of Mr. Vasari's picture?"

"That is exactly what we are doing, Fruin."

The white-haired old man shook his head.

"Why, what have *you* got to say about it Fruin?" asked his master with considerable surprise.

The old servant shook his head once more.

"You hate ghost stories, Sir Hugh. That's why I've never spoken to you about these goings on."

"These goings on! Heavens! what's the man talking about? Let's have your ghost story, Fruin, and I'll suspend my criticism and laughter till—you are out of the room," he added aside.

"There's something very queer about that picture."

The Weird Picture

This was my opinion too, and I listened with breathless interest to the butler's words.

"My bedroom—as you know, Sir Hugh—is over one end of the gallery, and ever since that picture of Mr. Vasari's was put into it I have heard at night sounds as if some one were walking to and fro there, and faint cries now and then. Before going to bed I always lock the doors at both ends of the gallery, and take the keys with me, so that how any one can get in at night is a puzzle. I have come down alone several times to see who was there." Fruin was not a timid character, if his own statement were to be received as evidence. "I always come with a lamp and a loaded pistol," he added, causing me to modify my opinion of his valour. "And on opening the door the sounds always cease and the place is always empty."

"A clear proof," replied Sir Hugh, "that no one had been in the gallery, and that the sounds, caused by the wind probably, must have proceeded from some other quarter."

Fruin's air implied that he was not going to be imposed upon by this explanation.

"You hear cries?" said I. "What sort of cries?"

"I can't tell you exactly, sir, for I am never near enough to hear. Faint die-away sounds they are, like a mother crooning her babe to sleep."

"Granting, what I don't for one moment admit, that the sounds come from the gallery, what have they got to do with Mr. Vasari's picture?" the Baronet asked.

"I have been butler in this house for twenty years, Sir Hugh," said the old fellow gravely and respectfully, "and there were never such sounds in the gallery until that picture came here."

"Do you hear them every night?" my uncle asked.

"Oh no, sir, only at intervals. They may occur for two or three nights running, and then perhaps they won't be heard for a week."

"Well," said Sir Hugh testily, "since you are sure the sounds are real and that they *do* come from the gallery, give us your explanation of them, that is, if you have any to give."

The Weird Picture

"It isn't what you might call an explanation," said the butler, who maintained a quiet but firm manner throughout, "but I can tell you a little more. One evening last week I was passing along the gravel-path outside the gallery windows, when I chanced to look up, and there, staring at me through the panes, was a face. Though it was dusk at the time, there was light enough to see every feature of it, and I will swear that it was the same face as in the picture."

"What did you do when you saw it?"

"I went close up to the window."

"And then?"

"It wasn't there."

"And you heard no sound from within?"

"Not a sound. I came into the Abbey at once, taking Brown with me, and found both doors of the gallery locked. We searched the gallery, but found no one in it."

"Did you examine the picture, Fruin," said the Baronet, "to see whether Imperial Cæsar exhibited any traces of having lately walked out of the canvas?"

"I did examine the picture, Sir Hugh, and I am certain it had been disturbed, for I will swear that it was not hanging at the same angle as it had been in the morning."

"Cæsar didn't speak, I presume, and ask you how you were?"

But the butler, whose air of quiet and sober dignity almost atoned for the absurdity of the story, was not to be moved by his master's gibes.

"Don't you think it was fancy on your part, Fruin?" said I. "Just think how impossible it is for a figure painted on canvas to move from its frame and peer through a casement!"

"What I saw on the other side of the window was a real thing," replied the butler firmly. "It was the very face in the picture, and so would you say had you been there to see it."

"I wish to goodness we had!" said Sir Hugh. "Well, well! you may go, Fruin, unless Mr. Leslie or Mr. Willard wishes to ask you any more questions."

The Weird Picture

We had no more to put, and when the butler had withdrawn, I asked the Baronet his opinion of the story.

"Pooh, pooh, my dear boy! Outside the pale of serious discussion. I must have stronger evidence than the solitary testimony of a superstitious and dim-sighted old servant, who in the twilight mistakes some shadow across the stained panes for an apparition."

And he waved his hand with a deprecatory gesture, as if wishing to hear no more of the absurd business.

I was silent for a time, reflecting on the story I had just heard. If it had stood alone—had been the sole remarkable thing related of the picture—it would not have been entitled to consideration; but so many strange things had occurred in connexion with Angelo's masterpiece that I hesitated before pronouncing Fruin's narration to be a fable, destitute of any foundation whatever. Though at present the affair seemed coloured by the supernatural, it might have a groundwork of fact to rest upon.

"Well, Sir Hugh," remarked my uncle, "we must certainly view this mysterious picture in the morning."

"Why not now?" I said, jumping to my feet. "Let us see it to-night. I shall not be able to sleep if I go to bed without seeing it."

But the Baronet shrugged his shoulders with a good-humoured smile.

"No, thank you. We are warm and comfortable here. A walk in a cold picture-gallery by the pale light of the moon is an affront to these cigars and this port. Let us defer our visit till the morning."

I was loth to wait till then. The picture had eluded us so long that I thought it quite within the range of probability for it to walk off during the night.

"Did Angelo ever speak to you of his stay at Rivoli?" said I to the Baronet.

"Never knew he had been there till you mentioned it."

"He's a native of the place. He never told you, then, of a little incident that happened in the cathedral of Rivoli?"

"You are talking Greek to me—at least, that is," coughed the Baronet, reserving to himself the credit of a classical reputation, "er—Chinese, I should say. What is the little incident to which you refer?"

I satisfied Sir Hugh's curiosity by giving him an account of Angelo's expulsion from the Communion.

"Did you not ask him the cause of it?" inquired he.

"We have never seen him from that day to this," I replied.

"Humph!" remarked the Baronet gravely. "Expelled from the Sacrament, was he? I don't like that, you know: it looks bad. I wish I had known this before I asked him to spend his Christmas here. Of course, for aught we know to the contrary, he may only have been guilty of some little trifle which we men of the world"—he swept his arm towards me as he spoke, and I felt quite proud of the title conferred on me—"think nothing of; but still it looks suspicious. A shade rests on his character, and till it be cleared off I would prefer him at any other table than mine. I ought to be certain that he is a person of fair repute—that is a duty I owe my guests; but I don't see what I can do now that matters have gone so far. I cannot, in the circumstances, ask him point-blank to produce a certificate of good character, so I must display the hospitality of the Orientals, and entertain the guest without inquiring too closely into his character."

"'For thereby,'" quoted my uncle, "'some have entertained angels unawares.'"

"You are not very likely to do that," I said to the Baronet, "and—"

The sound of carriage-wheels rattling over the gravel-path beneath the library windows checked the rest of my remark.

"That must be Angelo," said the Baronet, referring to his watch.

"Talk of Lucifer," said I, rising, "and he rustles his wings. With your leave, Sir Hugh, I'll retire for the night. I've no wish to see Angelo till the morning." And with these words I departed, leaving the representative of the Wyvilles and the head of the house of Leslie to welcome, perhaps it would be more correct to write receive, the late comer.

The Weird Picture

The bedroom allotted to me was, like those of the other guests, in the eastern wing of the Abbey, the western wing being appropriated to the servants' quarters. The front and central portions of the building contained the principal apartments; and the picture-gallery was at the rear on the ground-floor, connecting the two wings.

My room was a large old-fashioned chamber, whose oaken panels were draped with figured tapestry. An oriel casement with lancet-shaped panes of stained-glass gave me a fine view of the moonlit park, with the Nuns' Tower—Angelo's studio—rising grey and solitary above a dark clump of cedars.

There was a fire in the grate and its dancing caused strange shadows to quiver upon the walls and ceiling, seeming to invest the grim figures on the tapestry with life and motion—an illusion heightened by their rustling with the draught from the open door.

The supernatural element introduced into my mind by the butler's story played the wildest tricks with my imagination, reducing me to so tense a state of nervousness that I almost hesitated to look around, lest some eerie shape should meet my gaze. The sight of my face in the glass mirror so startled me that I turned the mirror round to the wall, in order that I might not be compelled to contemplate my own reflection, to which I felt attracted, not from vanity, but from a weird fascination that made me think it was another person in the room mimicking my movements. The brass knob of the door, too, was a source of annoyance, till I hung my handkerchief over it—it looked so like a gleaming eye. And when I had thus absurdly disposed of its glitter, I discovered many other eyes staring at me with maddening persistency from different parts of the room.

Anxious to chase away if possible the morbid fancies that were fast crowding into my mind and threatening to render my sleep the reverse of pleasant, I looked around for some book to divert my thoughts, and, suddenly remembering that at the bottom of my trunk was a volume of *Pickwick*, I drew it forth, and, having raked up the fire into a cheerful blaze, was soon laughing heartily over the drolleries of that immortal work.

How long I continued turning over page after page I cannot tell; my reading was brought to a sudden stop by a scream which rang long,

The Weird Picture

loud, and piercing through the corridors of the Abbey. I flung down *Pickwick* and darted to the door to listen. The scream was repeated, and I recognized Daphne's voice.

"Oh, Frank, Frank!"

Even in the excitement of that terrible moment a feeling of pleasure came over me. Why should Daphne, in her fear, call upon my name, unless I were the first person in her thoughts?

There was an ancient-looking sword hanging over the fireplace, and I took it down and rushed along the corridor in the direction of Daphne's voice.

Coming to the room which I knew to be hers, I dashed open the door, and saw Daphne sitting erect in bed, her eyes staring wildly around, her face and manner expressive of the extremity of terror. I at once ran to the bedside.

"Oh, Frank, don't leave me, don't leave me till some one comes!"

She followed up this appeal by a flood of tears, and clung tightly to my arm with both her hands, while staring about her on all sides.

"Why, Daphne, what is the matter?"

"There's something in the room." She paused, and looked fearfully around her. "I don't know what. A black shape—a shadow. It was bending over me."

I cast a glance over the room, but nothing unusual met my eye, and I concluded she had been dreaming.

"You are dreaming, Daphne. Do not cry so. There is no one here but you and me."

"Yes, yes, there is!"

All the guests, roused by the screams, had risen from their slumbers, and in various stages of dressing were thronging around the open door, becoming round-eyed as they took in the character of the scene.

"Heyday! what's the matter here?" exclaimed my uncle, entering at this juncture; and all the rest, imitating his example, entered too.

"I came because I heard Daphne calling for help," I replied.

"Oh, papa," said Daphne, withdrawing her arms from me and placing both hands in his. "I have been frightened, and could not help screaming out, and Frank came."

"Frightened? What was it that frightened you?"

"I—I don't know what it was," she stammered. "I opened my eyes, and there was a black thing bending over me. I could see a pair of gleaming eyes staring straight into mine. I screamed out, but the thing remained bending over me, and didn't move till Frank's step sounded outside."

"What?" I cried in amazement. "Didn't this shape, whatever it was, take its flight through the door?"

"No; there was no opening of the door till you came. It's here now in the room somewhere. As you opened the door it darted off on this side," motioning to the left with her hand.

There was a sensation among the ladies, and they drew closer to one another. The gentlemen, with a valour born of numbers, peered into wardrobes and cupboards, and looked beneath the bed and behind hangings.

I could see my uncle and the Baronet exchanging curious glances, and I knew that both were connecting the cause of Daphne's fright with the apparition supposed to haunt the picture-gallery. It was the opinion of every one else that she had been dreaming.

"Oh, you silly girl!" cried Florrie, coming to the bedside. "To fancy you saw a ghost, and frighten us all out of our beds!"

Daphne shivered visibly. The search into every corner of the apartment had done very little to remove her terror.

"Oh, Florrie," she cried, "do stay with me for the rest of the night! I dare not sleep alone. I shall die of fright if it comes again. If you could but have seen those gleaming eyes!"

The Baronet's niece expressed her perfect willingness to share her sleep with Daphne.

"Leave me that sword," she said to me. "I only hope that ghost *will* return: if it is one of flesh and blood it had better not venture too near me!"

And Florrie waved the blade above her head with the serio-comic air of the pretty lady-hero in the Christmas pantomine when she bids the wicked demon come on and do his worst.

"Florrie is an Amazon," smiled the Baronet, "and doesn't fear man, ghost, or devil. I think, Miss Leslie, you will be quite safe in her keeping."

We made no longer tarrying, but, bidding the two girls "good-night," withdrew—the ladies to their rooms, the gentlemen to the broad landing, at the end of the corridor, there to discuss the affair for a few minutes.

"This is a very mysterious house," said my uncle to the Baronet.

"Egad! I'm beginning to think so myself."

Among those who had stood silent spectators in Daphne's room was a doctor of great renown.

"Did you not detect," he said to my uncle, "a peculiar odour hanging around the dressing-table?"

"I did. Perfumes for handkerchiefs, I suppose."

"Perfumes for handkerchiefs—Oh?" replied the doctor in a curious tone of voice, and sniffing as if the odour still remained in his nostrils. "Hum! I shouldn't advise the young lady to sprinkle her handkerchief too freely with that sort of essence, unless she wishes to be a member of 'kingdom come!'"

CHAPTER XII THE FIGURE IN THE GREY CLOAK

On descending next morning to the drawing-room, I found Angelo there before me, the idol of a crowd of æsthetic young ladies who adored art (and especially the artist) without understanding much about either. He was exhibiting to their admiring gaze the contents of his portfolio and unless my eyesight deceived me, it was the identical portfolio he had displayed to me on that memorable wedding morning.

It had been my intention to question the artist on that singular utterance of his when he first parted from Daphne: "You are nearer to him now than you have been for months;" but as I saw that he purposely ignored me, I imitated his example, and ignored him.

I was curious to see how he would receive Daphne on this occasion—their first meeting after her refusal of him; but he manifested no signs of embarrassment when she appeared, and acknowledged her presence with an air so grave and stately that none, seeing him, would ever have guessed that he had at one time made passionate love to her.

Daphne was confused and blushed a little, and was not sorry, I think, when, at the sound of the breakfast-bell, I relieved her of his presence by escorting her to the table, taking care to put as many feet of mahogany as I could between her and the artist, who had for his partner the lively Florrie.

During breakfast the conversation turned on the mysterious apparition of the preceding night, and Daphne was twitted by the ladies for her fright; but the Baronet, noticing how agitated she became and how distasteful the subject was to her, came to her aid, and, declaring that he would not allow her to be teased, diverted the conversation to another channel.

"When do you expect to finish your picture?" he said, turning to Angelo.

"Within a few days: perhaps a few hours."

The Weird Picture

Perhaps a few hours! Such an answer implied that it was within the range of probability for the completion of his picture to take place on Christmas Day—that is, on the very anniversary of the day on which he had finished his last masterpiece. This coincidence of dates was certainly remarkable, and my uncle could not help reverting to it.

"Christmas is a favorite time with you," he remarked. "Your last great work, if I remember rightly, received its final touch on Christmas Day."

"Yes," replied the artist, "because both pictures represent death scenes; and the brilliant sunshine and blue skies of summer-time are too joyous to allow me to think of anything sad. I am like that poet who could never write good verse unless he was in an elegant and tastefully-appointed study. Similarly, I find the gloom and darkness of your English Christmas a more appropriate time than any other to portray my conceptions of death."

"Egad! there's something in that," said the doctor with a nod of approval. He seemed to have taken a great fancy for Angelo. "The weather has a wonderful effect on the mental faculties."

"The want of a suitable model has delayed your work, I think you said," said the Baronet to Angelo. "Did you procure in London what you wanted?"

"Yes; I have—found a—a—" he seemed to hesitate as to the choice of a word—"a lovely figure. The very ideal of what an artist's model should be."

"What is the subject of your picture?" inquired Florrie.

"I am going to call it 'Modesta, the Christian Martyr.' It represents a scene in the Coliseum. A Christian maiden is breathing her last on the sands of the arena. A Libyan lion stands proudly over her, with one claw fixed in her breast."

"What a ghastly subject!" said Florrie.

"Ghastly? Yes; yet such things *have* been, and 'tis well to recall them," replied the artist gravely. "You must judge my picture by the end it is meant to accomplish, which is not mere vulgar sensationalism. It is intended as a contribution to religion—an aid to morality; for it is my object to show the character of ancient paganism, and from the contemplation of the sweet girl-martyr men will derive nobler ideas of the great battle which their ancestral Christianity had to fight."

His eyes sparkled and his cheek glowed with the fire of enthusiasm.

"Angelo posing as an exponent of morality is a new character," I murmured to my uncle, who sat beside me.

The artist was now in his element. A multitude of questions relative to his new work were addressed to him from all sides. Nobody was more attentive to his words than the doctor, or more curiously interrogative. I marvelled to see him taking such an interest in Angelo's painting.

"It was Italy," explained the artist, "that furnished me with the blue sky of my picture. I spent months there experimenting on canvas till I had caught the lovely transparent azure of the Italian atmosphere. The amphitheatre I painted sitting on the arena of the Coliseum itself, picturing to my mental eye the place as it existed in the palmy days of the Empire. From Rome I transferred my canvas to Paris. They have a magnificent African lion there in the Jardin d'Acclimatation. I took a photograph of him. It was a difficult matter for the keepers to compel him to assume the pose I wanted, but it was managed at last; and, working from the photograph, I got the image of the lion fixed on the canvas. Since my arrival at the Abbey here I have been filling in the minor details and working at the figure of the girl-martyr, which I am hoping will prove the crowning-piece of the whole picture."

"Well," said the genial Baronet, when breakfast was over, "what is to be the programme for to-day? I would propose a ride over the moors, but I fear the weather is scarcely propitious."

"Oh, we can't ride out to-day," said Florrie. "We all solemnly promised the Vicar yesterday that we would help him to decorate the church with flowers and holly this morning."

"And he says that he must keep you to your promise," smiled a clerical-looking young man, the Rev. Cyprian Fontalwater, curate of Silverdale, who, having come with that very message from the Vicar, had been compelled by the hospitable Sir Hugh to stay to breakfast.

"Our Dissenting brethren"—he called them brethren, but he didn't mean it—"are beautifying and adorning their—er—meeting house, and we must not be outdone by them in floral decorations any more than we are in the—ahem!—spiritual portion of the service."

He coughed slightly, as if apologising for bringing this last point before the notice of the company.

The conversation now took an ecclesiastical turn under Florrie's lead, and we were soon discussing such topics as the decorations, Christmas carols, and the anthem to be sung at the service in the morning.

"Well," said the Baronet, giving the signal for rising, "suppose before setting off for the church you spend an hour in the picture-gallery, and view my latest addition to it."

Expressions of delighted assent arose.

"When I tell you that the addition I allude to is the great masterpiece of Mr. Vasari," he added with a gracious wave of his hand towards the artist, "the masterpiece that set all Paris talking last summer, we shall require no other reason for visiting the gallery at once."

Remembering Angelo's curious dealings with regard to his famous work of art, I thought to see him betray some little confusion when it was mentioned by the Baronet. He manifested no such embarrassment, however, but gravely bowed his acknowledgments; and Sir Hugh led the way from the breakfast-table. The artist and curate each offered an arm to escort Florrie. Preference was given to Art, and Ecclesiasticism retired confounded.

"I shall put myself under your guidance," said Florrie, taking Angelo's arm. "You must be my cicerone, and point out the beauties of the picture for me. I haven't seen it yet, you know."

"The beauties? You do me too much honour. Say the defects, rather."

"Very well, the defects, then," said the irrepressible Florrie. "I daresay that sounds uncomplimentary, but it isn't meant to be so. I'm no connoisseur, and what you artists consider defects I may consider beauties, and what you know to be beauties I may think defects. I never go into an art-gallery and become enraptured with some sweet

The Weird Picture

interesting painting without being told by some frowning critic that it is a very mediocre performance, worth nothing at all. But if I come to some ugly daub, whose perspective is all at fault and whose figures are so comically drawn that I feel tempted to laugh, I am told that I must reverence and adore because it is a Cimabue or a Fra Angelico. I am deficient in taste, I suppose. What is the title of your picture, Mr. Vasari?"

"I have entitled it 'The Fall of Cæsar,'" replied the artist, a little confounded, I thought, at the idea that there should be any one in existence ignorant of the title of his famous work.

"'The Fall of Cæsar?' Oh, how interesting. What did he fall from?" she asked with an assumed ignorance. She uttered this rather loudly; and then, dropping her voice, she whispered in Daphne's ear: "Now hear Mr. Fontalwater give us a lecture. He's sure to. Mad on history. Read nothing else from his cradle upwards."

And sure enough the Reverend Cyprian, on hearing her question, at once proceeded to satisfy her curiosity.

"Caius Julius Cæsar, Miss Wyville, was stabbed by conspirators in the Senate House at Rome, and fell at the base of Pompey's statue covered with twenty-three wounds. According to Plutarch the conspirators were Marcus Brutus, Metellus Cimber, Cassius, Casca——"

"My goodness, Mr. Fontalwater, what a memory you have!" cried Florrie, cutting him short with a look of mock admiration. "You surely don't expect me to remember all those names? You are worse than my old governess. Have you introduced all those classical fogies into your picture, Mr. Vasari?"

"No, Miss Wyville; my picture contains but two figures—Cæsar lying dead at the foot of Pompey's statue. I have represented this statue pointing downward with its lance, figuratively intimating thereby the fate that befalls a too lofty ambition. Personal vanity has induced me to represent Pompey with my own features, a proceeding for which I can quote a notable precedent—the immortal Haydon, who, in his famous picture, 'Curtius leaping into the Gulf,' gave to the Roman hero his own countenance—a fact mournfully prophetic of his own sad downward destiny."

"And so," replied Florrie, "in the figure of Pompey you represent yourself as triumphing over the dead. Fie, Mr. Vasari!"

"I am pointing a moral, you see."

"What a curious idea to introduce one's own face into a picture! I should not like to offend you: you would paint some wicked historical woman, and then give her my features. But tell me, have you given to your Cæsar the face of a friend? Come, don't deny it; I am sure you have. Whose features served as a model? Oh, do tell us!"

"You are mistaken," he replied. "I did, indeed, procure an ancient bust of Cæsar, but finally I abandoned sculptured fact for my own imagination, and endeavoured to paint ambition's ideal face."

"I am quite dying to see it," said Florrie. "Is it true what they say, Mr. Vasari, that your way of painting is a secret?"

"Quite true. I am not aware that my method is employed by the artists of to-day. Yet my method is no new thing; it is simply the revival of an idea buried in the dust of ages."

"And are you not going to reveal it?"

"And raise a crowd of imitators? Pardon me—no. None shall rob me of my laurels. If it were possible to patent my idea, I should have no hesitation in disclosing it. But the secret shall not die with me. At my death I will leave papers showing how my effects were wrought."

I attributed all this to the vanity of the artist, not knowing how much truth there was in his boasted secret.

The doctor nodded approval, as if he understood all that the artist meant. He had been walking close to Angelo all the way from the breakfast-table, listening to his utterances as though they were so many gems of wisdom that deserved to be treasured in the memory.

By this time we had entered the gallery, a magnificent hall—long, broad, and lofty. On one side only was the light admitted, and that through high and deep embrasured casements. The spaces between the windows were adorned with the family portraits all arranged in chronological order, beginning with a fearfully weird daub of Richard III.'s time, and ending with a splendid portrait of Sir Hugh.

The Weird Picture

The wall facing the windows was covered with pictures of a general character, and was penetrated at regular intervals by deep alcoves containing suits of mail and mounted knights armed *cap-à-pie*, illustrating various periods of English history; for the Wyvilles had been an ancient family long ere they received from the hand of Mary Stuart's son the patent of baronetcy.

We proceeded leisurely down the gallery, I listening, in shame be it written, with very little interest to the Baronet's genealogical discourse, because all my thoughts were running on Angelo's painting.

"I understood," said my uncle, turning to the artist, "that your great picture had gone to Spain, and never expected to meet it in the Abbey here."

"What gave you that idea?" inquired Angelo with a smile of amusement.

"Yourself, I believe. Don't you remember telling us at Rivoli that you had sold your picture to a Spanish nobleman?"

"I certainly do *not* remember saying so," replied the artist with a decided emphasis on the negative adverb, and speaking in the tone of one who was quite sure of the truth of his statement.

"Oh, yes, you did," I returned quietly. "De Argandarez was the name of the nobleman—an old hidalgo of Aragon, you know."

"I think I remember it, too," said Daphne timidly.

"We are three to one, you see," remarked my uncle.

"Far be it from me," said Angelo, "to differ from Miss Leslie, but I certainly have no recollection of ever saying any such thing. I was guilty of falsehood if I did. How could I have said so, when Sir Hugh was the only one who offered to purchase?"

This argument was of course unanswerable. The doctor offered us the tribute of a pitying smile, as if to say, "This is how a man of genius is liable to be misinterpreted."

We had now reached the middle of the hall, when a sudden exclamation broke from Sir Hugh, and on looking up I saw that

The Weird Picture

worthy Baronet staring at a certain extent of oak panelling in the wall that faced the windows. There was nothing remarkable about this extent of panelling: it held no pictures, that was all; but the Baronet's words soon showed us what was wrong.

"Why, how's this?" he cried in a voice that was almost a shout. "The picture's gone!"

"The picture? What picture?" cried Angelo, dropping Florrie's arm in his excitement, and hurrying to the side of the Baronet.

"Why yours! 'The Fall of Cæsar.'"

"Are you sure?" cried Angelo breathlessly.

"Quite. And it was hanging here last night, I will swear."

There was a deep and painful silence, followed by the usual commonplaces evoked by a surprise.

"Where can it have gone?" cried Angelo, his voice expressing the deepest concern. "Sir Hugh, I trust nothing has happened to that picture. Though yours in point of law, I still regard it to some extent as mine. I would never have parted with it, if I had thought it would be destroyed. My picture! my picture! Some one must have stolen it."

He sank down on a seat, and lifted his hand to his brow with a bewildered air, as if scarcely realising the situation.

"This is the work of an enemy," he murmured.

If his words were true, the enemy was certainly one who knew how to strike home. No mortification—not even Daphne's refusal of his love—could have been more bitter to the artist than the knowledge that his adored masterpiece was in the hands of an enemy capable of destroying it.

"Let all the servants be sent for," cried the Baronet. "What does all this mean? First it is a book that vanishes, then a picture."

"And next—*a lady*," murmured a voice.

It was the doctor who spoke, but his tones were so low that they reached no ear but mine. I stared at him, wondering what he meant.

"A book? What book?" cried Florrie.

The Weird Picture

The Baronet described the missing volume, relating the circumstances under which he came to lose it. The guests shook their heads. They could give no account of its disappearance.

All the servants, young and old, male and female, now came trooping into the hall, with wonder depicted on their faces at being thus strangely summoned.

"Now, Fruin," said the Baronet, addressing the butler, whose duty it was to see that the gallery was locked at night, "let me ask you if the fastenings of these windows," and he pointed to the long line of casements, "were all as secure when you examined them this morning as they were when you left them last night?"

The butler murmured an affirmative reply.

"You locked the doors at both ends of the gallery?"

"I did, Sir Hugh."

The Baronet turned to his housekeeper.

"There was nothing, I suppose, Mrs. Goldwin, in any part of the house this morning to lead you to suspect that the Abbey had been entered during the night?"

The good dame asserted that there had been nothing to lead her to that suspicion.

"Very well, then," continued the Baronet, scanning the faces of the assembled servants with a keen eye; "let me ask if any of you can account for the disappearance of a picture—a very valuable picture. It was hanging on this part of the wall last night. It is not here now, you see."

The servants began to interchange significant glances, and I knew that in their own minds they were connecting the disappearance of the picture with the ghostly figure supposed to haunt the gallery.

"The thing couldn't go without hands, you know," resumed Sir Hugh; "and as you are certain that no burglars entered the place last night, it follows that the picture must have been removed by some one in the Abbey. Can any of you tell me what has become of it?"

The Weird Picture

"It always was an uncanny picture," remarked a little housemaid. "When I was dusting it the other day the figure stared at me with its dead eyes. I am sure they moved once."

"Uncanny! How dare you?" exclaimed Angelo so fiercely that the poor little maid shrank behind the others in dismay. "Your dislike of it exposes you to suspicion. You, or some of your fellow servants here, from an absurd fear, have destroyed it. Produce the picture, you gaping pack of menials! My picture! my picture!"

And he sank down again on the seat, the very image of despair.

"What Mr. Vasari says is perfectly correct," said the Baronet. "Suspicion rests on you all till the picture be produced. There is a silly story going the round among you that a ghost is seen in this hall at night. I need not tell you I do not believe it; but even if it were so, what has that to do with the picture's disappearing? A ghost, according to your own theory, you know, is nothing but air: now a being that is simply air cannot carry off a heavy picture, any more than the sunbeams shining through that casement can lift this chair. No; human hands have been at work here, that's quite clear."

There was silence for a time, and then Fruin, stepping forward and clearing his throat, said:

"Sir Hugh, I ought to have spoken before, perhaps, but knowing how much you hate ghost stories, I didn't like to speak."

"Well, speak now," said the Baronet impatiently—"that is," he added, "if your story is a fresh one, and not a mere repetition of last night's nonsense."

"My bedroom, as you know, Sir Hugh, is over one end of the gallery."

It was with this very sentence that Fruin had begun his story of the previous night. Evidently it was a stereotyped formula with him when recounting his ghostly experiences, not to be abandoned any more than the orthodox "Once upon a time" of the fairy stories.

"This morning about three o'clock I fancied I heard a noise as if some one were walking up and down here; I got up and looked out of the window, and I could see a light shining through the casements below on to the lawn. This light kept appearing and disappearing, as if the person in the gallery were walking to and fro with a lamp. I put on my things and came downstairs— —"

"Didn't you wake some of the others?" interrupted the Baronet.

"No, Sir Hugh."

"Why not?"

"Because I knew none of them would come. It isn't the first time nor yet the second that we've heard queer sounds coming from this hall at night, and once when I did try to persuade the others to come down with me to find out what the matter was, not one of them would leave their beds, so I didn't try last night."

"Cowards! Why did you not come to me, Fruin?"

"Or to me?" groaned Angelo.

"It would have taken me some minutes to reach your room, Sir Hugh, and by that time the thing might have gone, and a pretty fool I should have looked at having called you up for nothing. Well, as I was saying, I crept downstairs and stood outside that door. I had the keys in my hand, but I don't mind confessing I was afraid to enter. A man, a burglar, anything in human shape I'll face, but this on the other side of the door was a different matter. I listened and heard steps moving softly to and fro— —"

"Was there more than one person, do you think?"

"I can't say, Sir Hugh. I thought at first there was only one; afterwards I thought there were two."

"What made you think there were two?"

"I am coming to it, Sir Hugh. As I was saying, I listened, and could hear footsteps. After a time they ceased, and there came sounds as if two persons were whispering together, but it may only have been one person talking to himself. Then there was a long silence, and at last there came a cry—such a cry! My blood ran cold to hear it. I dropped on one knee, and peered through the keyhole, a thing which, strangely enough, I hadn't thought of doing before, and there—and there— —"

The Weird Picture

Here the butler paused as if conscious that his next item was a little too extravagant for belief.

"Well, go on. You saw ——?"

"Mr. Vasari's picture was hanging in its usual place there," pointing to the black panel, "but," and the speaker dropped his voice to an awed whisper, "lying on the floor was a figure—the moonlight was shining clear upon it—a figure in a long cloak, a grey cloak. I jumped to my feet at once. 'Good God! there's a murder been done!' I thought. I forgot my fright in the desire to see if I could give the poor fellow any help. I unlocked the door, flung it open, and—" He paused once more. "The picture was still there, but the figure was gone. I came a little way into the gallery, but I could see nobody. Then all my fright returned. 'It must have been a ghost,' I thought. I dared not stay any longer, and I bolted off to bed as quick as my legs could carry me. For a long time I lay awake, but I heard nothing more."

I offered a chair to Daphne, for she seemed on the point of fainting. The mention of a figure in a grey cloak had revived all the memories of that night by the haunted well.

Strange as Fruin's story was, it was told in a way that made it impossible to dismiss it with a sneer. Sir Hugh seemed to feel this; seemed, too, to be angry with himself for feeling it. He looked in silence at his guests, whose faces reflected his own uneasiness. The empty space on the wall was a disquieting fact.

"Your story," he said, "does not explain in the least how the picture comes to be missing." Turning to the other servants, he continued:

"The picture has been removed by some one within the Abbey, and not by any outsider: of that I am certain. If any of you has taken it, he had better confess at once, and I will overlook the offence, or rather I will inflict no other punishment than that of dismissal from my service. I will give the guilty party, whoever he may be, an hour to consider the matter. If at the end of that time no confession be forthcoming, I will make a thorough search of the Abbey from end to end and from roof to basement, for I am certain the picture must be concealed somewhere within it. And I promise you whoever shall be

The Weird Picture

found to have taken it shall not be leniently dealt with. What's the matter with that girl?"

This last question was occasioned by the singular conduct of the little housemaid before mentioned who had so evoked Angelo's wrath. She was staring at the artist, and had been staring at him ever since his outburst, as though there were some strange attraction in his face. Several times she had seemed on the point of speaking, but had hesitated as if from fear. At the Baronet's question, however, her emotion at last bubbled over and took the shape of words. She pointed to the artist with her forefinger, and cried, as defiant of grammar as the monks of Rheims when they beheld the kleptomaniac jackdaw:

"That's him! that's him!"

Her arm dropped from a horizontal to a vertical position on receiving a smart tap from the housekeeper's hand.

"How dare you point in that rude fashion? Have you no manners? What do you mean?"

"That's the face!" cried the girl—"the face in the picture!"

"Oh, that's what you mean, is it?" said the Baronet. "Yes, yes; we know that." And turning to the artist, he explained the housemaid's words by saying: "She recognises you to be the Pompey of the picture."

"And there's the other face," cried the girl, pointing at me.

This observation startled me. Surely the artist had not adopted my features as the model for the face of his Cæsar?

"Don't be stupid, girl!" said Sir Hugh impatiently. "The other face is no more like Mr. Willard's than—yes, it is, though, now I come to look deeply at you," he continued, regarding me a moment. "There is a faint resemblance—not much. The girl has a quick eye. How she stares at you, Angelo! Upon my word," he said with a grim smile, "I believe she thinks you have stepped out of the canvas. Don't stare so at Mr. Vasari, girl. You must be out of your mind!"

"Then what's he laughing for, and staring at me with his wicked eyes—frightening me so?"

The Weird Picture

"Jane," said the housekeeper, administering as mild a shaking as the dignity of her position and the presence of her guests would allow, "how dare you make an exhibition of yourself in this manner? I'll send you home to your mother this very day! How dare you? You shall not stay here another hour!"

"It's his fault!" cried the girl, rendered desperate by fright. "He keeps staring at me and smiling wickedly. I won't be looked at like that!"

Her manner almost led one to believe that Angelo had been casting the "evil eye" upon her, and that the operation hurt. All looks were turned towards him; but whatever peculiarity his eyes may have displayed had quite vanished now: they manifested only their usual quiet dreamy expression.

"The girl is as mad," he said with a scornful air, "as your curiosity of a butler, who takes the caterwauling of a tom-cat for the cry of a banshee."

He had quite recovered from his outburst of excitement, and seemed by far the calmest person present.

"Egad, you're right!" replied the Baronet. "They both seem anxious to qualify themselves for Bedlam."

The doctor said nothing, but rubbed his hands with the air of a man who has arrived at a satisfactory solution of some problem that has been puzzling him.

Well, the picture was gone, nor could it be seen in any part of the gallery. The ladies expressed a wish to retire, and, headed by the whispering servants, we all withdrew.

I was the last to leave, lingering awhile to explore the recesses of the hall in the vain hope of lighting on the missing picture. On gaining the drawing-room I found Daphne alone waiting for me. The rest of the company had retired to dress for their expedition to the church.

"Oh, Frank, I feel so frightened!" she said, referring to the incident of the missing picture, and laying both her hands on my arm.

"And I am not very easy in my mind," returned I. "Silverdale seems more mysterious than Rivoli."

The Weird Picture

"What can it all mean? There was some one in my room last night; and now the butler declares that he has seen a figure in a grey cloak in the gallery. Can it"—and her voice sank to a whisper of awe—"have anything to do with—with George?"

This was the first time she had mentioned his name to me since our leaving Rivoli. While pronouncing it she gave a shiver of terror, and I saw clearly that of all persons on earth, the one whom she was least desirous of meeting was—George!

"There is a tide in the affairs of men," etc. I resolved without delay to take advantage of the tide, that seemed to have turned full in my favour.

"No, no," I said. "You mustn't let that stupid fellow's ghost story trouble you. He's a fool! All butlers are," I added, with a hasty generalisation; "they're always so old, you see."

"Then what can it all mean?" repeated she. "We seem to be leading haunted lives. I have become so nervous of late. I look in the glass every morning to see whether my hair is turning grey. I live in daily dread of—I don't know what, and at night I am as afraid of the dark as a little child."

She was trembling like a leaf. She looked so pretty and interesting in her grief that I could not resist the temptation of placing my arm sympathisingly around her waist. She did not resent the action. On the contrary, the new light that sprang up in her eyes could only be caused by one feeling.

Now I had not intended to make love to Daphne for some weeks to come, but the present occasion was too tempting to be thrown away. As Angelo himself had very justly remarked on a similar occasion, "Who can forge chains for love, and say, 'To-day thou shalt be dumb; to-morrow thou shalt speak?'"

"Daphne," said I, "I am going to let you into a secret."

"A secret?" she repeated.

"Yes; you have always taken me into your confidences"—this was scarcely true, but it served to pave the way for what was to follow—"so I am going to take you into mine."

The Weird Picture

I paused to admire the look of mystification in her bright eyes.

"What will you think," I continued, speaking very slowly and deliberately, "when I say that I have fallen in love with one of the ladies here at the Abbey?"

"Are you in earnest?" she asked, trembling all over, and gently endeavouring to free herself from my embrace.

"So much so," I replied gravely, "that I am going to propose to her this very day."

Daphne's tongue seemed frozen.

"Well," I said, "aren't you going to wish me success?"

"Tell me her name. Who is she?" she gasped.

"I have her portrait here—somewhere—in a locket—that I'm going to give her as a Christmas gift," I replied with apparent unconcern, fumbling in my pockets for it; and while I was doing so Daphne contrived to withdraw from my embrace.

I drew forth the locket and handed it to her. It contained, instead of a portrait, a tiny mirror, whose convexity of surface diminished the objects reflected by it.

"You have made a mistake," she replied coldly, returning the locket. "There is no portrait here; nothing but a little mirror."

"No; I do not mistake. If you look again you will see the face of her I love."

She gazed at me for a few seconds before my meaning became clear, and then gave a little cry:

"Oh, Frank!"

And Eros and Anteros at last kissed each other.

I was alone in the drawing-room, the happiest mortal beneath the roof of Silverdale. Daphne had gone off to change her dress. She was going to help the guests in their work of decorating the church with holly and other Christmas emblems. As the party were to lunch at the Vicarage, they would be absent a considerable part of the day.

The Weird Picture

My language implied that I was not going to form one of this party. Such was the case. With many expressions of regret for my seeming want of gallantry on this day of all others, I had claimed indulgence of Daphne to remain behind at the Abbey on the fictitious plea that Sir Hugh was desirous of consulting my uncle and myself together with some speculator from London, on the formation of a company for the purpose of working a vein of lead recently discovered on the Silverdale estate. The truth was that the Baronet had determined to avail himself of the absence of his guests to make a thorough search for the lost picture, and I was desirous of helping him.

It was not without a mental struggle that I consented to forego the pleasure of Daphne's companionship for several hours, but my anxiety to penetrate the mystery surrounding the missing picture was so great that it overcame the fascination even of love.

The sound of approaching voices told me that the doctor and the Baronet were entering the drawing-room.

"And so," remarked the latter, "you have made up your mind to go to the church?"

"Yes," replied the doctor, drawing on a pair of gloves; "though not from any particular wish to aid in the decorating."

"No?"

"No! A very different motive takes me there. Your young friend, the artist Vasari, is going."

"Yes?"

"I have taken a deep interest in him."

"Ah! how is that?"

"He is a psychological study."

And with these words the doctor walked away, flourishing his cane in a mysterious manner.

CHAPTER XIII WHAT THE ARTIST'S PORTFOLIO REVEALED

The company departed for the village church; and the Baronet, my uncle, and myself, aided by the servants, whose zeal had been stimulated by the promise of a liberal reward to whomsoever should discover the picture, proceeded to search the length and breadth and depth of the Abbey. Every room, including the bedrooms of the guests, was subjected to a careful inspection; places the most unlikely to be selected as the hiding-place of the famous *chef-d'œuvre* were examined by keen eyes, but all in vain. We might as well have looked for the Holy Grail, said by poets to have vanished somewhere in this very neighborhood.

Late in the afternoon of the day—it was Christmas Eve—we stood on the terrace overlooking the undulating extent of woodland that formed the grounds of the Abbey. The sun was now low down on the horizon. Its dying splendour tinged with red hues the ivy-mantled Nuns' Tower, that rose in solitary grandeur on one side of the Abbey. The Baronet's eye was resting on this tower, and his thoughts reverted to the tenant of it.

"Angelo can explain the disappearance of the missing picture," he said suddenly.

"You think so?" returned my uncle.

"I am loath to suspect him, but I cannot help thinking that he carried it off in the night."

"He carried it off well in the morning, then," responded my uncle jocularly. "Who would have thought from his surprise and agitation that he himself had removed it!"

"His surprise and agitation were assumed, to disarm suspicion."

"Perhaps. But what is his motive for the removal?"

"From certain things you have told me, I believe he is determined that neither you nor Frank shall see his great masterpiece."

The Baronet's opinion was one that I had long held.

"Why not, in Heaven's name?" cried my amazed uncle.

"Ah, that is a reason best known to himself. I fancy—it seems absurd to say it—that the picture, when seen by you, will reveal something that is entirely passed over by others: something detrimental to himself, I mean—what, I cannot undertake to say."

"What can he have done with it?"

"It is inside that tower," replied the Baronet confidently.

"Why there? Why in existence at all? If he is so anxious, as you say, to prevent us from seeing it, the safe plan would be to destroy it altogether."

"That would be the course of a wise man—yes; but Angelo is a fond parent, you see; his picture is his favourite child, and he cannot bring himself to destroy it. Perhaps he intends after your departure to return it to me uninjured, concocting some cock-and-bull story as to where he found it. I trust to goodness he will do something of the kind," continued the Baronet. "So valuable a thing is no trifle to lose. If I could obtain proof that he *has* taken it, I would certainly bring him to book before the law."

"Can't we search the tower?" I said; "Angelo is absent."

"Exactly; but he takes care to lock the door every time he leaves it."

"Have you no other keys that will fit the lock?"

"The key of that lock has peculiar wards. There is no other like it in my possession."

"Well, let us go to the tower," I said. "He may for once have left the door unlocked—who knows?"

"Not very likely, but we may try."

The tower, octagonal in shape, was situated at a little distance from the main body of the Abbey, to which it was joined by a covered walk consisting of a wall on one side and a row of pillars on the other. It contained but one story, lighted by a large Gothic casement twelve feet at least from the ground. Access was gained to the tower by a flight of steps surmounted by an oaken door studded with iron nails.

"The Nuns' Tower," I murmured, as we walked down the cloister; "how came the place to receive that name?"

"Tradition says that when this place was a convent, nuns who broke their vow of virginity were tried in this tower by their ecclesiastical superiors—or, if you will, inferiors—and were led hence by a subterranean passage to their doom."

"Which was——?"

"Precipitation down a deep chasm. The book I spoke of last night—a book I firmly believe to have been stolen, and not mislaid—will tell you more about those dark days than I can."

On reaching the foot of the steps leading to the tower, we mounted them, and, having tried the door, found it locked.

"It would have been strange, indeed," smiled the Baronet, "if Angelo had left his studio accessible."

Bending down I applied my eye to the keyhole.

"What do you see?" asked my uncle.

"It's impossible to see anything," I returned. Something dark within—it may have been a folding screen, the back of a chair, any piece of furniture, in fact—standing immediately behind the keyhole, prevented me from obtaining a glimpse of the interior.

"A cold cell to paint in during the depth of winter," remarked my uncle. "Does he work without a fire?"

"Scarcely," responded the Baronet. "A servant makes up the fire every morning, and brings in coal enough to last the day; but Angelo takes good care to stand by all the time, with a curtain drawn over his easel, and his artistic paraphernalia covered by a cloth, and does not begin work till he is alone."

The concealment displayed by Angelo over his new work of art made me only the more curious to obtain a glimpse of the studio; so I clambered up the ivy towards the Gothic casement, and peeped through its diamond panes, to find that a curtain of violet silk had been drawn across.

"Upon my word," I called out, "Angelo takes precious good care that no one shall discover his art-secret—if secret he has. There is a piece of violet silk stretched across the casement!"

"You can't open the window and get in, I suppose?" said Sir Hugh.

Mounting still higher, I stepped upon the windowsill, and, holding on to a mullion by my left hand, shook the casement with my right; but the fastenings were too secure to permit my forcing an entrance, so I scrambled down again.

"He hasn't put up that curtain exactly as a screen of concealment," remarked the Baronet, stepping backwards to take a view of it. "In this new picture of his the amphitheatre, so he tells me, is represented as being partly screened from the glare of the sun by a purple velarium. The curtain that you see up there faces the south. Angelo has no doubt been trying an experiment: studying the effect of violet-coloured rays upon the sanded floor; for he has had it sanded," the Baronet explained, "to make it resemble the pavement of an arena."

If Sir Hugh really believed that this was the reason why Angelo had covered up the window, he had greater simplicity than I gave him credit for.

As we were turning to go away, my unsatisfied curiosity induced me to take a second peep through the keyhole. An ejaculation of surprise escaped my lips, and I rose to my feet in perplexity.

"When I looked through the keyhole just now, there was something dark within that prevented me from seeing anything. That dark something—whatever it was—has vanished. I can now see nothing but a white surface."

The Baronet and my uncle, stooping down to the keyhole, satisfied themselves of the truth of the last part of my statement, and then both looked at me with a half-doubting expression.

"There is something white in front of the door now," said Sir Hugh. "Are you certain it was dark before?"

"Quite certain. There's some one inside."

"Can Angelo have come back?" the Baronet whispered. "You remember he said at breakfast that he might finish his picture within a few hours. Is he at work now?"

This idea made us look rather mean. It is not nice to be caught playing the spy upon a man in his supposed absence. Only the oaken door separated us from the cell within, so that the artist, if he *were* there, must have overheard our suspicions of him. We all three listened with our ears pressed close to the door, but could not detect the faintest sound within.

"Angelo, are you here?" cried the Baronet, rapping on the door; "we have come to see how the picture is going on."

There was no reply, and all our words and knockings failed to evoke any.

"You must have made a mistake, Frank," said my uncle, as we relinquished our efforts, and turned to go away.

"I think not," I replied, having my doubts on the matter nevertheless.

"Angelo can't be painting now," remarked Sir Hugh. "This dim twilight would not permit it. And if he has been at it earlier in the day, his fire would surely have been lit; but," glancing back and pointing to a little chimney-turret on the battlemented roof of the tower, "we have seen no smoke."

"Yes," returned I; "but if Angelo wishes to keep his presence there a secret—and secrecy seems to be a *sine quâ non* in all his undertakings—he won't have a fire."

"Well, then he'll be confoundedly clever if his chilled fingers can handle the brush with any delicacy of touch in this cold atmosphere," said the Baronet with a shiver, for the air was extremely damp and cold.

"Sir Hugh," said my uncle, "if you are certain that the picture is concealed in this tower, why not force an entrance?"

"Well," replied the Baronet doubtfully, "there is just the possibility that it may *not* be there, which would be rather awkward; for Angelo on his return would see the broken lock, and learn that we have been playing the spy on him, which is exactly what we have been doing," added he with a cynical smile, "but there's no need for him to know it."

Evidently the Baronet regarded espionage very much as the ancient Spartans regarded theft. There was no dishonor in the act—the dishonor consisted in being found out.

"I shall tell Angelo," Sir Hugh continued, "when he returns, that as we have thoroughly examined the Abbey, including the apartments allotted to my guests, without coming upon the picture, we must, in common fairness, subject even *his* sacred studio to the same investigation."

"And supposing he refuses to submit to this?" said my uncle.

"Then I shall assert my authority as master of Silverdale, and order an examination of the tower. Ugh! how cold it is!" he added. "Let us get back to the library fire. I feel frozen."

Twilight was coming on apace, and a dim silvery mist was gradually veiling the landscape from our view as we turned to enter the Abbey.

My visit to the Nuns' Tower made me anxious to learn whether the artist had returned. I questioned some of the servants on this point, but none of them had seen Angelo since the morning, so I was forced to the conclusion that I had been mistaken in supposing any one to have been in the tower.

On repairing to the library I found my uncle and the Baronet discussing the technicalities of some Parliamentary Bill of the past session, a topic that was speedily cut short by the entrance of Fruin, the butler, who carried under his arm an artist's portfolio filled with papers and sketches.

"What have you there, Fruin?" said the Baronet.

"A portfolio, Sir Hugh. I found it hidden under some leaves in one of the vases on the West Terrace."

"A queer hiding-place for it," remarked the Baronet, taking the portfolio and examining it. "How came it there, I wonder. Vasari's, of course. He was showing the ladies some sketches this morning before breakfast, and suddenly closed the portfolio and would not allow them to see any more. He said they must be tired of them, but Florrie declared he had shut it up because there was something he did not want her to see, and she seized the portfolio and ran off with it. I suppose she must have hidden it where you found it, Fruin. Thank you for bringing it here."

The butler withdrew, and the Baronet pushed the portfolio over to me.

"Here you are, Frank," he said, "if you are interested in Vasari's sketches."

"Not at all," I replied carelessly, and then a thought struck me. "Stop, though! You say Vasari would not let all of them be seen. More secrecy. What's the game this time? Let me try to find out."

I drew a chair to the table and began to examine the contents of the portfolio. They consisted of sketches—ink, pencil, and crayon—in every stage of execution, some being unfinished outlines, and others finished to perfection. They embraced a vast variety of subjects— single objects, landscapes, sketches for historical pieces, and copies of statuary from the antique. Like a detective seeking for evidence I examined each sketch suspiciously, holding it near the light and turning it over to see whether there was any mark or writing on the back. I came at last to twelve sketches of different heads, and unfastening the tape that kept them together, I laid them out on the table and drew my uncle's attention to them.

"You see these twelve heads? They have been in this portfolio a year, for Vasari showed them to me last Christmas and asked me whether I recognised any of them. As a fact I did not, but I fancied at the time he had an interested motive for the question, and now I am pretty certain he had."

My uncle looked at them carefully.

"You don't see a likeness to any one you know?"

"No," I replied.

"Try again."

The Weird Picture

There was one face that seemed familiar. It was that of a man about thirty years of age, but the head was quite bald, and the face destitute of beard and moustache.

"I may have seen this fellow," I said. "I seem to have a faint recollection of him."

My uncle laughed.

"Your recollections of your brother are growing very faint indeed if you do not recognize that face. Can't you see that it is George?"

"George?" I cried.

"Yes. That is George's face, minus hair, beard, and moustache."

Now that the likeness to George had been pointed out I could see it clearly enough, but the absence of all hair had imparted so different a look to the face that I doubt whether I myself would ever have discovered it.

"And why the deuce should he sketch George like that?" I asked, thoroughly perplexed. "I remember how relieved he seemed when I did not recognise it."

"Can't say," replied my uncle. "It's another of those little mystifications which he delights to put upon his friends. By the way, wasn't Cæsar bald, and beardless?"

"'Like laurels on the bald first Cæsar's head,'" I murmured. "Yes, at the time of his death he was. But I don't quite see the relevancy of your remark."

"Merely a passing thought," he said lightly. "It's not much of a portrait of George; it's like him, and yet not like him. And there is a most uncanny expression about the eyes."

He threw aside the sketch, which the Baronet took up. As soon as his eyes fell upon it a half-repressed exclamation escaped his lips, and setting his gold-rimmed glasses upon his nose he took a long and careful look at the drawing.

"Do you say this is Captain Willard?" he asked, elevating his eyebrows in surprise.

"Yes," I replied. "That is my brother."

"He is a handsome man," said Sir Hugh, studying the sketch as if it were some puzzle offered to him for solution.

"Do you know him?" I asked.

"I have never seen Captain Willard in my life," he replied, laying aside the drawing.

It would have been wrong to doubt his word, but if any one else had spoken in the same curious, halting way I should have hesitated to believe him. I was on the point of asking him the reason of his evident surprise, when my attention was caught by a series of remarkable drawings that my uncle had just taken out of the portfolio. There were completed sketches of gravestones and monumental pieces, which I supposed had been drawn by Vasari at the request of some cemetery mason in want of new designs, or else were the result of some competition at an art school. Whatever their origin, they had provided Vasari with an opportunity of displaying his inventiveness and taste, and the result was a collection of from twenty to thirty funeral monuments of various graceful shapes, decorated with broken columns, reversed torches, urns, crosses, wreaths, and other objects emblematic of death and immortality.

But what interested me most in this collection was a sort of grim humour, which had taken the shape of placing on these monuments the names of many distinguished men, and from my knowledge of the artist's character, I readily discerned that the persons thus selected were those from whose opinions he differed. I suppose his eccentricity found a kind of pleasure in thus consigning to the tomb men whom he disliked. Some of the epitaphs served only to display the morbid vanity of the man, as, for instance:—

"SACRED TO THE MEMORY OF

FREDERICK, LORD LEIGHTON,
P. R. A.,

WHO WAS SUCCEEDED IN THE PRESIDENTIAL CHAIR
BY THE EQUALLY EMINENT IF NOT
SUPERIOR ARTIST,

ANGELO VASARI."

The Weird Picture

A future Walpole in search of "Anecdotes of Painting" must not overlook the following curious incident:—

"IN MEMORIAM,

ALMA TADEMA,

THE STAR AMONG ARTISTS,

WHO DIED WITH GRIEF AT THE ECLIPSE OF HIS NAME
BY THE RISING SUN,

ANGELO VASARI."

"Egad!" said the Baronet, who was looking on with the half-abstracted air that he had displayed since the discovery of George's likeness. "I don't wonder he shut the portfolio up when he came to this exhibition of his vanity. What a conceited fool the fellow is!"

Casually turning over the rest of these drawings, we came upon the following singular epitaph, inscribed on a monument crowned with a piece of sculpture representing the Crucifixion:

"TO THE MEMORY OF THE SUBLIME
GIOTTO,

WHO, IN HIS ZEAL FOR ART,

SET AT DEFIANCE THOSE FANTASTIC NOTIONS WHICH
CASUISTS CALL MORALITY,

AND WHOSE EXAMPLE INSPIRED THE GENIUS OF
ANGELO VASARI,

WITH THE IDEA THAT GAVE BIRTH TO THAT NOBLE
MASTERPIECE,

'THE FALL OF CÆSAR.'"

"Giotto? Giotto?" repeated the Baronet with a thoughtful air. "He means *the* Giotto, of course."

"Without doubt," responded my uncle. "But what does he mean by the words, 'setting at defiance those fantastic notions which casuists call morality?'"

"Can't say, I'm sure," replied Sir Hugh. "I'm not sufficiently versed in Giotto's history to understand the allusion. But perhaps Frank can explain it."

"I'm sorry to say I'm exactly in your position," I returned.

"Learned gentlemen we are!" laughed the Baronet; and then, after a brief interval of silence, he continued:

"I would like to know what this allusion is—for a reason," he added in a grave tone. "It refers undoubtedly to some incident in Giotto's career; if we knew what this incident was, it might furnish us with a clue to the mystery that surrounds the production of Angelo's picture."

"Well, let us try to solve the enigma," said I, going to a bookcase, and taking therefrom a volume entitled *The History of Early Italian Art*. "Here's a book that is sure to contain a biography of Giotto."

I turned to the index, and having found the pages referring to Giotto, I glanced hastily over the biography of the great "Fa Presto," stopping now and then to read aloud, for the edification of the Baronet and my uncle, some item that I deemed worthy of notice. At length, in the course of my reading, I came to the following passage:

"A horrible story is told in connexion with his picture of 'The Crucifixion.' It is said that Giotto persuaded the man who acted as his model to be tied to a cross, and while in this helpless state he stabbed him, in order that he might be the better enabled to limn with ghastly fidelity the dying agonies of the Saviour."

"What do you think of that?" said I, looking up from my reading. "If that isn't setting morality at defiance, what is?"

"You've hit on it," said the Baronet. "That's the story Angelo's alluding to, for see! he has put the Crucifixion scene on the tomb. But what does he call Giotto's deed? 'A zeal for art?' Surely he doesn't approve this horrible act?"

"It would seem so from his language," I returned blankly.

"'Whose example,'" said the Baronet, reading from the epitaph, and tracing the words with his forefinger, "'inspired the genius of Angelo Vasari with the idea that gave birth to that noble masterpiece, "The Fall of Cæsar."' What can he mean, Leslie?" he continued, addressing my uncle. "Not," he added with a grim smile, "that he, too, stabbed his model for the sake of an artistic effect. That would be too much of a joke, to murder a man for the sake of producing a realistic picture. And yet," he concluded with a perplexed air, "that's the only meaning one can give to his words."

He stared uneasily at my uncle, who stared uneasily at me.

"I don't know what to think of it," said my uncle. "He certainly seems to approve Giotto's act, and intimates that he copied his example in painting his own picture. This must be the language of a madman!"

"There's method in his madness, then," remarked the Baronet. "He had wit enough to hide this from the ladies this morning."

We read daily of terrible murders committed by men who are mere names to us. In the columns of the newspaper such crimes do not seem out of place—they are quite natural; we almost look for them; but to learn that a person within our own circle—who has sat at our table, and is on familiar terms with us—has his hands stained with the blood of his fellow-man; this is so new an experience that we can not bring ourselves to believe.

For a long time we sat looking at each other in silent surprise, not knowing what to make of the singular effusion to the memory of Giotto.

"It must be, it must be!" murmured the Baronet at length. "It's quite clear to me that Angelo stabbed his model."

"No, no, it can't be!" exclaimed my uncle, unable to keep his chair in his excitement, and nervously pacing the apartment. "You do not really think that Angelo would murder a fellow-mortal merely to produce a realistic picture?"

"Why not?" replied the Baronet coolly, as if the supposititious act, were the most natural one in the world. "Such instances *have* occurred in the history of art—science, too, has had its murders. Did not Vesalius on one occasion dissect a living man?

The Weird Picture

From his boyhood Angelo has thirsted for fame as an artist. His long line of early failures, therefore, may have had the effect of disturbing his mental balance. Constant brooding over the neglect offered to his genius may have so obliterated the line that divides right from wrong as to have led him, in despair of obtaining success by any other method, to imitate the example of Giotto."

"Good God! And this man might have been my son-in-law!" cried my uncle.

"Let me congratulate you upon your lucky deliverance from such a relationship."

"If Angelo is an assassin," said my uncle, "who was the victim?"

"That is the question which the picture will answer."

"You mean that Angelo has transferred the features of the dead without alteration to the canvas?"

"That is my meaning—yes."

"And yet," remonstrated my uncle, "he exhibits his picture at Paris in a public gallery open to all. That is the very way to betray himself."

"Exactly, if the dead man were a well-known person, which probably he was not."

I sat silent, revolving in my mind the whole history of the strange picture, as I was by no means disposed to accept the Baronet's theory that Angelo was an actual assassin. I remembered the date assigned by the artist for the completion of his work. It was Christmas Day— the day of my brother's departure for the Continent. I recalled the red stain on his vest. Could it be that both George and Angelo were concerned in a murder? But why should one remain and the other become a fugitive? Was it the more guilty of the two that had fled? and had Angelo for his own purpose simply taken advantage of a deed that George alone had committed? Was the officer who had caused the fracas in the Vasari Gallery at Paris none other than George, who, angry with the artist for having painted a picture that might lead to the detection of the crime, had attempted to destroy it. Was the silver-haired old man—Matteo Caritio—an accessory to the deed? Touched with remorse, had he confessed his part in the plot to

The Weird Picture

the priest of Rivoli, only to meet with death a day later at the hand of the man whose secret he had betrayed?

I turned to listen to the Baronet, who was holding forth to my uncle.

"You see now, Leslie," said he, "why he exercised such secrecy over the production of this picture, and why he kept his studio-door locked while painting it. It was because the model that he painted from, the model for his fallen Cæsar, was, in point of fact, a dead man."

My uncle's reply was startling in its suggestiveness:

"That may have been the reason why he kept his studio-door locked then; but why does he keep it locked now?"

"Yes—over this new picture of the girl-martyr?" said I.

The Baronet had not considered this point.

"Why—does—he—keep—his—door—locked—now?" he repeated, pausing in a curiously deliberative manner between each word. "Ah, why?" He made a long pause. "Not for a similar reason, surely? And yet—" he made another long pause. "He said at breakfast, you know, that he might finish his picture to-day. He was playing with his knife, very curiously at the time. What could he mean? Good God! what could he mean? Not that——"

He paused, afraid to give utterance to his suspicions. For a few moments we durst not speak, for a dim presentiment of some awful tragedy to come had stolen over us.

The Baronet was the first to break silence.

"That tower must be watched to-night," he said in a hoarse voice.

"Sir Hugh," said my uncle sternly, "if Angelo be the fiend you think him, he must be arrested at once."

"That will require a magistrate's warrant," I said.

"Right; and we will procure it without delay," observed the Baronet, rising. "Colonel Montague is the nearest magistrate. He lives at the Manse—five miles from here. The carriage can take us there and back in an hour, and——"

His further words were checked by the sudden appearance of Fruin, who, without having waited to knock, entered the room, and, brimful of excitement, cried:

"I've found the picture, Sir Hugh!"

"The devil you have! Where on earth was it?"

"In the Nuns' Tower, to be sure!"

"The Nuns' Tower! How did you manage to get in there?"

Fruin's manner changed at once from excitement to soberness.

"Well, Sir Hugh," he began with the air of a penitent, "it was wrong, I admit, to play the spy on a gentleman, but—but— It's this way, you see. I have always been suspicious of Mr. Vasari and his doings, so—so that's how it was, you know. I haven't been doing exactly what's right, but—but—you see——"

He hesitated and stammered so much that the impatient Baronet, with a deprecatory wave of his hand, cried:

"There, there, go on. I forgive beforehand everything you've done in consideration of your having found the picture."

Highly gratified by this plenary indulgence, the butler began again in a more confident tone:

"Well, Sir Hugh, you remember that Mr. Vasari hadn't been here a week before I said to you, 'That Italian gentleman has come here for no good?'"

"I remember it, Fruin; and I told you not to pass remarks on my visitors."

"So you did, Sir Hugh, so you did," replied the butler, nodding, as if the reprimand were a decided compliment; "and I went off in a huff, determined to keep my own counsel for the future; determined, too, in spite of your rebuff, Sir Hugh, to keep a watchful eye on the foreign gentleman. Foreigners are always suspicious characters," he added digressively. "What first made me suspicious of Mr. V.," he continued, "was your telling me that he had chosen the Nuns' Tower as a studio. Why couldn't he take a nice cheerful room in the Abbey, and not that cold stone cell? 'You've got a motive for living in that

The Weird Picture

place,' I thought to myself. 'You're up to something queer, and you want to get as far away from us as you can, so that we shall not be able to overhear anything.' Then, when I learned that, with the exception of Adams, who lights the fire in the morning, no one must enter his studio, not even you, Sir Hugh, I grew more suspicious still. 'What's your little game?' I thought. Why, do you know, I've looked out of my bedroom window at one, two, and three in the morning, and I've seen a light burning in the tower! What's he doing there at that unearthly hour? He can't be painting. No one paints by lamplight. I've long had a desire to have a peep in at that tower, to learn what goes on there; and so the other day, when Mr. Vasari had gone to London, I got the blacksmith to examine the lock of the door for the purpose of making a key to fit it. Here it is," he continued, holding it aloft on his forefinger. "I received it only a quarter of an hour ago, but as soon as I got it I went at once to the tower to have a look at the place before Mr. Vasari should return. Brown and Tompkins were with me, carrying dark lanterns. We tried the key, and the door opened easily. Brown and Tompkins didn't like to enter—they were afraid—so they stood at the head of the steps and turned the light of their bull's-eye into the place, for of course it was quite dark, while I went in. I looked round—there was no one there—and while looking round, my eye was caught by something peeping out from under the fringe of tapestry. I lifted the curtain, and there was the picture behind the tapestry, reared up against the wall."

He paused, out of breath, for he had been talking very fast.

"It was well for you that Angelo was not there," remarked the Baronet gravely, and speaking with a knowledge of the artist's character gained only within the past few minutes. "He might have resented your intrusion with a pistol-shot. He's quite capable of it."

"Ah! that he is," cried the old servant, surprised and delighted to find his master coming round to his way of thinking—"that he is! Angelo may be his name, but Devilo would suit him better, and so would you say, Sir Hugh, if you had seen his face this morning when you were accusing us servants—*us*!" protested Fruin, emphasizing the word with some dignity, "of stealing the picture. I was watching him, and if you could have seen his wicked looks and the sparkle of his eyes you wouldn't have wondered at that girl's fright. Others of us noticed his manner, but we didn't like to speak out. I am certain he was laughing in his sleeve at you, Sir Hugh, and saying to himself, 'Don't you wish you may find the picture again!' It struck me at the time that it was he who had removed it."

I interposed with a question which I was burning to put:

"What did you see in the studio besides the picture?"

"I was so delighted at finding the picture that I didn't stop to examine the place, but hurried here at once to tell Sir Hugh of my discovery."

"But you couldn't enter the place without seeing something of it," I persisted. "Tell us anything you did see. What's the place like?"

"Well, sir, there was the usual furniture—the table and the chairs of carved oak. The walls and floor are of stone, you know. There's tapestry round the walls, and the floor is covered with yellow sand—why, I don't know. It's a whim of his, I suppose. There was an easel with a picture on it, which I didn't look at, brushes, paints, palettes, and things of that sort on the table, and—and that's all I can remember," he added.

"Did you see nothing more?" I asked. "Where was the artist's model that Angelo spoke of at breakfast this morning—the lay figure that he paints from?"

"I saw nothing resembling a lay figure. But then I wasn't in the place above a few seconds, and it was in half-darkness all the time."

"Is 'The Fall of Cæsar' damaged in any way?" asked the Baronet.

"Not in the least, Sir Hugh."

"What have you done with it?"

"I told Brown and Tompkins to carry it to the gallery."

"Quite right. Place it somewhere in the gallery—anywhere will do for the present. See that it's done, Fruin, and then lock the place up and bring the keys here. Give me the key of the Nuns' Tower. I will examine that place to-night myself."

Fruin, laying the key down on the table, departed on his errand.

The Weird Picture

"I'm off to the gallery," said I, preparing to follow the butler; "I must see that picture."

"No, no, not now," said the Baronet authoritatively, and laying a restraining hand upon my arm. "Time flies, and every moment is of value. Never mind the gallery for the present, unless you wish Angelo to escape us. I want you to take up your station at the entrance-hall of the Abbey, so as to be ready to 'shadow' Angelo the moment he returns. Keep a watchful eye on him, for should he overhear that the picture is found—and I daresay the servants are talking of nothing else at this present moment—he will be sure to seek safety in flight, knowing well that his crime is discovered. Detain him at the Abbey by every means in your power till we return with a constable and the warrant for his arrest. Should he show a disposition to bolt, give the servants orders to seize him. Don't hesitate; I will take the responsibility."

"Supposing the guests should return without him, what then?" I asked.

"Then you may depend upon it that he has fled. In that case, off to the railway-station at once; make use of my name; telegraph a description of him to the Chief Constable of Penzance: say that a warrant is out for his arrest; and you may be in time to check his flight. Come, Leslie."

"Stay a minute!" I cried, as both moved towards the door. "What will the warrant charge Angelo with?"

"With murder, of course."

"Stop! How can a warrant for murder be issued against a man unless you know the name of the victim?"

"But I do know the name of the victim."

"What!" I cried in amazement. "You do? How have you found out? Who was it?"

"You yourself have told me."

And with these words—a complete enigma to me—the Baronet darted off, accompanied by my uncle, who looked every whit as bewildered as myself.

The Weird Picture

I was on the point of going to the hall, there to await Angelo, when Fruin came into the room.

"Has Sir Hugh gone out?" he asked.

"Yes, but only for a little while," I answered. "Do you want him particularly?"

"Only to give him these keys," the butler replied, laying them on a table.

"Have you put the picture back in the gallery?"

"Yes, sir; stood it on a table in the middle of the hall. Mr. Vasari must be very strong to have been able to carry it off by himself. It takes two of us to lift it."

"Ah! Have the company returned yet?"

"No, sir, they will not be back for a long time."

"Why, how's that?"

"We've just had a boy from the vicarage to say so. Miss Wyville has persuaded them all to accompany the church choir in a round of carol singing."

I found the news particularly agreeable. Sir Hugh could now procure the warrant without Angelo's having any idea of what was in store for him, and I should have ample time to study the weird picture and to examine the interior of the Nuns' Tower, two occupations in which I resolved to have no companion. A vague feeling of peril gave a charm to the idea. I did not know what form the peril might take, but determined to be prepared for it in any shape, I took the liberty of borrowing a brace of loaded pistols which Sir Hugh kept in a drawer of his writing-table.

"One for the ghost in the gallery," I said cheerfully to myself as I slipped it into my hip pocket, "and one for the artist in the studio," and I slipped the second into the other hip pocket. "And now for the masterpiece."

CHAPTER XIV THE MYSTERIES OF THE STUDIO

Taking up a lighted candle and the keys both of the tower and of the picture gallery, I directed my steps towards the latter place. It was situated at some distance from the library, and, the house being new to me, I had some difficulty in finding it.

In the distance the sound of jovial carols told me that in the servants' quarters due homage was being paid to the spirit of the season. Floating faintly along the corridors came the snatches of a refrain—

"Come, bring with a noise,
My merry, merry boys,
　　The Christmas log to the firing;
While my old dame she
Bids you all be free,
　　And drink to your hearts' desiring."

I hummed over a few bars myself as I made my way along.

At last, after losing my way several times, I stood in front of the thick oaken door that I knew to be the entrance of the picture-gallery. Half-a-dozen keys inserted into the lock one after another failed to open the door. The seventh caused the steel tongue to spring back with a sharp click. I was on the point of turning the handle when a sound on the other side arrested my act. A moment's reflection induced me to believe that it was merely the night breeze sighing through the elms and yews outside, but in my first start I had likened it to human footsteps stealing softly away from the door. So strongly had I been impressed with this fancy that I had at once turned the key in the lock again, so as to keep two inches of solid oak, at least, between me and the something on the other side.

Up to this time I had always considered myself fairly brave, but I now began to question my right to the title. Should I return whence I came, safe in limb, sane in mind, but baffled in my quest by my own fears, or should I invite one of the servants to accompany me? No! I determined to venture by myself. What a fine thing it would be, if, alone and unaided, I should succeed in solving the mystery that gave this chamber the reputation of being haunted! I should be the hero of the hour, eclipsing all the male guests of Silverdale and receiving the smiles and praises of the women. While the men were singing carols at a safe distance, I should have been keeping a solitary vigil in a moonlit hall surrounded by ghostly perils. Vanity rather than courage inspired me to proceed.

I could still hear the carolling of the servants, and the sound, remote though it was, gave me a sense of safety. Once more I turned the key, and then flung wide the door. Before entering, I gazed down the gallery, but no sound came from it now, and nothing moving was to be seen.

It was a superb night. The moon was at the full, and its bright rays, falling upon the tall casements, flung parallelograms of light across the polished oak flooring, causing the gallery to present a chequered appearance, silver alternating with ebony in regular perspective. A more weird place to spend a night in could hardly be imagined, and I quite forgave the servants for believing it to be haunted. Mailed warriors and mounted knights shimmered in the moonlight apparently on the point of starting into life and action; the eyes of the portraits on the walls seemed to stare at me with a marvellous resemblance to those of human beings; mysterious shapes seemed to be lurking in the alcoves, whispering and pointing at me as I advanced with beating heart.

I had not taken more than ten steps when the great door swung to on its hinges with a clang that gave me a sudden start and called forth strange echoes from the gallery.

There is nothing remarkable in the clanging of a door, if it be due merely to a current of air or to automatic action; but when neither of these causes is in operation it is apt to create an uneasy sensation, especially when, as in the present instance, it is accompanied by what sounds very like a laugh, coming it is impossible to say whence.

I felt afraid almost to turn round to discover the author of the laugh, but when I had turned and could perceive nothing to justify my belief that it was a laugh, I was equally afraid to turn the other way, and so stood rooted to the spot for a few moments, not wishing to retire, nor yet overbold to go forward.

The Weird Picture

At length, despite the frowning faces of the portraits on the walls and the threatening lances of the knights, I advanced, with one hand on the pistol in my pocket. I could have wished myself for the time being one of those students of the black art who, successfully passing through the fabled hall in Padua, are said never afterwards to have cast a shadow; for, as I moved before the moonlit casements, a black shape moved with me along the floor of the hall, and when I had passed out of the moonlight, the candle I carried in my trembling hand caused the shadow to start up on the adjacent wall as though it were some sable familiar attendant on my movements.

In the middle of the gallery, upon a small table and reared up against the wall, I could perceive in a massive frame a large picture, which I took to be the thing I was in quest of, but before I had got near enough to obtain a glimpse of it an unfortunate accident occurred. I dropped my candle, and the moon at this moment being obscured by clouds, I was left in darkness.

The superstitious fancies of my overwrought mind were for the moment overcome by the annoyance I felt at being thus baffled on the edge of discovery. Here was I at last standing before Angelo's great picture, the picture that had lifted him to fame, the picture that some critics had assigned to a hand other than his, the picture he had been so anxious to conceal from my view, the picture whose principal figure the Baronet averred was copied from the murdered dead, the picture whose figure, so the servants whispered, had the power of descending from the canvas, and yet beyond the fact of its size I was precluded by the darkness from learning anything about it.

It stood glimmering faintly through the gloom, and eluding my power to penetrate its secret. I strained my eyes to the utmost, and after a time they became accustomed to the darkness; but all I could discern on the canvas were two figures, one erect, the other prostrate, both which seemed to be returning my stare like faces in a mirror. Faint whisperings seemed to be trembling on the air around, and more than once I thought I heard a subdued laugh.

I passed my hand over the canvas, not without the weird fancy that it might be seized in a cold clasp. It is needless to say that my sense of touch did not add anything to my knowledge.

Just as I was preparing to return for another candle the moon emerged triumphantly from an array of defiant clouds, and its light, increasing almost to the brightness of day, enabled me to obtain a clear view of the picture.

My first feeling was one of disappointment.

What I had expected to see I do not quite know: something alarming, probably.

There was, however, nothing alarming on the canvas before me. It was a painting that Gérôme himself might have been proud to own, so classic and finished was its character. Indeed, I cannot give a better idea of it than by saying that in the pose of the two figures, and in the arrangement of the details, it bore a considerable resemblance to the work of that great master on the same subject, save that in Angelo's composition the figures of the conspirators were wanting.

The principal features of the picture (to quote the language of the *Standard* correspondent) were: "The fallen Cæsar with his toga wrapped partly round him, the statue of Pompey rising above, a tesselated pavement stained with blood, here and there a discarded dagger, columnar architecture in the back-ground: such were the simple elements presented by this *chef-d'œuvre*."

I fell back a pace or two to contemplate the picture as a whole, and, despite my dislike of the artist, I could not repress a feeling of admiration for the man who had produced such a masterpiece.

Desirous of verifying the Baronet's suspicion that the picture might reveal to me something that would be entirely passed over by others, I proceeded to examine it in detail.

I first directed my attention to the statue of Pompey, and saw that Angelo had given his own regular and haughty features to this figure, which was represented as being crowned with a laurel-wreath, and armed with spear and shield. The centre of this shield was set with the helmeted head of Minerva—a gem of minute painting—and it required no second glance to tell me that the face of the goddess was simply a miniature portrait of Daphne. The Baronet had never made any reference to this fact. How the likeness could have escaped his notice was a marvel to me. Perhaps a lover's eyes were more discerning than his.

From the statue of Pompey I turned my attention to the figure at the base of the pedestal. Angelo had not strictly adhered to the minutiæ of history in this portion of his picture, for he had given a full view of Cæsar's face instead of veiling it in the folds of the toga.

From the space between two lofty columns there slanted a flood of sunshine, painted with a technique so marvellous that the beams seemed actually to quiver on the canvas. In fact, so beautifully was this sunlight managed that I was impelled to touch it with my hand, almost expecting to see it tinged with a golden hue. These rays formed the principal beauty of the picture, suffusing the dead body of Cæsar with a transparent veil of light.

The bald and beardless head of the fallen Dictator became next the object of my study.

Standing close to the canvas, my eyes could detect nothing but a confused daub, but on receding gradually from it the effect was curious, not to say startling. The features of Cæsar, which appeared but dim and vague at first, became gradually clearer and more distinct, till at length each curve and every line of the painted countenance stood out in relief through the cascade of yellow beams. I could quite forgive the little servant-girl for supposing that the eyes of this figure moved, for more than once I was seized with the same impression.

The thought, suggested by the epitaph in the artist's portfolio, that a murdered man might have contributed to the deathlike realism displayed by this face invested it with a weird interest; and I continued to gaze at it as though it were the embalmed head of Orpheus, celebrated in classic legend, whose dead tongue could whisper things past and to come. The filmy, glazed eyes fascinated me with their dreadful stare. The face had a mournful, surprised expression—the very expression, so far as I could imagine (for happily I am no judge of such matters), of a man who, without warning, had been cut off out of the land of the living. It was not, however, the face that meets us in the coins and busts of art-galleries:

it seemed to have a much more familiar look. It seemed a face well known to me—one, too, that I had seen but recently.

Minute after minute passed, and still I stood there contemplating the dead face, with the secret consciousness that ere long I should recognise it. A sudden movement on my part to the left, seemingly, as it were, to set the face in a new point of view, caused the light of knowledge to flash into my mind.

A loud cry broke from me, and I reeled back into the middle of the hall.

For my brother's face was staring at me from the canvas in lineaments not to be mistaken—in lineaments so startling in their fidelity to the original that I marvelled how I could have failed at the first to detect the resemblance. The beard and hair were wanting to complete the likeness: it was this omission that had delayed my recognition of it, just as it had prevented my recognition of the portrait sketch that Angelo had exhibited to me.

Overwhelmed with amazement I stood staring at the picture, rooted to the spot, without power to move from it. Whence had Angelo derived the marvellous art that had enabled him to limn my brother's face so faithfully, and yet to transform it so as to make it seem like the very image of death?

I lifted my eyes to the figure of Pompey mounted on his lofty pedestal, and as I gazed at the proud face, over which the changing moonbeams seemed to impart a smile of mockery, the picture assumed a new and terrible significance. An ordinary spectator might regard it simply as a splendid work of art, and see in it nothing more than was implied in its title—"The Fall of Cæsar;" but to me, familiar with the artist's aspiration, it was full of a latent symbolism expressive of his hopes at the time of painting it. It was no longer the conqueror of the East triumphing over the conqueror of the West, but Angelo in his own person exulting over the rival whom he had slain. The laurel-wreath on his brows represented the crown of fame which the exhibition of this very picture was to bring him; and the setting of Daphne's head in the shield that was braced tight to his arm expressed the confident conviction that she was destined one day to be linked to him. The artist's secret was revealed:

The Weird Picture

he had killed my brother! In his morbid desire of fame, and in a spirit of hideous realism sometimes, though rarely, exemplified in the history of art, Angelo had murdered a fellow-mortal for the purpose of having by his side a dead man to serve as a model for the fallen Cæsar, even proceeding so far as to retain in his picture the very features of his victim.

The commission of this terrible deed, and the thought that now that his rival was dead Daphne would be his, had imparted to the mind of the artist a sort of diabolic inspiration—a tone of fiendish exaltation that had enabled him for the time being to rise superior to his ordinary mediocre powers, and to surprise the art-critics by producing a work far surpassing all his previous efforts.

He could expose this painting to public view with little fear that its exhibition would be attended with the discovery of his crime, owing to the fact that his victim (to represent faithfully the person of Cæsar) must be delineated as both bald and beardless, a fact that had imparted a very different look to the painted face; and moreover, since George had spent the years subsequent to his twentieth birthday in India, he was not known in Europe except to his own small circle of kinsfolk.

The only persons, then, whom the artist had cause to fear were the relatives of his victim, and returned Anglo-Indians.

I now understood his motive in calling my attention to the pen-and-ink sketch of George's face. It was to ascertain whether, in the event of seeing his picture, I should detect any resemblance to my brother in the bald and beardless head of Cæsar: hence his satisfaction at my want of perception, for he felt pretty certain that if I failed to recognise the likeness, other persons would be equally or more obtuse.

Yet, despite the apparent safety which my mental blindness had promised him, he had feared after all lest the picture should betray him, and the *fracas* that had occurred in the Vasari Gallery at Paris was a result of this fear.

The Indian officer, whom Angelo had ordered to be expelled from the gallery, was doubtless a friend of George's, belonging, perhaps, to the same regiment, and who, if permitted to see the work of art, might have discovered in the same more than was intended by its author.

Hence Angelo's reason for withdrawing the picture from the public view. Too fond of his handiwork to destroy it, he thought that by consigning it to the private collection of the Cornish Baronet his safety would be assured.

Vain hope! Avenging Nemesis was pursuing him, bringing to the chosen asylum of his masterpiece the very bride of the man he had slain—the one person above all others who would be swift to detect in the face of the painted Cæsar the features of her lost lover; and so, in order to avert the penalty which such a recognition would bring, the artist had been compelled to resort to the desperate expedient of carrying off the picture during the night.

Such were the thoughts that went whirling through my mind!

Then, with a sudden revulsion of feeling, I laughed at these wild ideas, and at the fright they had given me.

"No, no. It can't be. I'm out of it altogether," I muttered. "This picture was exhibited last spring: the *Standard* newspaper's a proof of that. But George was seen at Rivoli by Daphne in the autumn: clearly, then, he can't have been killed last Christmas in order to minister to the success of Angelo's art."

It was a relief to believe that George might still be living and that Angelo was not his murderer. But the affair was still as great a mystery as ever—nay, rather, it was enhanced. The question still remained: Why had the artist employed George's features in painting his Cæsar?

The human mind is not content with simply accepting facts: it must endeavour to account for them. Men will theorise, as confident to-day as ever that they can solve every problem presented to them, whether it relates to things in heaven above, or in the earth beneath, or in the waters under the earth.

Flinging myself on a seat within an embrasured casement, I tried to devise some new theory to account for the admission of my brother's face into Angelo's picture.

"Angelo had George before him in his studio while painting this picture: of that I am certain. But how came George to be there? He would never of his own free will consent to pose as an artist's model—of that, too, I am certain. Besides, if it were so, Angelo would have nothing to fear from our discovering the fact; but that he does fear our discovering it is manifest by his behaviour. It's quite clear that something suspicious has attended the production of this picture. There's only one conclusion left as far as I can see. George, on account of his fine athletic figure, was inveigled into Angelo's studio; and, in order to produce a state requisite for the artist's conception, he was compelled to drink some drug which subdued his natural powers, and gave him every appearance of death. And since Angelo could never by his own strength overpower George, it is clear he must have had others to help him in this plot. That silver-haired old man, Matteo Carito, may have been one; and perhaps that mysterious veiled lady was another.

"But what happened after the picture was finished? George would never permit himself to be quietly and contemptuously dismissed from the studio without making the affair public, or seeking redress. Nor would Angelo be such a fool as to permit George to go forth to the world, proclaiming the ignominious treatment he had received. Ah, I have it! That drug must have so disordered his senses as to leave him without intellect and without memory of the past. Angelo would have no difficulty in removing him in that state to Rivoli, and detaining him there—a harmless lunatic—in his old nurse's cottage. What cared he so long as his rival in love was out of the way, and his fame as an artist established? Yes, yes; I see it all now.

"'In some secluded part of Europe I shall live out my days a lonely recluse.' That letter was a forgery of Angelo's. The damnable villain! I now understand his words to Daphne when parting from her at Rivoli: 'You are nearer to him now than you have been for months.' Of course she was. George was living, a sort of prisoner, at Rivoli. He must have contrived to escape from his place of captivity that very day; and, perhaps with some faint glimmering of reason left, he determined to have vengeance on all who had taken part in the plot against him. That is why he hurled the old man over the cliff. He was mad, quite mad, there can be no doubt, and that is why he took no notice of Daphne when he saw her by the haunted spring."

As I thought of the old man's awful death I muttered, "It will not be well for Angelo if George should find him out."

Scarcely had this idea occurred to me when I recalled the butler's stories of the wild face he had seen staring through the casement in the dusk of evening, a face like that in the picture; of the figure in the grey cloak, and of the terrible cry of the previous night—a "death-cry" the butler had called it.

Now the butler knew absolutely nothing of my brother's history; how came he, then, to connect this picture with a figure in a grey cloak, unless, indeed, he had seen such a figure lying on the floor of the gallery?

Could it be that George, having secretly gained access to the Abbey with intent to kill the artist, had been himself killed by the very man whose life he sought—struck down in the dead of night in front of the picture that had been the cause of all the mystery?

Was it possible that only a few hours ago this gallery had rung with my brother's death-cry as Angelo struck him down? Oppressed by this new idea I turned quite faint, becoming alternately cold and hot.

"If so, what can Angelo have done with the body?" I thought. "Is it in the tower?" From the casement where I sat a view could be obtained of the Nuns' Tower. I turned, and to my surprise beheld a light shining from the window of the artist's studio.

Too impatient to await the return of the Baronet with the constable and the warrant, I determined to make my way to the tower, and force from the artist an explanation of the mystery that overhung George's fate.

With a final glance at the painted image of my brother's face, whose mournful eyes and mute lips seemed appealing to me for justice, I left the gallery, and hurrying over the lawn reached the tower, bareheaded, breathless, and excited.

"Angelo," I cried, hammering at the door, "I want you. Something really important. I know you are inside. Open the door. I won't go away until I've seen you. Angelo, do you hear?"

It was not my fault if he didn't, for I delivered at the door a succession of kicks which not only hurt me frightfully but made a most tremendous noise. Then remembering that I had the key of the tower with me, I thrust it into the keyhole and turned the lock. I hesitated before actually opening the door, thinking that the artist might be ready on the other side to offer armed resistance to me or to anyone who should invade his sanctum by force. But I thought of the pistols, and taking one from my pocket, I softly and slowly pushed the door ajar, standing a little on one side as I did so in order that I might escape the full force of a frontal attack if one were made.

But no voice or sound of any kind greeted me, and venturing to peep inside I found to my surprise that the room was unoccupied. As soon as I was satisfied that this was really so, I slipped in and locked the door behind me in order to secure myself against the return of the artist.

The chamber, like the tower which contained it, was octagonal. The roof was beautifully vaulted. From the eight angles of the octagon eight pointed arches sprang towards a common centre, meeting in the capital of the solitary pillar that supported the roof. The walls were hidden by tapestry, and the floor was strewn with yellow sand.

A mediæval monk of the most ascetic tastes could not have found fault with the appointments of this cell. A carved oak table littered with an artist's paraphernalia, a carved oak chair, and an iron lamp affixed to the central pillar constituted all the furniture of the place. The only other conspicuous object was the easel with its canvas. No fire had been lighted that day, though materials for one were laid in the grate, and the chilling atmosphere of the room sent a shiver through me.

It was evident that the artist had been in the studio since our afternoon visit. For the lamp was alight, and the purple curtain had been taken down from the casement and now hung over the back of one of the chairs. All this I noticed at a glance, and then I eagerly

The Weird Picture

approached the easel, and throwing off the sheet that covered it, I turned it so that the light from above fell full upon the canvas.

The picture was a representation of the Flavian Amphitheatre in the days of its wicked old glory, when the balconies gleamed with mosaic-work of precious stones, and clouds of purple incense rose in the air. The galleries were crowded with spectators, and in the expression of the various countenances ample scope was given for the display of the artist's skill. Every character typical of the times was represented, from Imperial Cæsar viewing with cold disdain the death of the enemy of the gods, down to the secret Christian slave shuddering at the fate of his co-religionist. A purple velarium was drawn above the amphitheatre as a shield against the sun's rays, and the painter had displayed with artistic effect every object tinged with a faint violet hue.

But the spectator of the picture felt at once that all these details were mere accessories. The arena—dotted here and there with helmet, shield, and spear, or the gilded net of the retairius—was intended to be *the* feature of the picture. A magnificent Libyan lion, lashing his tail on the sands, was standing proudly erect, his flaming eyes fixed on something beneath his forepaws. That something was nothing; or, to be less paradoxical, what was to be there was not yet painted. The picture was in an unfinished state, and the dying martyr was not yet outlined upon the canvas.

It was disappointing to contemplate the picture with what was evidently intended to be the central figure absent. I did not doubt that were it completed and exposed to public view it would create as great a furore as his last masterpiece.

I was puzzled to find the work in so unfinished a state, for Angelo himself had said that most of the details I now beheld had been painted before he came to the Abbey. It was clear that he was a dilatory worker, and the picture gave the lie to his assertion that since his arrival he had been engaged upon the figure of the girl-martyr, for not a trace of her was visible upon the canvas. He may, of course, have been dissatisfied with his work and have effaced it, but if that were the case there seemed no justification for his saying so late as this morning that he expected to complete the picture in a few hours. Some characters at the foot of the canvas in one corner attracted my notice, and bending low I saw that they gave the title of the picture and the name of the artist. Prompted by the appearance of the letters, I drew my forefinger heavily over them, and, as I had expected, they were immediately converted into a long smear.

The paint was wet, a proof that it had been but recently laid on. My action had completely effaced the title of the picture, but not before I had read it. That title was "Modestus, the Christian Martyr."

"*Modestus!*" This was singular. It was only this very morning that the artist had called it "Modesta." Why this sudden change of title? Was he going to represent a man, and not a maiden, as the martyr? Why had he abandoned his original project—abandoned it, so it would seem, within the past few hours? Was it because he had failed to delineate to his own satisfaction his ideal of beauty?

I was unable to answer this question, and turned from the easel to the table, on which lay a medley of articles. First, there was a white woollen tunic such as the antique Roman was wont to wear, a girdle, a pair of sandals, a short Roman sword, and a buckler of oblong shape. In my dulness I at first thought that these were to form Angelo's costume for the fancy-dress ball to be held at Silverdale on Twelfth Night, but they were of course the "properties" in which the model for his picture was to pose. Perhaps, on the principle of killing two birds with one stone, this costume was to unite both purposes. At any rate it furnished an additional proof that the artist had abandoned the title of "Modesta," since these articles, though suitable enough, perhaps, for an Amazon, would have been out of place as the equipment of a Christian maiden.

But who or what was to be the model? I looked around for the lay-figure of which the artist had spoken. I lifted different portions of the tapestry, thinking that the model might perhaps be in some recess behind it, but failed to discover anything suitable for the artist's purpose. Was he going to employ the human form once more? and if so, whose? Had last night's tragedy in the gallery furnished him with a ready means of completing his picture without delay? Was this the real reason of the change of title, and of this sudden preparation of artistic material? I say sudden, because it had evidently been introduced into the cell since Fruin's visit to it, otherwise the gleam of the sword and buckler would surely have attracted his attention,

The Weird Picture

and have been mentioned by him. If we delayed the arrest of Angelo for a few hours in order to peer through the casement of the studio with the first gleam of daylight, should we catch him at work upon his canvas with a dead form before him, completing his picture, by a singular coincidence of dates, on the very anniversary of the day on which he had finished his last masterpiece?

A short dagger was the next object that engaged my attention, a double-edged and pointed weapon. Taking it up for closer inspection, I saw a red stain on it. Was it paint or—something else? The dagger seemed familiar to me, and I now remembered to have seen its painted image in "The Fall of Cæsar." The artist had evidently copied its antique shape in his picture; the stain on it was probably some colouring matter, and not blood, as I had supposed in my first start of surprise.

By the side of this poniard was a curious article representing a lion's paw with claws projecting out. The paw was of ivory, exquisitely carved; the claws were of bright steel. I could not help connecting this curious object with the lion in the picture on the easel, yet utterly failed to perceive the links of the connexion. The artist had not employed it in delineating the paw of the lion—such a supposition was absurd; and, besides, on glancing at the painting of the animal, I saw that its claws were curved in a manner very different from those of the model before me. As I could not conjecture what its use was, I began to examine the next object to it, a small cut-glass phial containing some dark liquid.

Removing the stopper, I applied my nostrils to the orifice. An extremely fragrant odour arose—so pungent, however, that it caused my eyes to water, and set me coughing for several seconds.

Of course it was impossible for my nostrils to detect off-hand the nature and composition of the contents of the phial; and, though not gifted, perhaps, with any large amount of wisdom, I was not quite so foolish as to attempt to gain any knowledge of the liquid by tasting it. Replacing the stopper, I put the phial in my pocket with a view to subjecting its contents to an analysis at the first convenient opportunity.

The Weird Picture

At this point I sank into a chair, for a strange drowsiness was stealing over me. I could not account for it at the time, but I know now that it was due to the volatility of the liquid, which was operating on my mind with a stupefying effect.

Scarcely knowing what I was doing, I lifted up a purple-bound volume from the table, and turning mechanically to the first page, found a fresh surprise in the title of the work, *Silverdale Abbey: Its History and Antiquities*.

Why, here was the very book that had disappeared from the library, the book whose loss had so much fretted the Baronet! The contents of the book were not printed, but written with a pen, in a hand beautifully clear and flowing. This manuscript, according to Sir Hugh, had been compiled by an eminent archæologist; but there was at the end an addendum of a few pages which were evidently not by the hand that had penned the body of the work. I recognised the crabbed characters to be those of Sir Hugh's predecessor, whose autograph I had seen.

This addendum contained matter that the last Baronet for obvious reasons would not wish to be generally known. It gave an account of certain secret panels, hidden corridors, and subterranean chambers, made in the days of the Commonwealth, when loyalty to the House of Stuart meant confiscation and death.

The present Baronet had never read the book, and was ignorant of the existence of these secret rooms, in which his Royalist ancestors had been wont to take refuge from the search of the Puritan soldiery.

Not so Angelo. The book had fallen in his way, and by its perusal he had become master of secrets unknown to the household of Silverdale—unknown even to the white-headed old butler, who had passed all his days at the Abbey. It was this knowledge that had enabled the artist to remove his picture with such secrecy during the night, for, as I read on I came to the following:

"The Nuns' Tower is connected with the picture gallery by a subterranean passage, which — —"

I could get no farther. The letters were dancing wildly on the page, and all efforts on my part to persuade them to behave like quiet, respectable members of the alphabet were useless.

I found myself mechanically repeating this fragment of a sentence, and then, with the sudden consciousness that I was falling asleep in a very dangerous place, I staggered to my feet, but the soporific drug had done its work, and I sank back again into the chair in a state of coma.

CHAPTER XV THE DENOUEMENT!

I believe it is not an uncommon thing for a sentinel to slumber at his post, and wake to find himself still in a standing posture. To the ordinary mortal, however, this would certainly be a novel experience.

Judge, then, of my surprise, on returning to a state of consciousness, to discover that I was on my feet in an erect position with my back against what seemed to be a stone pillar. It is not quite correct to define my attitude as "erect:" leaning forward would more aptly describe it. My balance was maintained by a contrivance of somewhat sinister significance. My hands were extended almost horizontally behind me, one on each side of the pillar, my wrists being firmly secured to each other by something which, judging by the sense of touch was a silken sash so twined and twisted as to serve the same purpose as a strong cord. My arms ached with the pain arising from the unnatural position in which they were sustained; and my head throbbed acutely, probably from the effects of the drug exhaled by the phial.

In what place I stood it was impossible to tell, for there lay a darkness all around as black and oppressive as though a pall had been flung over me. Fear imparts the wildest fancies to the human mind. My first impression was that I had awoke on the other side of the dark river that parts this world from the next, and that my eyes, so soon as they were able to pierce the gloom, would discover scenes more terrible than those imagined by the genius of Dante.

Reverting, however, to the train of events that had brought me to the state of unconsciousness, I came to the more rational conclusion that I was still in the Nuns' Tower. The stone column to which I was attached was without doubt the pillar that upheld the arched roof of the studio-cell; and the silken fabric that bound my hands, I felt intuitively, was the purple curtain that, earlier in the day, had been hung over the casement.

My eyes, becoming by slow degrees accustomed to the darkness, discerned through the penumbra around me a grey oblong object elevated in air and crowned with a triangular apex, which finally resolved itself into the shape of a Gothic casement; and then little by little the whole perspective of the studio-cell became dimly outlined on my vision; and there, by the side of the table, within the oaken chair, sat a figure.

My first impulse was to shout for help, but I checked myself lest such cry should be the signal for my mysterious captor to despatch me. How he had gained access to the cell was evident.

At a point equidistant from the window and the door a slab of stone that formed a part of the flooring was raised, and reclined obliquely against the wall. Beneath the place where it had lain an opening yawned, and the faint outline of steps going downwards proved the truth of the statement contained in the addendum to the antiquary's book that there was another mode of communicating with the tower besides the ordinary way of the door.

I turned my staring eyeballs towards the shape at the table. It was too dark at first for me to distinguish his features, but the contour of the figure seemed to suggest the personality of Angelo. By and by the obscurity of the cell became faintly illumined by the withdrawal of some dark clouds from the face of the sky, and I saw that my captor was indeed the artist. Clad in a dark velvet jacket, he sat with his hands clasped at the back of his head, and one leg thrown carelessly over the other.

I had not expected my captor to be any one else than Angelo, and yet the recognition seemed to come upon me as a surprise.

I shall not pretend to be a hero, and say that the recognition brought with it no fear. It did indeed bring a very great pang of fear. I felt such a sensation then as I never before felt and never wish to feel again.

I was a captive in the power of a rival who hated me with all the hatred of a hatred-loving race. I had sneered at him and at his adored art. I had robbed him of Daphne, depriving him by that act of a figure whose beauty would be an acquisition to his studio. I had little to hope from his mercy.

Preserving with difficulty my presence of mind, I manipulated the silken bands on my wrists in the hope of releasing myself, but

The Weird Picture

Angelo had performed his task too well to permit this. It was evident that my earthly salvation was not within my own power. It must come—if it should come at all—from without. With a terror that increased moment by moment, I recognised how hopeless was my situation.

True, the Baronet and my uncle would miss me on their return, and, conjecturing that I had gone to the Nuns' Tower, might come to seek me, but their aid would be of no avail, for, even if they should come with a body of servants armed with axes, it would take them a minute at least to force open the strong oaken door—ample time for the artist to compass his work of vengeance and escape by the secret passage.

What men usually do when nothing else is left for them to do, I did. The first really fervent prayer that I ever breathed rose to my lips.

As I could see Angelo's eyes quite plainly, I concluded he could see mine, and hence he must have perceived that I had recovered from my state of lethargy. He did not speak, however, but continued to look at me, as if my captivity were a luxury too rich for words. Several minutes passed, and at last the silence became so oppressive that I could bear it no longer, and I said:

"Was it you who bound me like this?"

"It was."

A brief reply—delivered in a cool tone of voice, too, as if the seizure and binding of a gentleman to a Gothic pillar was an every-day event with him, and of too trifling a character to require any comment or apology.

"Confound your ill-timed jest! Cut these cords at once, before my cries bring assistance."

The artist took up from the table the poniard with the red stain on its blade, and proceeded to sharpen the edge on a square slab of marble that did duty occasionally as a palette. Silly that I was! I actually believed that my bold manner had frightened him, and that he was going to comply with my request. The noise produced by the sharpening process was not a pleasant one, and it set my teeth on edge.

"Oh, that'll do!" I cried impatiently—that is, impatiently for a captive, dependent on the pleasure of another for his release. "That'll do. It's sharp enough for the purpose."

"Pardon me, no," he replied, lifting his eyes from the dagger to contemplate me for a moment. "It's not sharp enough for the purpose."

Something in the intonation of his voice drove out the last traces of the drug, and restored me instantly to the full use of my faculties, as drunken men are said to become sobered by a sudden shock.

"What are you going to do?" I cried.

As if there could be any doubt in the matter!

"Immortalise you by my art."

If he had said that he was going to take vengeance on a rival whom he hated I should have understood him, but this speech of his was unintelligible.

"What are you going to do, I ask?"

"I have told you: make a sacrifice on the altar of art."

"What on earth do you mean?" I cried, tugging at my bonds.

"That picture," replied the artist, pausing in his occupation to point with his dagger at the canvas on the easel; "that picture is at a standstill for want of an appropriate model. *I have found my model.*"

With parted lips and dilated eyes I gazed at the speaker, wondering whether he were in earnest. His easy air of unconcern inspired me with false hopes. He was only acting the part of a would-be assassin, I thought. It was a jest of his to frighten me. A trick to compel me perhaps to forswear all claim to Daphne.

"Do you hope to frighten me by these tricks?" I cried, assuming a courage I did not feel. "I have but to raise my voice——"

"Raise it, then."

There was a look in his eyes, a motion of the dagger that convinced me I had better not.

The Weird Picture

"You are wise. Your silence has added a few moments to your brief span of life."

If there had been a tremor in his voice, if his features had relaxed from their set expression, I could have hoped then that his humanity might yet triumph over the impulse of crime. But this cold, mechanical calmness—it was even a more frightful thing than the deed he was contemplating.

"Would you murder me for the sake of a picture?" I asked in as quiet a tone as I could assume.

"Killing in the interests of art is not murder, any more than the burning of a heretic in the interests of holy religion is murder."

It was evident that the Italian was in deadly earnest, and that his whole soul was absorbed by one passion—devotion to his art. In the interests of that fetish, crime even was excusable. This is the age of realism—of a realism that too often dispenses with morality. Angelo's æsthetics of death was but the logical outcome of the realistic school.

The artist had imparted the necessary edge to his weapon, and reclined once more in an easy attitude, fingering the blade with a delicate touch, and surveying my form with a critical eye.

"I cannot say that you are quite the *beau-ideal* for an artist. A little more massiveness in your figure, a little more muscular development of the limbs, would be more in accordance with the canons of physical beauty. Still, these little imperfections can be rectified on the canvas."

The mockery of this remark was not accompanied by any relaxation of his features. He might have been wearing a stone mask, so little mobility did his face display.

"Nor can I say that your present expression is precisely that which a dying Christian ought to assume. There is an appreciable want of resignation in it. Still, it is within the power of my pencil to transfigure your face with the divine light of martyrdom, thus conferring upon you an immortality on canvas—an eternity of fame which assuredly you would never gain by the productions of your pen, though literature, we know, be your *forte*."

This last was a mocking allusion to a boast of mine made at Rivoli.

A devilish motive prompting these remarks was obvious. He wanted to apply torture to the mind before applying it to the body. He felt that the captive was the true victor; for though he might slay me, yet the deed would never make Daphne his. I longed to taunt him with this, and to hurl back gibe for gibe. Prudence restrained me, however. A rash retort might precipitate matters, and cause him to execute his deadly work sooner than he intended; and delay was of value to me, for as the human mind abandons hope only with the last breath, so did I cling to the expectation that rescue might come in a shape I did not dream of. Therefore I listened to the artist without saying a word.

"Some weeks ago I learned that you and Daphne were to spend your Christmas at the Abbey. I prepared for the event. I had vowed that, living or dead, Daphne should minister to the success of my picture, and since I could not have the living woman, I resolved to have her dead form; it would suit my purpose equally well—perhaps better. I have learnt a little of the topography of the Abbey. A secret passage connecting this tower with the bedchambers furnished me with the ready means for carrying her off to my studio in the darkness of the night. This phial here," holding up the bottle that he had evidently removed from my breast-pocket, where I had placed it—"you have had some experience of it yourself—applied to her pretty nostrils would be an instant balm for hysterics. However, my scheme of last night miscarried—through you. Therefore you take her place. You have prevented me from adequately realising my conception of the sweet and sad death-beauty of a girl-martyr. Art demands, then, that you atone for your intervention by becoming the substitute. Behold, martyr, your attire!" he added, turning to the table and lifting up the different articles composing the Roman costume.

Replacing them, he took up the ivory paw whose use had so much puzzled me.

"You see this? To lacerate your naked body with—to give to its quivering white the very wounds that a lion's claws would inflict. My own invention—exclusively my own."

The Weird Picture

He spoke of his projected task in as cool a tone as a scientist might use in speaking of the dissection of a dog.

"You see," he continued, laying down the claw, "this is the age of realism. Nothing is now accepted in literature, art, or the drama that does not bear on its front the stamp of reality. Art, if it is to hold the mirror up to Nature, must not shrink any more than medical science from experimenting on the living frame, and analysing with delicate eye its varying phases of agony."

He paused for a moment, and then, with the air of a man arriving at the end of a set oration, he said:

"You now have my secret. Know, then, how I intend to produce on that canvas the dying agonies of Modestus the martyr—the picture destined to create an epoch in the history of modern art. So soon as the church-bells chime the hour of midnight you are dead. Such is Daphne's wish."

"Daphne's!" I ejaculated.

"Ay! She wishes for your death. She has promised to marry me to-night. Did you not know?"

He spoke in so natural a tone that I could but stare fixedly at him, wondering what his motive could be in fabricating so wild a statement. My look of perplexity was so great that the artist laughed aloud. This was the first time his facial muscles had relaxed. The transition from rigidity to mobility was not an agreeable one.

A terrible metamorphosis was coming over the artist. It seemed as if some part of his nature, that he had long kept hidden, was rising up to the surface. It did arise—fast. It revealed itself in his unearthly laugh, in the distortion of his mouth, in the wild light of his eyes, in the goblin attitude he had suddenly assumed with his head sunk forward on his breast and his crooked fingers clawing at the air.

ANGELO WAS MAD!

Mad! Why had I not guessed this before? A thousand circumstances—curious facial expressions, odd sayings, tricks of gesture—came welling up from the depths of the past. Trivial, considered apart, in the aggregate they were significant, and tended to confirm my terrible discovery.

This revelation of Angelo's character imparted a fresh element of horror to my situation, and reduced to a minimum my chances of escape. Angelo sane might perhaps be diverted from his deadly purpose by the thought that discovery would be certain to attend the commission of his crime. But no such reason could prevail with a madman.

Flinging back his dark locks with a defiant gesture, the maniac fixed his glittering eye on me, and commenced to chant some Italian refrain composed in a very mournful key, keeping time to the air with the motions of his hand. I recognised the refrain. I had heard it once at Rivoli. It was a funeral hymn.

The foreign words imperfectly comprehended by me, the plaintive character of the refrain, united to the melancholy voice of the maniac, made this singing the most awful and unearthly thing I had ever heard, thrilling me to the very centre with the most eerie sensations. Every now and then he would pause to take a drink from a spirit-flask, resuming his wild song immediately afterwards. Usually a foe to intoxicants, he was now taking draughts of brandy in a reckless fashion, and I knew that he was working himself up for his fiendish task. The cold grey cell, the dim light, the gibbering thing at the table chanting my death song, formed a picture that has lived in my memory ever since, and often have I started from sleep with a cry of terror, shivering at the recollection of this night.

The cell had been gradually growing brighter, and at last on one side of the casement, through the tangles of ivy, appeared the silver arc of the moon whose arrowy beams slanted to the floor, adding a still greater sense of weirdness to the scene. The moon seemed to have a disturbing effect upon the artist's disordered mind, for he turned uneasily to the casement.

"Too much light. Too much light. I hate this silvery glare," and raising his arms he exclaimed tragically, "Oh, Endymion, why sleepest thou? Rise with thy white arms and draw Cynthia down to thy embrace."

As he spoke the moon actually was veiled by a passing cloud.

"I knew he would obey me," he exclaimed triumphantly. "Am not I lord of the night and of its shadows?"

Had there remained in my mind any doubt as to his sanity this absurd effusion would have effectually removed it. The sound of the church clock chiming the half hour now smote on my ears. If the maniac adhered to his threat I had but thirty minutes left to live, and I concentrated all my faculties upon the difficulties of my position. My uncle must by this time have returned with Sir Hugh, and on finding myself as well as the keys of the Nuns' Tower and the gallery missing, would guess where I was and they might even now be on their way to seek me and to arrest the artist. If they were listening outside they would hear Angelo's voice and would understand the peril I was in. They could not easily force the door, nor, if they had any suspicion of the artist's insanity, would they be so rash as to try, but one blow would shatter the window and give them instant admission into the tower.

Buoyed up with the hope that help might arrive at any moment, I resolved, if possible, to soothe and flatter the maniac, with a view of gaining time and of getting him to postpone his self-imposed task beyond the midnight hour. I would persuade him to talk of his last picture, of his brother artists, of his early days at Rivoli—of anything, that would divert his attention from me, and delay the fatal stroke.

"Angelo, listen to me," I said, forcing my voice to adopt the slow deliberate tones I have heard hospital nurses employ in order that they may the more readily find lodgment in the disordered brain—"I am quite willing to die."

Even while saying this, the incongruity of telling a falsehood when so near the point of death occurred to me, but I repeated the falsehood:

"I am quite willing to die."

"It is sweet to die for art," cried the artist gravely, as if the remark were an indisputable axiom.

"I will not struggle with you."

This at least was true, for the silken bands would not let me.

"Daphne wished you not to struggle," remarked the madman.

"But before I go, tell me—tell me—" I hesitated, not knowing what to say next. "Tell me—what has become of my brother George?" I cried, on the spur of the moment. "You must know," I added.

"Your brother?" cried the artist, his eyes lighting up, as if some new chord in his memory were touched. "Your brother?"

He was silent for a moment as if reflecting; and then looking all around, as if to ascertain that we were alone, he whispered:

"You will never reveal to any one what I am going to tell you?"

"It will not be within my power to reveal anything after you have finished with me," I replied with a smile that was the essence of ghastliness.

"True, true; I am forgetting that."

Taking up the stained poniard, he bent forward in his chair and whispered between his white teeth:

"You see this red stain? *His!* It is a twelvemonth old—a twelvemonth this very night."

Making a stab at an imaginary figure, he looked at me, and said: "Wait. I'll show you how I did it presently."

"I am quite willing to wait." My trembling lips could scarcely frame the words. "Let me have the whole story—every word. I shall not mind if you take hours over it."

"You shall have the whole story. Oh, you shall not lose a syllable of it! Ho! ho! it was a master-stroke of craft. Was Borgia or Macchiavelli ever more cunning? I glory in the deed. I love to dwell on it. I act it every night. In the secrecy of my chamber, in the quietness of the picture-gallery, I rehearse the whole tableau of that glorious time. They would not permit me to do this in the day-time, you know," he said, exchanging his excited manner for one that was quite grave and confidential. "They would call me mad: they would take me away— far away from my studio and my easel, and they would put me in a padded room, and I should paint no more. But I am too cunning for them," he cried, his eyes lighting up once more with the fire of madness. "I baffled them. They know not that in the still hours, while they sleep, I am occupied in the work of killing Captain Willard. He takes a deal of killing, too!" he added, resuming as if by magic his quiet air again. "Each night I slay him; yet each night he returns again, clamouring for the death-stroke. I would not believe it if I did not see it for myself. Strange, is it not?" he concluded, turning to me.

"It's extraordinary!" my white lips gasped. Which, if it were true, it most certainly was.

The maniac stared at me a few seconds with a most bewildered air, looking as if he had forgotten something, or as if he did not quite understand how I came to be in my present position, and then went on:

"Yes, this red stain is his. I slew him. Why? Let me think," resting his elbow on the table and pressing his forefinger to his brow for all the world like a sane man. "Let me think; I had a motive for it. What was it? Love of my art? Yes, that was it — art."

He paused again, as if he found it difficult to collect his shattered memories.

"From the first hour of my calling as an artist it became an object with me to woo and win a woman whose face should be all that a painter could desire. No vulgar model who displays her charms for hire would do for me; my inspiration must come from a pure and beautiful maiden who, fired with the spirit of my enthusiasm, would be devoted to all that was high and noble in art for its own sake. Her lovely shape, delineated in various attitudes on the canvas, should be the making of my pictures. In short," he added, "I was a second Zeuxis in quest of beauty."

He made another stop, and then resumed:

"At last, after long years of waiting, I found what I had sought. Imagination could not picture a form more lovely than that of Daphne Leslie, and I resolved to make her the handmaid of art. But there was an obstacle in the way. That obstacle was Captain Willard. No matter. He must die; art demanded it, and I took an oath that the eve of his wedding should be the last day of his life. But how was I to set about it? I knew what suspicions would arise — what a hue and cry would be raised by society — if a distinguished officer, who had come all the way from India to wed a rich and lovely bride, should vanish mysteriously on the very eve of his intended marriage. All the machinery of the law would be set in motion to discover the

The Weird Picture

author of the deed. Suspicion would be sure to fall on the artist who was known to entertain feelings of love towards the bride. 'It was Vasari that did it,' men would say, 'and jealousy was the cause.' I must act with caution. Ah! I would forge a letter in Captain Willard's handwriting—easy task this for an artist!—purporting that he had fled of his own accord to the Continent. Ho! ho! it was bravely done—bravely. No one ever dreamt that he was dead, and that Angelo had killed him."

He put on an air of savage pride which plainly implied, "Now what do you think of that?"

Like a trembling child flinging a cherished eatable to a dog of which he is afraid, I flung the maniac a propitiatory falsehood, despising myself for it the minute afterwards:

"I always thought you were a clever fellow."

He accepted this tribute of admiration with the air of one who quite deserved it, and continued:

"Yes; I would so arrange the affair that none should ever discover what had really happened. I would kill him and travel in his dress to Dover, making it appear as if Captain Willard had really departed for the Continent. I was not unlike him in build and features, and by painting and disguising my face I could transform myself into his very image. I tried the experiment beforehand. The mirror showed me what an actor the stage has lost. Even you were deceived when landing from the steam-packet last Christmas morning. It was I whom you saw on the pier amid the falling snow."

My amazement at this point was so great that it made me forget the perilous situation I was in. Spellbound at the revelation, I stood like a spectator gazing at some actor who enthralls him.

"His death furnished me with a noble idea in connection with the picture I was then painting, 'The Fall of Cæsar.' Did not Parrhasius when he wished to paint Prometheus chained to the rock and tortured by the vulture, order one of his slaves to be fettered, and the bosom of the shrieking captive to be laid open, that he might paint the agony of Prometheus in all its glorious reality? Gods! what a picture that must have been! Oh, that I, too, could have by me a man just slain, with the red blood distilling from the wounds! What a glorious model it would be! Its image transferred to the canvas would be the making of my picture. What realism it would exhibit! This work at least would not be called mediocre by the cold critics. Ah! bright thought! Captain Willard shall be my model. The very stroke that deprives a rival of life shall be the means of elevating me to fame. Could vengeance take a sweeter, a more subtle form?"

It seemed an age since Angelo had begun his recital, but as the church-bells had not pealed the quarter, I knew he had not yet been fifteen minutes over it. My ears were keenly alert for any sound that might indicate that help was approaching, but everything was still and quiet outside the tower.

"I met Captain Willard late on Christmas Eve returning from Daphne's house. I asked him to come to my studio for a few minutes: 'I have a surprise for you,' I said. So I had. As I spoke I had to turn my face from him to hide the light of triumph in my eyes. He came willingly enough, talking of the happy morrow. We were alone. I led him to a picture on an easel. 'A present for your bride; do you like it?' I said, standing behind him. Oh, what a thrill was going through me! 'Yes,' he replied—his last word! 'Well, how do you like *that*?' I cried as my weapon descended. Hatred—love—fame nerved my arm with a triple power, and I struck him down—down—down. This is how I did it."

At this point the maniac sprang to his feet with the rapidity of lightning, and, lifting the dagger on high, made a swift downward stab at an ideal figure. My heart gave a great leap, for I thought he was going to strike me.

"With one loud cry he dropped—thud! Oh, that cry! It rings in my ears still. It was the sweetest music to me. I stood over him with my dripping weapon ready to deal him a second stroke, and a red drop fell on his vest. I wanted him to cry, to move, to rise, that I might have the pleasure of striking him down once more. But he never moved after that one stroke, and I took him up in my arms and flung him down again that I might enjoy the luxury of the sound."

The Weird Picture

Dropping the dagger, he illustrated his words by going through the motion of flinging a body to the ground. Anything more devilish than his manner I had never seen.

"And he fell thus, and lay in this manner—*so*."

And here the maniac flung himself backward with his arms aloft, and dropped to the floor so swiftly and naturally that I marvelled he did not hurt his head on the yellow-sanded stone. And there he lay in silence for a few seconds, with his eyes closed and his limbs rigidly extended in imitation of a dead body.

I thought of the figure in the grey cloak that Fruin had seen lying on the floor of the picture-gallery. That figure had been none other than the mad artist, whose diseased imagination gloried in the still hours of night in rehearsing the terrible drama of last Christmas Eve. His monomania, in fact, had taken the shape of a subjective reslaying of the slain, united to an objective wearing of his victim's dress. Instead of destroying that evidence of his guilt, he had retained George's clothing, and, as his subsequent ravings showed, regarded it as a memento of his own cleverness.

The artist rose to his feet, and flung himself back in his chair again, apparently exhausted by his emotion.

"Cruel?" he gasped, staring at me, and striving to palliate the deed by the example of others. "Cruel? If Giotto stabs his living model on the cross that he may paint a crucified Christ, if Parrhasius damns his slave to torture that he may produce the agony of Prometheus in all its realism, may I, too, not have my victim? Cruel? It was a sacrifice to art. Churchmen have burned each other for the glory of God. Art is my god."

And the maniac lifted his clenched hand aloft as if defying Heaven.

"My rival was lying at my feet, dead. I wanted his clothing for my purpose, so I stripped him. Gods! what a figure for an artist! But he had received only one wound as yet—Cæsar had many—so I dealt him some six strokes or more. How the red blood spouted up! Oh, those wounds! 'Poor dumb mouths!' How eloquently they will speak from the canvas! What a divine picture I shall produce! 'Il Divino' will deserve his name at last. Already I hear the voice of the public saying, 'What a genius this Vasari is!' Ah! that reminds me. You have not yet seen my noble work of art. You shall. 'Tis behind that tapestry."

Evidently the maniac did not know that the picture had been removed. I trembled lest he should rise and discover its absence.

To my mental agony was added physical suffering, due to the unnatural position of my arms. For the sake of relief I had often moved them to and fro and up and down at the back of the pillar. I was now moving them farther round than they had been before, when my wrists came in contact with something sharp. Feeling with my fingers as well as I could, I discovered that a part of the column had crumbled away with time and presented a rough, ragged edge. An idea darted into my mind. An idea? Say an inspiration rather. My wrists were not in contact—the breadth of the pillar prevented that—there was a distance of about a foot between them. The silken band that secured me was drawn in a tight slip-knot round one wrist, and, proceeding to the other, encircled it in the same manner, and then hung downwards trailing on the floor.

Now if I could but bring the band connecting my two wrists across the sharp edge of this stone, steady attrition would tear it into two portions, and I should be free. With some difficulty I worked the twisted silk into the requisite place, and then began as vigorous a friction as my cramped position would allow, dreading every moment lest the madman should perceive my motions and detect their cause.

Though bending all my energies to the task before me, I tried at the same time to give a listening ear to the artist, but I am of opinion that my further report of his utterances is far from being a faithful one.

"I donned my rival's attire. I was no more Angelo: I was the Captain. How well his dress became me! Observe my military cloak, my martial stride! See my painted scar—my brown hair and beard! I had prepared for all this weeks beforehand. Who that saw me now would take me for poor 'Il Divino,' whose pictures are always a failure? But I had no time to lose—the Dover train would be starting soon—and, leaving my divine model locked up in the studio, I hurried off to the station, posting on my way the forged letter that was to tell Daphne that her bridegroom had fled to the Continent. Now for Dover to prove the truth of the letter. The booking-clerk, the guard of the train, the ticket-collector, could all swear that an officer in every way resembling Captain Willard had travelled to Dover on that Christmas morning. I stood on the pier-head expressly for you to see me! I knew that you were coming in by that steamer, for Daphne had told me the hour of your intended arrival. Ho, ho! his own brother thrown off the scent, and ready to swear he had seen George at Dover, at the very time that George was lying dead in my studio! It was rare glee afterwards to listen with grave face to the various theories propounded in my presence to account for Captain Willard's flight. And the world calls me mad!"

I was not aware that the world did so; but if it did, it had ample reason in his wild laugh, and demoniac glee. However, as his eyes were off me, I worked away desperately at my silken manacles.

"I must not return to London in the same attire: that would be to contradict the letter; and I must not return in my own: that might involve *me* in suspicion, and give rise to awkward questions if it were known that I had been at Dover on the morning of Captain Willard's flight. No! I would return disguised in a woman's dress. Ha! ha! how often have I heard you discuss the identity of the veiled lady who travelled with you from Dover to London! Learn now that the veiled lady is before you. Now you know why she was dumb. I could not disguise my voice so effectually but that you might recognise it next morning at the wedding."

To say that I was amazed at this revelation is but a feeble way of expressing it. Great as was my amazement, however, it did not check for an instant my working for freedom.

"There was living then at Dover an old friend of mine from Rivoli— Matteo Carito by name. He was caretaker to an Italian family who were spending their winter abroad. I had paid him a chance visit the previous week, and he had casually told me that he meant to spend his Christmas with some Italian friends in London; he thought he might safely leave the house for a day or two. It would be empty, then, on Christmas morning. Good! Unknown to him, I procured a key that would open the front door; in the secrecy of this house I would assume my female disguise. Do you remember finding me outside old Matteo's house? You came on me as swiftly and silently as a ghost. I was startled, for I knew you were his brother—Daphne had many a time pointed out your portrait to me—and I thought all was discovered. But I baffled you—I eluded you—how adroitly you know. Matteo's house was my asylum. But Matteo had not gone to London after all, and discovered me in the very act of changing my attire. He wanted to know how I had gained access to the house, and why I was masquerading in two different disguises. For a minute I hesitated; I thought of braining him on the spot. It would have been rare sport. But I pitied him—he had known me from childhood—and I concocted some story that seemed to satisfy him at the time. Would now that I had slain him there and then! It would have saved me a world of trouble. He discovered it all!"

I was still tearing away fiercely at my bonds, confident that if the artist continued his ravings for a few more minutes my hands would be free. The friction of the silk on the jagged edge of the pillar produced a sharp rustling noise, but the artist noticed neither the sound nor my motions, so taken was he with the story of his own cleverness. He seemed to be orating more for his own satisfaction than for my information.

"Yes, he discovered it all," continued he. "I had thought myself safe, for had I not effectually disposed of the body? Steeping it in chemicals and wrapping it in asbestos, I had in the dead of night, in the secrecy of my cellar, committed it to the flames. Ho! ho! A true classical funeral that, as became the subject, for was he not the pagan Cæsar of my picture? 'Vulcan, arise! Vasari claims thine aid.' Ah! what a glorious night that was as I moved round the funeral pyre, pouring on oil and chanting an ode from Horace! What a splendid picture it would have made—'A Pagan Funeral!' How I regretted that I had not prepared my canvas for the event! But it was too late to think of that. Then, one dark night, on some lonely common, I scattered the ashes to the four winds. Not a trace of my victim left! And yet, after all my care and caution, that old dotard of a Matteo had discovered my secret—discovered it by accident. I was at Paris, exhibiting my picture to admiring thousands. Among those who thronged to gaze at my 'Cæsar' was a Colonel Langworthy, but just returned from India. 'That face is very like my friend Willard, who

The Weird Picture

disappeared so strangely last Christmas!' he cried. I turned to the speaker, and whom should I see at his elbow but old Matteo, with his great eyes staring at me. He had heard this chance remark: he at once divined my secret. I was so infuriated that next day, when the Colonel was coming to take a second view of my picture, I ordered him to be thrust out—a mad act, for it got into the newspapers, and confirmed Matteo's suspicions. Thenceforward I had no peace, for no bribe would stop his mouth. He was forever reproaching me. I had made him an accessory to a crime, he said. His conscience troubled him for having in a manner aided me to escape on that Christmas morning. He could not sleep at night. Poor fool! He could go no more to Mass with such a sin on his soul. He followed me to Rivoli. He must—he must confess all to the priest. Damn him! he did! That was why Father Ignatius refused me the Mass that morning, and Daphne present, too, to witness my humiliation! It was that that caused her to look with a different face on me, and to turn from my love with scorn. I marvel now that she is still living when I recall my fury at her refusal. She was nearer to death then—nearer to her lost George—than she had been since her bridal morning. My old nurse said I was mad that day; perhaps I was. No matter. Let Daphne refuse me, hate me as she will, she cannot recall her dead hero to life. There was consolation in that thought. That night, as I was making preparations to depart from Rivoli, I came across his grey cloak. I always carried it with me. It was a joy to gaze on it, to think how I had won it. It was a sign of my triumph—it was a proof that he would trouble me no more with his rivalry. I put it on, for I loved to act the scene over again, and sallied out in it. I remember now with what glee I climbed crags and cliffs, singing and dancing along. Aha! who is this in monkish garb that rises up before me in the moonlight? Old Matteo, as I live! Matteo! Matteo the betrayer! He sees me, he turns, he flees. Ha! ha! what feeble steps! I hear him. How he pants for breath! With one fierce leap I am on him. Ho! ho! my hand is on his old throat. How he struggles as I force him to the edge of the cliff! How he clings to me! 'Mercy! mercy!' he screams. Mercy? To him who had robbed me of my fair model? He could not tell any more tales after I had finished with him. From the cliff——"

The artist stopped abruptly, and assumed a listening air. Along the gravel path outside came the tread of many feet approaching the place of my captivity. My heart throbbed wildly with hope, for I made certain that it was the Baronet and my uncle coming to my rescue. It was not so, however. Sounds of laughter, the rough voices of men mingling with the sweeter tones of women, floated upward to our ears, and I knew then that it was the party returning from the vicarage. They passed quickly beneath the window of my prison—so quickly that I had scarcely time to realise the situation—and by and by were standing, so I judged, on the lawn at the rear of the Abbey. Then came a silence, followed by the twanging of strings, the faint puffings of wind instruments, and such sounds as are usually the prelude to music, and I knew that they were going to sing some carols for the edification of the Baronet and the other tenants of the Abbey.

I glanced at the artist. Should I give one loud shout for aid? I hesitated, lest the cry should cause him to sheath his dagger in my breast. I resolved first to make one more attempt to burst my bonds, and, exerting all my strength, I strained desperately at the twisted silk, plunging forward as far as its limited length would allow, careless almost as to whether the eyes of the artist were on me or not.

And now uprose an outburst of instrumental melody which lasted for a minute or so, and then, as the harmony subsided into fainter keys, the carol began. It was a solo.

Whose tones were those that now rose so clear and silvery on the still, frosty air? Was I doomed to die with Daphne's voice ringing in my ears? She thought, perhaps, that I was in the library listening to her voice, and she was singing with more than ordinary power and sweetness. How quickly her joy would have turned to terror had she but known my real situation!

"Aha!" screamed the maniac, so loudly that it could scarcely fail to attract the attention of those without. "Aha! The spirits! the spirits! I knew they would be here. They visit me every night. They know the work that is going on here. Listen—listen—listen to their voices! They are singing your requiem. How bravely they chanted at the foot of the grey old cliff the night I flung old Matteo over! What rare music! Ah! here they come, sliding down the moonbeams! God! what a throng!" he exclaimed, springing up excitedly and striking at the empty air, which his delirium was peopling with phantoms. "Off!

off! Do you not see them? One cannot move—breathe in this atmosphere!"

My confused mind heard as in some weird dream fragments of his mad ravings mingling fantastically with the words of the carol:

> Christ was born on Christmas Day,
> Wreathe the holly, twine the bay,
> *Christus natus hodie.*
> The Babe, the Son, the Holy One of Mary,
> He is born to set us free—

Laus Deo! the band that connected my two wrists gave way. I was free! And at the same moment the first stroke of midnight chimed from the village steeple.

At that sound the artist snatched up the dagger from the table, and turned towards me.

"The hour is come! Art demands her victim."

"Stand off, you devil, or I'll brain you!" I cried, springing forward with the ends of the purple silk trailing from my wrists.

The pistols I had brought with me lay on the table beyond my reach, for the artist stood between them and me, and in default of any other means of defence I snatched up the massive oaken chair, and balanced it aloft—a feat I could not perhaps have performed in ordinary moments, but now excitement imparted a magical strength to every fibre of my body.

"Come on! I am free now!" I cried, brandishing the chair. "Do you see me? Free—*free—free!*"

In the sudden joy of my recovered liberty I was ten times madder than my opponent.

The artist might have stood for an image of amazement. Silent and immovable he stood, staring at me with a vacuous look, evidently unable to comprehend how I had gained my freedom.

Then suddenly Daphne's voice was drowned in a loud tumult, and in the quick trampling of numerous feet. This was immediately followed by a succession of strokes on the massive panels of the door, dealt by some heavy implements, accompanied at the same time by the sounds as of persons scrambling up the ivy outside towards the casement. Rescue was at hand!

And now across the oblong patch of moonlight that lay on the stone floor between me and the maniac appeared some dark shadows, and, turning towards the casement to ascertain the cause, the artist beheld human faces peering in through the diamond-shaped panes. A moment more and there came a great shivering and shattering of glass. The cold night air swept with a rush through the broken panes, bringing with it the wild crash of the Christmas bells, a tumult of voices, and Daphne's thrilling scream.

Peril makes some men mad. It made Angelo sane. He realised the situation—realised that his hated rival was slipping from his power; but the knowledge of this fact only made him more desperate.

"Damn you! you shall not escape!" he cried fiercely. "I'll have your life, though I die the next moment for it!"

With the dagger gleaming aloft, he darted on me. Measuring him with my eye, I swung the chair round, and tried to bring it down on his head, but he eluded the blow by springing deftly to one side.

The robe of tragedy is often sewn with the threads of comedy. The chair intended for the artist lighted instead on his unfinished picture, and went sheer through the canvas, overturning the easel, and inflicting more damage to the painted Colosseum in two seconds than old Time has been able to inflict on the solid original in well-nigh two millenniums.

"My picture! Oh, my picture!" cried the artist. "You have destroyed it!"

Petrified with dismay, he gazed on the ruins of his work of art, oblivious for the moment of everything else. Taking advantage of his surprise, I sprang forward, and seized him by the throat with such force and energy that he toppled backwards, and measured his length on the floor of the cell. I fell with him.

"That's it! Bravo! Hold him down!" cried a voice, which I recognised as the Baronet's. "We'll be with you in an instant."

The Weird Picture

Sir Hugh, my uncle, and some others were standing on the window-ledge, striving to effect an entrance by forcing asunder the slender cross-bars of the casement.

The artist lay extended on the floor of the cell. My knee was on his chest, and with one hand I grasped him by the throat, and with the other pinioned to the floor his hand that held the dagger. I tried to keep him in this position till aid should come, but with a strength almost superhuman he rose to his feet, dragging me with him, and, grappling with each other, we swayed backwards and forwards in the moonlit cell.

"I always hated you," he gasped. "But for you I might have won the love of Daphne. You shall not escape me!"

He made frantic efforts to reach me with the dagger, but I clung heavily to the arm that held it, impeding his power of action. At length with a sudden effort of strength he flung me off, but as he did so the cross-bars of the casement gave way, and three human bodies were projected through it in a most ungraceful fashion, and fell on all-fours to the floor.

For one second the artist stood irresolute, and then darting towards the secret opening, he disappeared from view.

The cell seemed to swim around me, a mist passed before my eyes, and then dimly as in a dream I became conscious that I was reclining in an oaken chair, supported on one side by my uncle and on the other by Daphne. The door of the tower was wide open, hanging obliquely on one hinge. Someone was putting a lighted match to the wick in the antique iron lamp, and its bright flame lit up a crowd of faces that were bent upon me with wondering looks. At one end of the cell some men, a helmeted police-officer among the number, were kneeling, fingering and clawing at the stone slab which the artist had pulled down after him to cover his retreat.

"It must be chained down," I heard the Baronet saying. "Pass the crowbar. Damn it! the fellow will escape."

"His eyes are open," I heard Daphne saying. "Oh, Frank, you are not hurt, are you?"

She was now kneeling beside me, her lovely eyes full of tenderness and sympathy. It was worth all the agony I had endured to be the object of her sweet pity. I tried to speak, but emotion checked my utterance, and I could reply to her question only by an assuring smile.

"You are looking like the very dead," said the doctor. "Here, take a drop of this. This will revive you."

"Is my hair grey?" I murmured, putting my hand to my head, as if it were possible to ascertain by the sense of touch. "Do I look old? I feel like a captive liberated from the Bastile. How long have I been in this prison? Years upon years?"

In a few words I told my shuddering listeners of the artist's designs on me. From regard to Daphne, I reserved the story of George's end for another occasion.

"Ay, ay," remarked the doctor, gravely shaking his head. "I saw this morning that he exhibited all the symptoms of insanity. Genius and madness are often allied."

"Well, thank Heaven you are safe!" exclaimed my uncle fervently; "though more by your own efforts than by ours," he added.

"Have you only just returned from the magistrate's?" I asked him.

There is a good deal of ingratitude in human nature, and even in the first joy of my deliverance I felt a disposition to reproach my uncle for what I considered a very tardy rescue, totally forgetful of the fact that if my rescuers had appeared earlier on the scene there would have been an end of me, for the artist at sight of them would have effected his deadly purpose without my being able to offer any resistance.

"Yes, we have only just returned," he answered, understanding the motive of my question. "Everything that possibly could went wrong. The carriage broke down half way from the Manse, and when we set off to finish the journey on foot we missed our way on the moors and were a long time in finding it again. When we did reach the Abbey and did not see you about we guessed where you were and came at once to the tower. We heard enough to assure us that something very serious was the matter, and as we could not hope to make our way in empty handed we ran back for—"

He was interrupted by a shout coming from outside of the cell, and turning quickly I saw that the slab had been lifted up revealing a stairway beneath.

"Turn your lantern down here, Wilson," cried the Baronet excitedly, "and lead the way. Look sharp, or he'll escape after all."

The constable obediently went down the opening, followed by Sir Hugh, my uncle and two or three other men. Thinking that I had as good a right as any to join the pursuit, I rose with the intention of following them, but at Daphne's entreaty, I forbore, and, leaving the cell, we both walked across the lawn to the Abbey, all unconscious of the tragedy that was happening under our very feet.

For the steps down which the artist had fled opened into a stone passage, the walls of which were dripping with moisture and stained with horrid fungi. At the foot of the steps Sir Hugh came upon a recess, where they found a grey cloak, and a gentleman's dress suit. The Baronet, with a look of inquiry on his face, pointed out these things to my uncle.

"Yes," said my uncle, "those are his clothes right enough. They are what he wore the last time we saw him alive. It is clear that Vasari murdered him that night, and he has kept these clothes by him ever since. Look," he went on, "this is where he was stabbed," and he pointed to a cut in the back of the coat. As he was handling the garment something bright fell from the breast pocket, and stooping to pick it up he recognised the ring which Daphne had thrown into the well at Rivoli.

"We mustn't stop," the Baronet said. "Hold up the light, Wilson," and the whole party again stumbled forward along the passage.

"Where does it lead to?" the constable asked, peering cautiously into the darkness before him.

"I wish I could tell you," Sir Hugh replied. "I have never seen the place before. It must be the nuns' corridor of ancient days. I always understood it had been bricked up. By the way, we must go carefully. If I'm right, there must be a deep chasm ahead—the Nuns' Shaft, and if—hullo, what's that?"

Distant a few paces in front was a human figure crouching low against the wall.

"There he is," several voices cried at once.

"Take care," said my uncle. "Remember, he is a madman!"

At this, the whole party came to a sudden halt.

"Yield in the King's name," shouted the constable. But whatever effect the King's name may have upon the sane it cannot be expected to exercise much influence upon a maniac. Rising to his feet, with a wild laugh that sounded unearthly in the echoing passage, the madman ran on into the darkness, with the pursuit hot behind him.

Suddenly he checked his headlong pace, and, turning swiftly, confronted his pursuers. The light held aloft by the constable fell full on his despairing face, and to their dying day those who saw Angelo Vasari at that moment will never forget the sight.

With a gesture in which rage, defiance and hopelessness were all mingled, he sprang into the air. For one moment he was visible, in the next he had vanished. No sound broke from him. In absolute silence, more terrible than any cry, he was swallowed by the blackness beneath him.

"By God, he's gone!" the Baronet shouted, and there was fear in his voice. "Stop, stop, for Heaven's sake, or you are all dead men."

"What is it?" shouted some, catching the infection of his fear.

"He has leaped down the shaft of the old silver mine."

Thus died Angelo Vasari, and perhaps it was better that he should perish by suicide than be taken alive only to fall into the hangman's hands or drag out a long life in some asylum for the insane. That the story could be kept from the general public was, of course, impossible, and the sensation caused at the inquest by the telling of the manner of his death was enhanced by the account I had to repeat of how my brother came by his. Vasari's studio in London was examined, and evidence was discovered in the cellar corroborating his assertion that he had burnt the body of the man whom he had sacrificed to his insane desire for fame.

As for the picture itself, Sir Hugh at first thought of destroying it, but finally decided to keep it on account of its marvellous merit as a work of art. It was removed from the gallery, and hung by itself in a room where it could be inspected by the privileged few. Daphne could never bring herself to look at it. She did not want the idealised image of her lover to be marred by the ghastly presentment of his dead likeness.

Whose wife Daphne is now, it is hardly necessary to say. We were married in the spring at Silverdale, and quiet though we wished the wedding to be, the church was crowded with people from far and wide who were eager to see the girl whose beauty had been the cause of such a tragedy. To efface from her mind as far as possible the memory of that tragedy is the chief object of my life and I am glad to think I do not wholly fail. She wears in addition to her wedding ring a second golden band, the ring that she threw into the well at Rivoli. It is to be buried with her, she says. May that day be far distant, is my constant prayer.

THE END

By the Author of " The Weird Picture "

THE
SHADOW OF THE CZAR

By JOHN R. CARLING

Illustrated. 12mo. $1.50. *Fifth Edition*

"An engrossing romance of the sturdy, wholesome sort, in which the action is never allowed to drag," (*St. Louis Globe-Democrat*) best describes this popular novel. "The Shadow of the Czar" is a stirring story of the romantic attachment of a dashing English officer for Princess Barbara, of the old Polish Principality of Czernova, and the conspiracy of the Duke of Bora, aided by Russia, to dispossess the Princess of her throne.

It is not an historical novel — the author makes his own events after the manner of Anthony Hope, and the *Boston Herald* is of the opinion that it "excels in interest Anthony Hope's best efforts." "Rarely do we find a story in which more happens, or in which the incidents present themselves with more suddenness and with greater surprise," says the *New York Sun*.

"Mr. Carling has a surprising faculty of making it appear that things ought to have happened as he says they did, and as long as the book is being read he even succeeds in making it appear that they did happen so," says the *St. Louis Star*.

"The Shadow of the Czar" fairly captivated two countries. In England the *Newcastle Daily Journal* says it "transcends in interest 'The Prisoner of Zenda.'"

LITTLE, BROWN, & CO., Publishers
BOSTON, MASS.

*A New Romance by the Author of
"The Shadow of the Czar"*

THE VIKING'S SKULL

By JOHN R. CARLING

Illustrated by Cyrus Cuneo. 350 pages. 12mo. $1.50

A tale full of stirring surprises. — *Philadelphia North American.*

A capital tale of mystery and detection of crime and retribution. The ingenuity with which its intricacies are threaded is really wonderful.— *New York Times Saturday Review of Books.*

It is a remarkably lively story, with a novel mystery, wrought out of old Norse history, but the scene is modern England for the most part, and all the characters belong to to-day.— *Chicago Record-Herald.*

The reader who once becomes entangled in its meshes will sit up until the small hours to finish it. It is a romance pure and simple from the outset, and refreshing to a degree. — *Brooklyn Eagle.*

An engrossing tale of love, adventure, and intrigue, the reading of which makes hours fly on the wings of minutes. An ingenious, dramatic, interest-compelling romance. — *Boston Herald.*

LITTLE, BROWN, & CO., Publishers, BOSTON

At all Booksellers'

Mr. Oppenheim's most Romantic Novel

THE MASTER MUMMER

By E. PHILLIPS OPPENHEIM

Author of "A Prince of Sinners," "Anna the Adventuress," "Mysterious Mr. Sabin," etc.

Illustrated by F. H. Townsend. 12mo. $1.50

The dexterous craftsmanship in the manipulation of an absorbing plot that characterizes Mr. Oppenheim's work is here applied to the most romantic theme he has as yet conceived. The strange adventures that befel the young Princess of the imaginary kingdom of Bartena, who is kept out of the way in order that her place may be filled by her cousin, appeal strongly to the reader. Her temporary guardian killed, and knowing nothing of her parentage, the young Princess is befriended by three bachelors who stand Godfather to her, heedless of her high estate. The many intrigues to obtain possession of her, the part which the mysterious "Master Mummer" plays in the girl's life, and the perils which her lover encountered furnish material for an original modern romance of unusual interest.

LITTLE, BROWN, & CO., Publishers, BOSTON

At all Booksellers'

The Weird Picture

The New Novel by the Author of "Truth Dexter"

THE BREATH OF THE GODS

By SIDNEY McCALL

Author of "Truth Dexter"
12mo. Decorated cloth, 420 pages. $1.50

It is now four years since the sweetness, freshness, and tenderness of "Truth Dexter" captivated and delighted the reading public. The gifted author has devoted these years to the careful writing of a second story, which it is assuredly safe to call a masterpiece.

The greatest value of "The Breath of the Gods" lies perhaps in its unusual power as a story, with a strong, original, and unexpected plot, closely knit and vividly unfolded, and replete with surprises and striking situations.

The setting of the background, partly in Washington and partly in Japan, gives scope for the author's brilliant pictures and sympathetic interpretations of nature.

There is, however, in "The Breath of the Gods" no sacrificing of the dramatic story to an attempt at exposition; Japan is not an aim, but an incident.

LITTLE, BROWN, & CO., Publishers, BOSTON

At all Booksellers'